Lunatic Carnival

LUNATIC CARNIVAL

D.W. Buffa

POLIS BOOKS

Cover and jacket design by 2Faced Design

ISBN 978-1-951709-83-9
eISBN: 978-1-957957-41-8
Library of Congress Control Number: available upon request

62 Ottowa Road S
Marlboro, NJ 07746
www.PolisBooks.com

To Jason, Shel, and Kayla

"...THE NEAR-VOID IN EVERY MAN...THE LUNATIC CARNIVAL OF UNQUIET THINGS THAT DWELL THEREIN."

—Joseph Cropsey

One

Leonard Silverman got up from his black leather chair and walked the few short steps to the window. In the distance, beyond the busy narrow streets of San Francisco, a single span of the Bay Bridge glistened silver gray in the November midday sun. He stood there, his back turned to me, his hands shoved deep in the pockets of his dark tailored suit. When he was on the bench, presiding over a trial, he held himself in such a formal, dignified manner you would have had to stop and think about it had anyone asked you to give an exact estimate of his height. His hair, which had turned grayish white with the years, was cut close, the way they do it in the kind of barber shop where you walk in off the street and a haircut does not cost half a worker's weekly wage.

"Did you ever read Joseph Conrad's novel, *Heart of Darkness*?" he asked. "The best work of ninety pages in all of English literature, as far as I'm concerned."

He kept staring out the window, like some tourist on his first visit to San Francisco, caught, mesmerized, by something seen in a passing glance, something he wanted to make sure he would not forget. But Leonard Silverman had lived here all his life, and whatever he was seeing, it was not with his eyes.

"I read it first forty years ago, when I was in college, and even after all this time there is a line that still haunts me. It comes back to me every time I preside over a murder trial: 'All of Europe contributed to the making of Kurtz.'"

Slowly, and, as it were, reluctantly, Leonard Silverman turned away from the window and the cloud-shaded streets outside. For a moment, he seemed to measure me the way he might some unfortunate offender about to be sentenced for a crime he had not meant to commit.

"'All of Europe contributed to the making of Kurtz,'" he repeated. "You've read it. Remember who Kurtz was, remember what he became; how he turned his back on civilization, on everything he had been taught about good and evil; how he engaged in, and enjoyed, every form of violence and degradation."

He studied me with a strange intensity, as if my fate were, for some reason, entirely in his hands.

"'All of Europe contributed to the making of Kurtz,'" he again repeated, that line, somehow, the key to a mystery I knew nothing about. "You might remember that when you meet your new client; you might remember it when you get to know about all the others involved in this trial. You might remember to ask whether it might just be true, and if it is, what exactly it might mean, that all of America contributed to the making of Matthew Stanton."

I was almost too stunned to speak.

"When I meet my new client?"

He seemed to think my question irrelevant to anything we needed to discuss. He came back to his desk, but instead of sitting down, stood behind the chair and placed his fine, rather delicate hands on top of it.

"You've tried cases in my courtroom. I know what you can do.

Everyone—the whole country—knows what Joseph Antonelli can do. But I know more about you than what I have seen in court. Your partner, Albert Craven, is an old friend of mine." For the first time, Leonard Silverman started to smile. "Yes, I know: Albert is an old friend of everyone. There isn't anyone he doesn't know; no one, that is, who has lived their life in the city. It doesn't matter what charitable board you are on, the first question anyone asks when a meeting is about to begin is when is Albert going to arrive. Years ago, when Willie Brown was first elected mayor, Albert was the first person he invited to lunch. They still have lunch together. Whichever of them dies first, the other one will give the eulogy."

He laughed to himself, and then, suddenly, looked at me with a new interest. Moving across to a bookshelf on the wall, he took down the first of two thick matching volumes.

"The Greek drama," he explained, thumbing through the pages. "Everything, all the plays of Aeschylus, Sophocles, Euripides, Aristophanes, and...here it is."

For a few seconds he studied the page he had been looking for in silence, a moment's reflection on a favorite passage from an ancient playwright's ancient play. With a brief nod, an acknowledgement that he had remembered it accurately, he closed the book and carefully put it back next to the companion volume on the shelf.

"Euripides. You've read him, of course," he remarked as he sat down behind the gray metal desk. A thick wad of paper under one of the legs kept it in balance. The black leather chair, no doubt purchased at his own expense, was the only exception to the spare, budget-saving furnishings of an official's public office. "Albert told me that, unlike most lawyers—unlike almost everyone now —you are what used to be called a serious reader. You read Euripides. There is always a murder, a murder that involves the members of a family, a ruling family, a family that has power, or had power and lost it. There is something like that here. I know it; I can feel it. San Francisco, whatever the world might think, is really a small town; there are not more than a few dozen families with any real influence. They all know each other. They belong to the same clubs; they patronize the same charitable organizations. Their children go to the same private schools; they go to the same expensive places on vacations; and they end up, many of them, marrying one another. And they all knew the Stantons. Everyone knew Emmett Stanton, Matthew Stanton's father. Albert can tell you all about him, and all about both his wives. Euripides," he said, nodding to himself with a strange emphasis. "The Greeks had a fascination with Helen; a fascination with what a woman, a beautiful woman, can do. If we had a Euripides today, Victoria Stanton, Matthew Stanton's stepmother, would be the central character in the next play he wrote."

His eyes narrowed into a stare as penetrating as any I had ever seen, an inquisition, though into what I could not say. He watched me for a brief, decisive moment, and then nodded twice in quick succession.

"As soon as I heard about the murder of Matthew Stanton, the moment the defendant was arraigned, I knew you had to become the attorney for the defense."

"Attorney for the...? No, I'm sorry; I have too many other things to do, and, besides, I don't take court-appointed cases. I'm not—"

"I'm not asking you to represent someone who can't afford to hire an attorney! I'm asking you because I'm certain, absolutely certain, that the defendant, who everyone thinks murdered Matthew Stanton, is innocent! I don't need to tell you that I'm breaking all the rules. I'm sworn to be impartial; I'm not supposed to have an opinion, much less express one, about the guilt or innocence of someone on trial."

I should not have been surprised. If there was anyone who

would risk removal from the bench and even disbarment to do what he knew to be right, it was Leonard Silverman. But that did not explain why he was doing this now.

"I have no evidence, nothing at all, about who might have murdered Matthew Stanton," continued Silverman, "but I know enough—perhaps more than I should—about his father and his father's second wife, and about what happened after his father died. I know enough about the rumors, the strange suspicions about what went on, to believe that Matthew Stanton's murder had no connection to everything that happened before. Euripides! What do you learn when you read him? That everything that happens has some ancient cause. That is why you are going to take this case: because you are a serious reader, and only a serious reader knows how to read what isn't written on the written page."

Silverman bent forward and rested his arms on the old, tattered blotter that covered the middle of that government-issue desk of his. His voice became confidential.

"The defendant, T. J. Allen—Thaddeus John Allen. You've heard of him?"

The name seemed vaguely familiar, but only vaguely familiar, one of those names about which all you know, or all you can remember, is that you have heard it somewhere before.

"He has an attorney, a very good attorney," Silverman went on, determined, as it seemed, to tell me everything he could about why I had to take the case. "A very good attorney, but he doesn't do much criminal work and he has never taken a case like this to trial. He can't handle this; no one can. No one except you. The evidence against Allen seems overwhelming," he said, shaking his head with what seemed contempt. "Just what you would expect when the case is cut and dried, or when the evidence is manufactured."

Manufactured? How much did Leonard Silverman really

know, and how much was he holding back. He knew what I was thinking.

"That is all I can say about it," he said, nodding in a way that suggested there were things I would eventually learn myself.

I was starting to feel that I was being drawn into a conspiracy in which I would have to find out on my own the part I was expected to play. For all his obvious concern with making sure justice was done, I was being used.

"I'm sorry, but I won't do it. Allen has an attorney. He can hire another one. I told you before that I don't take court-appointed cases. I should have said that I decide who I am going to represent."

A curious smile, like the sly grin of a card player holding the winning hand, slipped slowly across his mouth. His bright, intelligent eyes filled with laughter.

"Of course you'll take the case."

It was absurd, it made no sense, the utter certainty with which he insisted I would do precisely what I had just said I never would.

"You have no choice." The laughter in his eyes was so obvious, so inexplicably exuberant, I could almost hear it. "Imagine what would happen if you didn't. A judge—the trial judge—asks you to represent an innocent man accused of murder. He tells you that the evidence against this innocent man is so great he is certain to be convicted; tells you that you are the only lawyer who can get to the bottom of one of the most incredible stories of power, ambition, and murder you have ever heard, a story only a Euripides could tell, and you are going to say no, that you won't do it? You'll never do that, not in a thousand years. Do you think that if I thought there was even the slightest chance you would turn me down, I would have told you what I have? That I'm going to preside over a trial in which I am already convinced what the verdict should be."

I felt like a coward, and I felt like a fool. It was true: I could not refuse a case in which I might be able to save an innocent man, especially when a judge I respected was willing to risk his own tenure on the bench by asking me to do it. Leonard Silverman had trusted me with more than his career and his reputation; he had trusted in the belief that I would not think there was any serious alternative to what he asked and expected. I promised to think it over.

"Think it over all you want," he replied. "Just make sure you're in my courtroom Monday morning when we start jury selection."

"You mean I have all weekend?"

"This is only Thursday," he reminded me. "I thought you might want to meet your client before the trial starts."

The laughter in his gentle eyes faded away. He looked at me with what seemed a warning, as if he thought he might have gone too far, or rather, not far enough.

"I told you he was innocent, innocent of the crime; I did not tell you he was someone you might like."

He started to get up, turning toward the shelves on the wall as if there were some other book he wanted, but he seemed to think better of it and sat down again.

"You might read it again this weekend, Conrad's *Heart of Darkness*." A slight, rueful smile creased the corners of his mouth. "'All of Europe contributed to the making of Kurtz.'"

I left the chambers of Leonard Silverman intrigued, and more than a little confused. Trial court judges had their biases, even, sometimes, their prejudices, but except perhaps among their closest friends, they never admitted it. Silverman was better than most of them, better by far than all the time-serving judges who had gotten on the bench because of their political connections. He was more than a judge, a scholar who studied the law. No one read, no one studied, serious things anymore; everyone watched television. Silverman read Euripides. He had read *Heart of Dark-*

ness, read it forty years ago, and still had that remarkable line in his head, the line that haunted him every time he presided over a murder trial. "All of Europe contributed to the making of Kurtz." A few words on paper, a single line from a now forgotten novel, had become the thought, the dominant experience, the central thread in how he understood things. He had changed only one word, replacing "Europe" with "America," to explain why he thought the murder of Matthew Stanton so fascinating, and so important. No one read Joseph Conrad anymore, but Leonard Silverman was right. *Heart of Darkness*, only ninety pages long, could make you doubt everything you thought you knew.

I kept hearing Silverman's remembered Conrad quote as I drove across the Golden Gate on my way home to Sausalito. A light rain had started to fall, not much more than a heavy mist. The rhythmic sound of the windshield wipers was like the drumbeat of a slow-marching parade. The headlights of the cars moving in both directions beneath the hanging cables of the bridge moved in such a steady, unbroken line that there did not seem to be any movement at all, and that, instead of getting closer to the other side, I was staying still in the same place. "All of America contributed to the making of..." What did it mean? How could a trial, even a murder trial, have that kind of significance?

Without quite knowing how I got there, I suddenly was home, the chocolate-colored, shingle-sided house high on the hillside above the bridge and the bay; the city, a brazen, brightly dressed harlot dancing in the darkness on the other side. I parked in the carport and started down the steep flight of wooden stairs to the front entrance. Through the window I saw Tangerine moving toward the door in a dance of her own. When she threw her arms around my neck, time lost all meaning—the future would never happen and I remembered nothing of the past.

"Have you missed me?" she asked as she pulled away just far

enough so I could see the soft, shining glow in her gorgeous dark eyes.

"Missed you? I can't remember being gone."

Barefoot, wearing a blue skirt and white blouse, she kissed me on the side of my face.

"It's nice you never change, nice you're still the lying lawyer you have always been. Now, come with me."

She took my hand and led me through the living room into the kitchen. Steam was rising from a large pot on the stove. A thick bunch of thin yellow pasta lay on a white plate on the counter next to it.

"We're having spaghetti?"

She threw me a quick, taunting glance. "Why do you think I'm not wearing shoes?"

She seemed to think the blank expression on my face hilarious. Then it hit me.

"Barefoot in the kitchen—keeping you barefoot and pregnant in the kitchen. Are you telling me that—?"

"No, not yet," she said with a droll look. "But maybe nine months from tonight—if you're willing...and if you're able."

She slid the pasta into the boiling water. The laughter in her voice became quiet, subdued, thoughtful.

"We haven't talked about having a child. I'm not getting any younger, so if we are ever going to..."

In the few short years we had been together, it had never occurred to me that she would ever change. She was too beautiful for that. It would have been like wondering what Helen of Troy would look like if she lived long enough to become an old woman. Like the age of everyone else, Tangerine's age had a number, but the number was an abstraction, a way to count time. It had no meaning; it signified nothing.

"Do you?" I asked gently. "Want a child?"

"I never used to. I was too selfish; there were too many things

I wanted to do, things I wanted to experience. I didn't want to be tied down; I didn't want to worry about someone else. It's different now. But if you don't want to, if you would rather not, it's all right. A child changes everything."

She stood there, barefoot and beautiful, stirring spaghetti sauce in a pan, and I tried to imagine what it would be like if the two of us became three. I had not thought about children; I had never seriously thought about marriage. I had...

"Do you remember what I said on what was probably only the second time I had ever seen you?"

She looked at me with a glance full of knowledge.

"You told me I should divorce my husband and marry you. And the moment you said it, I knew it was the only thing I wanted to do. I knew something else: I knew it was the same for both of us, that for the first time in our lives we knew what we wanted, and that before that moment we had not known at all. We fell in love, and we will always be in love, and if we have a child, it won't be because we made plans to have one. It will just happen, and if it does, we'll know it was always what we wanted, even though we had not known it. We'll just let love decide. We'll keep making love, over and over again—if you're willing...and if you're able—and see whether making love makes a child."

That was all that was said, perhaps all that needed to be said, about what might happen in the endless present in which we lived our own, very private, lives. A few minutes later, sitting at the dining room table, she asked me about Leonard Silverman. It took me a moment before I remembered.

"He presided over that trial, a few years ago, in which the first judge was shot to death on the courthouse steps," she remarked. "You did not need to be a lawyer to know that he knew what he was doing. You liked him, didn't you?"

"There is only one other judge I could compare to him," I said, remembering something I had not thought of in years.

"Leopold Rifkin, when I was just starting out, asked me to take a case, a case in which Rifkin ended up the defendant in a trial where I would have had to kill myself had I lost."

"Is Judge Silverman in trouble, too?"

"No; it's the Matthew Stanton murder trial. He wants me to take over the defense. You knew him, didn't you, Matthew Stanton?"

I glanced out the sliding glass doors at the lights of San Francisco, beckoning in the distance. There were shades of light, shades of meaning, everywhere; connections forming and dissolving in the relation of things, things that became visible only to vanish again, a moment later, in the dark night rain.

"Everyone knew Matthew Stanton," I heard Tangerine saying. She sipped on her glass of red wine and then smiled in the way of acknowledging a loss, someone she wished she had known better. "Everyone knew him; or rather, everyone knew who he was. I used to see him at those fundraising dinners for politicians, and those charitable events where everyone gives enough money to show everyone else how much money they have to give. You go to enough of those things and you get used to seeing the same people. You get to know them, in the sense of what they talk about, who they spend their time with, what they are really after. Matthew Stanton was different. No matter how often you had seen him, each time was like seeing someone who had not been there before. I don't mean that he seemed like a stranger, or that he was awkward or ill at ease. If you didn't know that he came from probably the wealthiest family in town, you might have thought he was a reporter, someone who always came to these things, but only as an observer, watching what the others were doing so he could later try to make some sense out of what he had seen."

Pausing, she studied the way the wine turned different shades of red as she twisted it slowly back and forth in front of the flickering light of a tall white candle, the only light we had.

"I once heard something strange about him, a rumor that he had once played Russian roulette with some other kids when he was in college, and that something happened, something no one ever talked about."

"Someone got killed?"

"I don't know. Only that something happened, and that, whatever it was, it got covered up, which in those circles meant someone paid to have it go away. It was a rumor. That's all I know. It may not even be true."

Her eyes had remained fixed on the slow, twisting glass, but now, finished with the story, she took a drink and looked at me across the table.

"You're going to do it, aren't you? Take on the trial?"

"Probably. Silverman asked... Asked! He told me I had to do it, that I could not say no."

"Because...?"

"Because the guy is innocent. He told me that, and by doing that, broke all the rules. He isn't supposed to have an opinion; he's supposed to be strictly impartial. It's more than that, more than the fact that he thinks someone innocent might be convicted. 'All of America contributed to the making of Matthew Stanton.' That is the line he used, a line that with only one word changed he had read in a novel forty years ago when he was still in college. What does it mean? All of America contributed to the making of Matthew Stanton. Who was Matthew Stanton? What made him so interesting? Yes, I'll take the case. There is too much mystery in it not to take it."

Something had been troubling me since I left the courthouse, something in the back of my mind. There was something else in Conrad's novel, something that, though I could not quite recall the exact words, helped clarify the meaning of that simple, enigmatic line: "All of Europe contributed to the making of Kurtz." I jumped up from my chair and hurried into my study, where I searched the shelves until I found it, an old, weathered paperback of *Heart of Darkness*.

"Listen to this," I said when I got back and found the page I was looking for. "'The conquest of the earth...is not a pretty thing when you look into it too much. What redeems it is the idea only, an idea at the back of it; not a sentimental practice, but an idea; and an unselfish belief in the idea—something you can set up and bow down before, and offer a sacrifice to...'"

I put Conrad's brief novel down on the table.

"All of America contributed to the making of... What idea was the moving force, what idea made it possible, what unselfish belief made it all happen, made Matthew Stanton what he was; what unselfish belief became the cause, the reason why he had to die?"

Tangerine's eyes glistened with the memory of a world she had left behind.

"It would be surprising if there was anything unselfish in anything that involved the people with whom Matthew Stanton spent most of his life."

"Do selfish people ever think they are selfish when they try to get what they think they need?"

"Never. But entitled, deserving of what they have? Always. I never thought I was selfish when I lived in one of the largest houses in San Francisco and drove expensive cars and spent more on clothes in a week than most people make in a year. I was living like everyone else I knew, and no one I knew thought anything was wrong with that."

"And now you're living here, with me, in a shack on the hill, close to destitution," I said with a sharp, teasing glance.

With an air of resignation, almost an act of contrition for her rich woman's sins, she turned up the palms of her hands and sighed.

"I even have to cook, barefoot in the kitchen. And I'm so poor, I'm not even wearing underwear."

Despite my sudden, breathless impatience, I refused to give her the satisfaction of an honest, heart-stopping response.

"But that wasn't how you dressed when you drove into the city in your Mercedes to have lunch."

"No, you're right," she replied. "I drove the Mercedes; I didn't drive the Porsche. And I wore a wool suit and lots of expensive jewelry. I even wore shoes. The difference, you see," she said as she got up and stared down at me, "is that I was having lunch with a girlfriend. I dress for women; I undress for you."

"That's too bad," I remarked with studied indifference.

"Too bad?" she laughed. "What do you mean, too bad?"

"I rather like you in shoes. Where are you going?" I asked as she disappeared into the kitchen.

"To get another bottle of wine. We might as well talk. And drink," she added as she came back, a look of triumph in her eyes. "Now, tell me more about your new case, the trial Leonard Silverman—he has money, too, you know; but with him, as you can imagine, the money doesn't matter. The only time you ever saw him with any of the rich and powerful was at a wedding or a funeral, and even then he never stayed to talk with anyone. I think he found most of them boring."

I knew she was right. Leonard Silverman was too serious to listen with any great interest to the mindless banter of the undeserving rich. If he stayed at all, it would have been to learn what he could about the changing manners and morals of his time.

"I told him I needed to think about whether I would take the case. He told me to think about it all I wanted, but that I had to be in court Monday morning when jury selection begins. He suggested I might want to meet my new client first. He said he did not think I would like him."

We kept talking about a trial that had not started and a client I had not met, and we seldom took our eyes off each other, until, finally, with little left in the bottle, Tangerine got up and took me by the hand.

"We have to go to bed now. If we wait much longer, that nine months I was talking about won't start until tomorrow."

Two

Leonard Silverman was right. I did not like Thaddeus John Allen, and he did not like me. I had not even sat down before he was telling me to leave.

"Why the hell would I want to see you?" he demanded in a harsh, strident voice.

I was a little over six feet tall, but he was six seven or six eight, with the longest arms I had ever seen. He was somewhere in his thirties, with a look of contempt in his angry eyes that seemed to dare you to hit him before he hit you. I almost laughed in his face.

"The real question, Mr. Allen, is why would I want to see you? I'm only here as a favor; not to you, but to someone who thought you might need an attorney who knows something about trying cases, especially cases in which the defendant has no chance to win!"

"An attorney who...!" With his hands on his waist, he bent toward me. "Jesus Christ! Don't you know who I am? I got more money than you'll ever dream of! I can buy any goddamn lawyer I want. My people are working on it; they'll get the best one money can buy. Who the hell are you, anyway? Some goddamn shyster who wants to get famous on my name!"

We were alone in a dreary holding room in the county jail, a room so small the chairs on each side of the square metal table would bump against the wall behind them if you did not suck in your breath when you tried to squeeze into them. Allen loomed over me, bigger than the door I had come through, a door that, with him in the way, I could not now see.

"When I quit playing, I was making forty, fifty million a year; and even now I make almost that much from all the endorsement deals I have, and all the commercials I make. So, whoever the hell you are, trust me, you ain't my lawyer and you ain't going to be!"

"You played basketball?" I asked with such innocence that it stopped him cold.

He looked at me to see if I was really serious. Everyone knew who he was; he was famous. How could anyone not know who he was? He almost felt sorry for me.

"You really don't know who I am?"

Six foot seven, six foot eight, and at least two hundred fifty pounds, he became almost gentle. He studied me the way the movies used to show a white explorer on his first encounter with a native tribe, only he was the black explorer and I was the last remaining member of a vanishing race: a white man who apparently knew nothing about professional sports. He shook his head in wonder.

"Man, that's just unbelievable. I never met anyone didn't know me. That's not true. I went to Europe a couple summers ago, after the season ended, there were people there...but here, in this country, hasn't happened. Didn't think it could. You really don't know me? Damn, that's interesting. But, listen, no offense, but, as I said, my people are working on this. They'll get me the best lawyer there is. But, thank you for coming. And, listen, next season—I still have connections with the team—we'll get you tickets. You really should see a game. You'll like it, you really will. Everyone does."

And then, before I could get in a word, he was pounding on the door, telling the guard the visit was over.

This was on Saturday morning; that afternoon, a little after five, he called collect from the jail. He was very formal.

"Mr. Antonelli, this is T. J., T. J. Allen. My people...they tell me you're the best there is, that there isn't anyone else; that you're the best, maybe the only, chance I have. I know I didn't treat you very well this morning, but I wonder—I would appreciate—if you could give me another chance. Would you mind coming back? I have to be in court Monday morning, so..."

I told him I would come the next morning, Sunday, at ten. I thought I would spend an hour with him; I was there almost all day. Instead of that airless, confined room we had met in before, he was waiting at a large round table in the back corner of the empty cafeteria. The jail guards were among his biggest fans.

"You probably want to know if I did it, if I killed Matthew. I didn't."

He said this before I had taken a chair. He had stood up when I entered the room, watching with nervous apprehension as I approached. The mean-spirited arrogance had disappeared, vanished so completely that I started to think the memory of what I had witnessed might have been exaggerated by my own reaction. It did not seem possible that he could have been as enraged, as potentially violent, as I had thought. He waited until I sat down, and then, in a single graceful movement, settled into a chair, not where he had been waiting on the other side of the table, but close to where I sat. He repeated what he had said just a moment before.

"I didn't do it; I swear I didn't do it."

I was at a serious disadvantage. I had not seen a police report, I knew next to nothing about the case, and, as I had shown to his astonishment the day before, knew nothing about him. I ignored what he said.

"You always wear a suit and tie?" he asked suddenly.

It seemed a strange thing to ask, the random inquiry of an undisciplined mind, the kind of question a child might innocently ask. I looked straight at him.

"Even at night, when I go to bed."

For half a second he was not sure I might not be serious.

"I mean, almost no one does that anymore. Actually," he went on, his enormous eyes growing bright, "about the only people who do that are the players. We had to. The league thought we had to set an example. Kind of funny, really; hardly any of us went more than a year or two to college; hardly any of us took any real classes while we were there. We play a game, make millions doing it, but we gotta dress like we're a bunch of bankers or lawyers. But really, tell me, why do you dress like that when you're visiting someone in jail?"

In all the years I had been practicing law, no one had ever asked me that question, and now that I had to think about it, I was not sure I knew the answer.

"Habit, I suppose—or my own form of rebellion."

"Rebellion? Against what?"

"The absence of formality, the absence of all standards," I heard myself say. There was something about T. J. Allen, the honest curiosity in his eyes, that made you want to talk to him. "When I first started out, a young lawyer trying to learn my way around a courtroom, all the jurors dressed like this. Men wore coats and ties and women wore dresses. A lot of people will tell you this is a good thing, that everyone should be comfortable, that they should wear what they like, but it makes it more difficult to be serious, and there are things that need to be taken seriously—a trial, for example; a trial when someone, someone like you, will have twelve strangers decide if he should go free or spend the rest of his life in prison. That is why I wear a suit and tie: it helps make the point that this is not some kind of grown-up game in which both the winners and the losers get to go home when the game is over."

The eyes of T. J. Allen grew larger and more focused as I spoke, and, at the same time, more distant and remote. He understood, or was beginning to understand, that this was serious, more serious than anything that had happened to him before. He had, of course, understood that the charge against him was serious, but this was the first time he had heard it from someone who knew from experience what he was facing. Read all you want on the internet about an illness you have, watch all the medical dramas on television you like, it is not what happens when a surgeon comes to your bedside in the hospital and tells you that the operation you are about to undergo does not come with any guarantees.

"But I didn't do it," he repeated, although this time more slowly than before, as if he wanted to be sure I had heard, and, hearing, understood.

They all said this, the guilty and the innocent. They tried to convince their lawyer they were innocent, because if their lawyer thought they were guilty, how could he convince a jury they were not. I decided to tell Allen the truth.

"I don't care what you did. Innocent, guilty, it makes no difference. All I care about—all you should care about—is the evidence."

His first reaction, completely normal and completely expected, was a show of indignation, anger that I would not accept at face value what he said and, even worse, dismissed it as somehow irrelevant. How could I think the question of his guilt or innocence not important? It was the only thing that was. Leaning on his large, heavy arms, he stared at me through narrow, doubting eyes.

"They told me you were the best, but if you don't believe me when I tell you that I didn't—"

"I didn't say I didn't believe you; I said it did not matter. And if you want to find another lawyer, one you think will believe whatever you tell him, go ahead. You may not have any choice. I haven't decided yet whether I want to represent you."

He was still staring at me, trying to figure out if I really meant what I was saying. It was a new experience for him. No one had ever turned him down; no one had ever not wanted to do everything they could for him. He was used to the attention of others, friends who wanted to stay friends, strangers who wanted to know him; everyone always eager to make sure he did not have to do anything for himself. Indifference was not just unusual, it was unique.

"Let me explain to you just how irrelevant your claim of innocence really is: it hasn't convinced anyone. The police obviously did not believe you when they arrested you. The grand jury did not believe you when they returned an indictment. The district attorney's office did not believe you when they charged you with first-degree murder. This is not a swearing contest, Mr. Allen; if it was, you would be on death row. Tomorrow morning you go on trial, and you can get up on the witness stand and swear to Kingdom Come that you're innocent, and even if the jury wants to believe you, they won't if the prosecution has enough evidence. So, no, it does not matter whether you say you're innocent; the only thing that matters is what anyone can prove."

Allen was moving his head from side to side, clenching and then unclenching his jaw. He was anxious, irritated, unwilling, and, perhaps, incapable of believing that any right-thinking person would refuse to take his word.

"You need to understand something," I said in a firm, even voice, "and I mean understand it well, because most people don't. Even when it is explained to them, they never quite believe it. A jury does not decide if someone is innocent. Never. They only decide if someone is or is not guilty. The verdict form gives two alternatives, and only two: guilty and not guilty. The question, the only question, is whether the prosecution has proved beyond a reasonable doubt that the defendant is guilty of the crime, or crimes, with which he has been charged. That's it! Nothing else! Now, start at the beginning: did you know Matthew Stanton?"

Allen blinked, and then blinked again. He took a deep breath, raised his chin, and nodded.

"I knew Matthew; I had known him for years. The Stantons owned the team."

"Matthew Stanton owned...?"

"His father, Emmett, bought the team, ten, twelve years ago. I liked him. Even when I was a rookie, he always had time for me. He treated everyone the same. That was what you noticed right away. I don't just mean the players. Everyone."

Allen's eyes lit up at the memory of something that had happened his first year with the team. He was not anxious or tense anymore; he was all smiles, his only fear there might not be enough time to tell the story in all the detail it deserved.

"He was off on the side of the court—I guess he had just come to watch practice—talking to one of the janitors. The guy—an old guy, probably in his fifties—was holding on to his broom. I don't know what they were talking about, but Artie Macklin—he was a big star then—came up to talk to Mr. Stanton, was real insistent about it. But Mr. Stanton just gave him a look, a look that said, 'Can't you see I'm busy?' and turned back to the old man and kept talking to him for another five or ten minutes. Hard not to like a guy like that. Macklin did not like it, but Macklin was a prick. They say—I don't know this for sure—that Mr. Stanton always flew coach. Probably the only guy who owned a professional team and did not have his own plane. That wife of his, on the other hand, wouldn't be surprised if she had more than one. Victoria Stanton," said Allen, rolling his eyes. "She's a real piece of work. If she had been talking to that janitor... That's stupid; she never would have been talking to any janitor. But, if she had been, she would have cut him off midsentence if Macklin had come up to her. I didn't like her; I don't like her, I don't like her at all. Mr. Stanton liked the game; she liked the crowds."

"What about Matthew Stanton? What did he like?"

"He liked to be alone. I don't think he ever came to practice; he almost never came to a game. You have to understand something. He wasn't one of those guys—the rich, white owners who were never athletes themselves, who were never popular in school; guys who somehow later on made money and started buying things so everyone would envy what they had; the guys who think the players really like them and want to be their friends. Matthew thought it was all a joke, a fraud. That's maybe the reason we got along so well."

"The reason you and Matthew Stanton...?"

"We were both, in different ways, part of what we both understood was one of the great scams of all time. Look," he said, leaning close, as if about to share some great, dark secret, "it's just a game. I was good at it; I was always good at it. Hell, that's not true," he laughed, "I was great at it, one of the best who ever played. But, you know, when you step back from it, it's just five guys trying to put a ball through a basket more times than the other five guys. And they pay us millions, tens of millions, to do it. And they can do that because millions of people think that if their team wins, it is the greatest thing that ever happened. You should go sometime. Forget the people sitting there at home, glued to their television sets, all rigid with anxiety; watch the crowd, watch their faces. I don't know much history, but what those Romans did, those gladiators who used to kill each other while the crowd went crazy—it's the same thing here. Go to a game when we're playing in another city. You should have heard some of the things I got called. I can't count how many times I got called a nigger, how many times some idiot in the crowd screamed at me to...well, never mind, I think you get the idea.

"Matthew saw it from the other side, the ownership; the way that, for all their money, most of these people are like needy little children. They want their team to win so they can hear the cheering of the crowd, so they can feel that they're more important than other people. I had not quite realized it before, not until Matthew explained it. The money lets you buy a lot of things, a bigger house, a more expensive car, but if you want everyone to know that you are one of the world's privileged rich, you have to own and control something everyone wants to be part of. If you own a professional football or basketball team, everyone knows who you are. That was what made Matthew so unusual: he did not really want anyone to know who he was."

Allen sat straight up, turned toward me, and slapped his huge hand hard on the table.

"There are a few people I've sometimes thought about killing, but kill Matthew? I loved the guy. It would have been like killing myself. We were friends, and if you don't count the guys I grew up with, guys I knew before anyone had ever heard of me, the best friend I had. And do you know why? Because he taught me things, helped me understand things I didn't know anything about. Look, I went to college, two years, before I turned pro, but I never took a class that meant anything. I played basketball. Matthew taught me how to read. I don't mean I didn't read before, but I had never read a novel, never read, to use your word, anything serious. That's what we did: read books, talked about what we read. Look, Matthew didn't have any friends. Same as me, and for the same reason. Everyone knew he had money, everyone wanted to get close. He told me he didn't trust anyone, and, except for his father and me, he meant it. He was one of the richest guys around and, other than me, he did not have a friend in the world."

I had not seen the police reports, I did not know anything about what kind of evidence the prosecution might have, but I knew that Leonard Silverman was right, I knew that T. J. Allen had not murdered Matthew Stanton. There were two questions that still had to be answered, two questions that would decide everything at trial; two questions that might never be answered until they were answered at trial: If Allen did not murder Matthew Stanton, then who did? And if someone else murdered Stanton, why had Allen been charged?

"You think it might have something to do with the fact that I'm rich and famous and black?" suggested Allen with a cynic's laugh. Folding his arms across his chest, he cocked his head and shrugged his shoulders at the predictable stupidity of the world. "People knew we were close, that we were good friends. No one could understand it. You have this shy guy with his polite good manners, always kind of withdrawn, and me, just the opposite. I never stop talking, especially when I'm playing. I push people around; I don't let anyone get in my way. No one could understand it, no one could figure it out. So, they did what they do every time they can't figure out why two guys so different spend a lot of time together: they figured we must be gay. Had to be; couldn't be anything else. Now, you got to understand, nobody was going to come out and say that to my face. Not that there is anything wrong with a couple guys being together, but there aren't too many gay guys in pro basketball. Let's just leave it at that. But there were rumors, and I didn't say anything about it, nothing, not a word. Why should I? Well, one guy did say something, one night after a game. Everyone was going to some party; I said I had other plans. And this guy says, 'Why, you going somewhere with your friend?' It was the way he said it. So I hit him, hit him pretty good, almost broke his nose. All it did was make everyone think the rumors must be true. They weren't. I'm not gay. But Matthew...I'm not really sure. I don't even know if he was interested in women. We didn't talk about that kind of thing, and we talked a lot. But Matthew was full of secrets. I couldn't even tell you what the secrets were about."

I started to ask another question, but Allen was not finished.

"Matthew was shot to death. I don't own a gun. I used to, but it was stolen. He was murdered in his apartment, late on a Saturday night. I was there that night; I had been there a lot of times. That night I came by around seven or seven thirty. We had dinner and talked for a couple hours and then I left. No one saw me when I left. There is a private elevator down to the street and the parking garage below."

"You were there, no one saw you leave, and Stanton is murdered later that night. There must be more to it than that, something that made the police think you did it."

"I found the body."

"You just said you left before the murder. You went back?"

"I wasn't going to go back, but Matthew was very upset, angry about something he did not want to talk about, and I got a little angry because he wouldn't. We got into an argument. I started yelling at him, telling him to grow up, act his age. We were friends, for Christ's sake! He's so goddamn depressed he can barely stand it, and he won't let me help. So I told him he could go to hell and I marched out of there, as angry as I had ever been. I calmed down after I reached the street and walked a few blocks. I realized I had acted the fool. You don't get mad at your friends, you let them get mad at you. I called to apologize, but he did not answer. He always answered when I called. I figured he must be really angry, or really depressed, about whatever it was that was bothering him, and then I started to think that maybe it was worse than I thought, that maybe, after what I had done, it might have been the straw that broke the camel's back, that maybe he might decide... So I went back, hoping he had not done anything, hoping I could stop him if he was still thinking about it, and that's when I found him, the side of his head all bloody, a gun laying on the floor. I thought he had killed himself, but then I realized that the gun was too far away, that someone had shot him and just dropped the gun and then run out of the room. It must have just happened; I could not have been gone for more than ten minutes or so. And then, before I could call for help, the police were there and I was being arrested."

"Did you pick up the gun?" I asked, watching his eyes, the feeling of confusion he still had about what had happened. "Are your fingerprints on it?"

"I must have. I don't remember picking it up, but I must have, because my prints are on it."

"You say he was angry and depressed, but you don't know what about. Was he often like that, angry and depressed?"

Allen did not answer at once; the question was not as simple as it seemed.

"Not like he was that night. I had never seen him that angry; never seem him angry at all. But depressed? It would be easy to think that, if you didn't know him very well. He wasn't one of those guys who likes to joke around. He didn't laugh all that often, and when he did, it was not much more than a smile."

Something came to him. He looked at me, certain I would understand.

"You and the suit and ties you wear. He was a lot like that; not so much in what he wore, but what he was. I never knew anyone that serious. It reminded me a little of the way players look in the minutes before a big game: the concentration, the sense of purpose, the knowledge, the belief, that nothing you will ever do will be this important. The difference was that Matthew was like that all the time. He was driven—I don't know by what—like no one I ever knew. We weren't that far apart in age, but he made me feel like he was all grown up and I was still a kid."

I had brought my briefcase, my legal pad, and my fountain pen, but I had not opened the briefcase and I had not bothered taking notes. I let the conversation go where it would. More than facts, dates, and places; more than a bare outline of T. J. Allen's singular biography, I wanted to get a sense of things, what he was like, how he thought, how he reacted. Every time he answered a question, I tried to imagine what he would be like on the witness stand; what he would be like when, instead of just the two of us sitting alone at a table, he would be facing the rapid-fire interrogation of a sharp-tongued prosecutor whose whole life and career had been dedicated to the complete and utter destruction of anyone fool enough to risk their life and liberty at trial. What would he be like, used as he was to the adoration of the crowd, suddenly subject to the hostile glances of a supposedly impartial jury that had just heard from a witness for the prosecution what a cold-blooded killer he really was?

What would he do when he finally realized that a murder trial was not a game? I was not sure. He was too different from most of those I had defended before; his personality was too unique, and too outsized, to fit any of the normal categories. Whatever the nature of his relationship with Matthew Stanton, it revealed a sensibility, an intelligence, that perhaps only Stanton had understood. He had given Allen serious books to read, and Allen had read them; read them and understood them, and, more than that, appreciated their value. He was, Thaddeus John Allen, a strange, or perhaps not so strange, enigma. He had read James Joyce, but he could not have told you the history of anything before his own birth. He was one of the most intelligent and, by the world's usual short-sighted standard, one of the least educated people I had ever met.

There was one more question that had to be asked. If he had not killed Matthew Stanton, who had?

"I don't know," he replied, puzzled by his inability to think of anyone who would have wanted his good friend dead. "He didn't have any friends, but he didn't have any enemies. None that he talked about."

"But he was angry and depressed that night?"

Allen's eyes grew wide with wonder. Stanton had been all that and more.

"It was like he had just found out something, something he had not known before, something that... If he had been married, or living with some woman, I would have thought he had caught her cheating, that he had been betrayed. It was that kind of anger."

We kept talking, and the more we talked, the easier it became. There was, I discovered, a remarkable generosity about him, what you see in the way a bigger boy looks after the kid all the others like to pick on. He had the kind of self-confidence that never doubted his ability or his courage. He was what every small boy wants to be when he grows up: a man of such great, overpowering strength, both of body and character, that no one would ever think to envy what he had. If only he could keep his temper.

The next morning, at precisely ten o'clock, I walked into Leonard Silverman's courtroom and announced that I was there, the attorney for the defense. Silverman did not seem the least surprised. The district attorney pretended she did not notice.

THREE

"Tell me, Mrs. McParland, have you ever thought of killing someone?"

The first question I asked on voir dire, and the district attorney was on her feet, shouting an objection.

"That question has no place in a jury trial! It has no place anywhere!"

There was no one quite as good at expressing outrage as Samantha Longstreet. Tall and willowy, wearing a dark gray skirt and jacket, her long, thin arms held straight at her sides, she clenched her hands tight, as if it were taking all her strength to control her scandalized emotions. She was so much the actress, always ready with her well-rehearsed lines, I almost applauded. They really were well-rehearsed, those few sharp, brittle words; learned by heart, the standard variations on a steady, consistent theme: anything she did not like was an unprecedented violation of the rules every lawyer was supposed to know and expected to follow. Leonard Silverman looked at her to see if she was serious.

"You don't think that if Mrs. McParland were to confess that she thinks about killing someone all the time, that might not be a reason to excuse her from serving on a jury?"

Glancing down at the jury box on his left, Silverman flashed a brief apologetic smile at the bemused, and mildly alarmed, Mrs. McParland, and then immediately turned back to the district attorney.

"You asked her if she could be fair and impartial. Mr. Antonelli has the right to assure himself that she can."

The moment Longstreet sprang out of her chair to object, I stood up, ready to respond, but Silverman just waived his hand. The issue had been decided. I sat down again at the counsel table closest to the jury box.

"Let me rephrase the question, Mrs. McParland. Have you ever thought about killing anyone—other than the lawyers who are asking you questions this morning?"

In her early fifties, with a round, pleasant face, Mary Ann McParland started to laugh. She looked up at Silverman.

"Am I under oath?"

"You are to answer the questions put to you honestly and to the best of your knowledge," replied Silverman in a firm, but kind voice that stopped the courtroom laughter before it could start. He had that kind of authority; a look, a glance, a single word had more effect than another judge's lengthy lecture from the bench.

"My first husband," admitted the good-natured Mrs. McParland. "Often wished I had," she continued, warming to the subject. "He was such a miserable, selfish, stupid, mindless... Spent most of his time drinking; could not hold a job, on those rare occasions when he had one. He—"

"Yes, Mrs. McParland; I think we get the picture," interjected Silverman, glancing up from a document he had been studying, probably a motion on which he had to rule in one of the other cases on his endless docket. "I think what you are trying to say, as

Mr. Antonelli asked, is that you sometimes had thoughts of murder." He started to go back to what he had been reading, but he could not resist. "Your former husband, you say. Tell me, is he still alive?"

"Sorry to say that he is, Your Honor!"

"So you didn't kill him after all. Glad to hear it, Mrs. McParland," he said, his voice trailing off as he went back to work.

I waited until she turned to look at me.

"You thought about killing someone, but you did not do it. Because you did not really think about it, did you? You did not plan to do it. Would that be the right way to put it?"

"Sure; I mean, that's correct. I thought about it, but I never thought about it seriously."

Twelve men and women had been called to the jury box, their names drawn at random from three dozen prospective jurors who had been brought into the courtroom. Each time I asked a question, they would look at me, and then look at the juror whose turn it was to answer. Jurors always looked comfortable and secure, ready to listen to all the evidence, ready to deliberate with all due consideration, ready to pass judgment, as if they had been doing nothing else all their lives. It was all theater, everyone an actor, each them trying to figure out how they were supposed to behave, what they were supposed to do, taking the measure, or trying to take the measure, of the others; hoping that when their time came to answer questions, they would do as well as those who had gone before. As nervous, or perhaps more nervous, as they had ever been, they tried to hide their fear behind fragile masks of stoic calm.

"You're scared as hell, aren't you, Mrs. McParland?" I asked with a sympathetic grin. "Here, in a crowded courtroom, with a couple of lawyers asking you questions, asking whether instead of serving as a juror you ought to be on trial for murder yourself."

Mary Ann McParland stared at me with the cheerful defiance of a would-be assassin.

"But I didn't kill him! He's still alive."

She was good, remarkably good. She bent forward, as if we were all alone and she was going to share a secret.

"You never asked me if I regretted it, that I didn't murder him."

Even Leonard Silverman had to laugh. I gave her a long, searching glance.

"This is a murder case, a murder trial. I ask all these questions because I need to make sure that you—that everyone on the jury—understand that words have more than one meaning. When you said, if you ever said to someone, 'I should have killed him,' or, 'I could have killed him,' or, 'I swear to God, I'm going to kill him,' that did not mean that you actually intended to do it. But, perhaps unfortunately, it's the way we sometimes express our anger, our frustration. We do not take such things literally."

She agreed. There was a difference between the literal and the actual meaning of words. I moved to the next question.

"You never seriously thought about killing your husband, your first husband, or anyone else, correct?"

"That's correct. Never seriously."

"But you have thought about the kind of situations in which killing someone would not only be permissible, but necessary. I'm not trying to confuse you. If someone kills someone because it is the only way to save their own life, it is self-defense, not murder. You would agree with that, would you not?"

I was not interested in the answer. I was not trying to find out what she thought; I was trying to get everyone to think about murder as more complicated, with more possible variations—with more excuses, if you will—than they had thought before. I must have spent close to half an hour going over the same ground with poor Mrs. McParland, exploring every kind of violent death, asking over and over again where she thought the line between what was and what was not justifiable homicide. Samantha Longstreet had had enough.

"Your Honor!" she protested, throwing up her hands in mock despair. "This isn't a law school seminar on the criminal law. This is a trial and—"

"Yes, I know," said Silverman. "Your objection is noted. Mr. Antonelli, it isn't clear to the court where this line of questioning is going; it isn't clear how any of it will help establish Mrs. McParland's fitness to serve as a juror."

"But of course it does, Your Honor," I remarked with all the false confidence I could summon. "The questions I am asking go to her ability to make distinctions, to appreciate the different degrees of culpability. They go to the issue of whether, after she has seen all the evidence, listened to all the witnesses, she is the kind of—"

"Really, Your Honor!" insisted Longstreet, her face turning red. "This is beyond belief! He isn't asking questions, he's telling the juror—telling the jury—how to think, how they should deliberate, how they should decide, and the trial has not even started yet."

I did not wait for Silverman; I knew what I was going to do next, and what would happen when I did.

"I'm sorry, Your Honor. The district attorney is right: I have asked too many questions about murder and what it means." I turned to Samantha Longstreet, standing at the counsel table on my left, less than five feet away. "I apologize to Ms. Longstreet for having become perhaps a little overzealous. But, as I'm sure she will understand, when you are representing someone charged with murder, a capital crime, representing someone you know is innocent, you—"

"Your Honor!" she cried, enraged at what I had just done. "I ask that be stricken from the record and that the jury—the jury we are supposed to be selecting—be instructed to ignore what the defense attorney has just said. He knows he is never allowed to express an opinion on the ultimate issue in the case. He knows—"

"That the defendant is presumed innocent as a matter of law. Is the district attorney saying that she presumes him guilty?" I asked, as if I were astonished at the possibility.

"He's been charged with murder," she reminded me with a withering glance of disapproval. "Of course I think he's guilty! Why else would we be...?"

She caught herself, but too late to undo the harm.

"The prosecution insists the defendant is guilty and we haven't yet heard from a single witness, but I'm not supposed to have an opinion on that same question? I must say, Your Honor, this seems like the classic double standard."

Leonard Silverman stared at the ceiling, but whether to search for patience or to stifle a laugh, I could not say. He turned to the twelve confused-looking people in the jury box.

"Mr. Antonelli is correct: The defendant is presumed innocent, a presumption that is to follow him throughout this trial, until, and unless, you determine that the prosecution has proven guilt beyond a reasonable doubt. Ms. Longstreet is correct: neither the defense attorney nor the prosecutor is permitted to express an opinion about the guilt or innocence of the defendant. They are only allowed to summarize the evidence during their closing arguments and show, or try to show, why it proves, or does not prove, the guilt of the defendant. Now, Mr. Antonelli, with this in mind, you may continue your examination."

I started asking the question while I was still standing.

"Mrs. McParland, does it make any difference to you—are you more inclined to believe the defendant must be guilty because the defendant is black?"

Longstreet had barely had time to sit down before she was flying out of her chair.

"Your Honor, I—"

But Silverman did not have to hear it.

"In chambers," he ordered in a brisk, efficient voice.

We had just settled into two armless chairs in front of Silverman's desk when Longstreet began to complain.

"I'm glad you at least had us come into chambers instead of doing this in front of all those prospective jurors. They have already been tainted by Antonelli's incredible disregard of the rules."

Leonard Silverman reached inside a black briefcase on the floor next to him, pulled out a blue thermos, unscrewed the cap, and poured himself a cup of coffee.

"It's better than what they make here," he explained. "Would either of you...? We have some other cups."

When he was sure we did not want anything, he took a long, slow drink of the still warm black coffee. The rain outside was coming down in torrents; the window looked like a ship's porthole in a storm at sea.

"You haven't tried a case against Mr. Antonelli, have you, Ms. Longstreet? Let me tell you what every prosecutor has discovered. He wins the case before the first witness ever testifies; he wins it on voir dire."

I sank lower in my chair, wondering what he was going to tell her next.

"By the time he is through asking questions, those people in there, people he has never met, will think he is the best friend they have ever had. None of those prospective jurors know anyone involved in the case, but they'll think they know him."

Longstreet was not impressed.

"He asks questions he has no business asking." Raising her narrow, rather pointed chin in an attitude of more than defiance, determination, she said what could only be considered a challenge. "No judge should allow it."

I thought Silverman would challenge her back, demand to know who she thought she was, telling him what he should and should not allow. Instead, he asked, quite calmly, "Why is that, Ms. Longstreet? Why do you believe no judge should allow Mr. Antonelli to ask what he asks?"

Intelligent, quick on her feet, a graduate of the Yale Law School, and before that a Rhodes Scholar, Longstreet had been trying high-profile cases most of her career. No one had to tell her what was permissible on voir dire. She was nobody's fool, but she could not even begin to guess what Leonard Silverman was talking about.

"I mean it, Ms. Longstreet. Why do you think the questions Mr. Antonelli asks should not be allowed?"

Tapping her fingers together, measuring her patience, she suddenly threw her hands open and laughed in bewilderment.

"For the reasons you just stated. They aren't intended to discover a bias; they are what you said they are: an attempt to ingratiate himself, to make the jurors think they can trust him, to convince them they should lean in his direction on any point in dispute!"

Silverman's head bobbed from side to side, a silent chorus to each of her complaints. He agreed with her, agreed with every word.

"You're right; that is exactly what Mr. Antonelli does. But that doesn't answer my question. What is wrong with it; why should it not be allowed? You don't believe me. I'm really quite serious. When you ask questions, what is it you are looking for? Not the answer. They all give the same answers. Ask anyone whether there is any reason they cannot be impartial. Once in a while someone will say they're not sure, but usually they say no. And yet you decide you don't want them on the jury. There is something about them you don't like, something that makes you think they might be more favorable to the defense. When you are asking questions, you are also answering questions they would like to ask you: Can they trust you? Should they believe you when you argue that the defendant's testimony is not credible? Mr. Antonelli does this with the questions he asks, and the way in which he asks them. I see no reason not to let him. As long as he stays within the bounds of propriety, I am perfectly prepared to give him all the time he wants and needs to complete voir dire. The defense, especially in a murder trial, should always be given the widest possible latitude in how it conducts its case, and in nothing more than in the selection of the jury. Don't you agree, Ms. Longstreet, now that you have had time to think about it?"

A brief smile, a triumph of self-restraint, slid sideways across her tightly closed mouth. With an even briefer nod, she remarked that she understood. I held the door open for her when we went back into the courtroom. She stared straight ahead and did not look at me once.

"You may continue, Mr. Antonelli," announced Judge Silverman as he took his place on the bench.

I began where I had left off.

"I asked you, Mrs. McParland, whether it might make any difference in your ability to be fair and impartial that the defendant, T. J. Allen, is black."

To everyone's surprise, she replied that it might.

"Not because he's black, but because I know who he is."

"You know him personally?"

"We've never met, but like everyone else, I know who he is. I watched him play for years."

The look in her eyes told me, and told everyone else, that she could never believe that T. J. Allen, who had been a star on a team she loved, could ever murder anyone. I might not have asked another question, but there were eleven other jurors yet to choose and she had given me an opportunity I might not get again.

"There are certain well-known facts that, without our

wanting them to, can affect the way we think about the issue of race. The percentage of black men in prison is three or four times their percentage of the population. What do you think the cause? Is it because black men are more likely to commit crimes, or are they more likely to be arrested and sent to prison because the system is racist?"

Samantha Longstreet slid to the edge of her chair. She could hardly stop herself from screaming an objection.

"I don't think it is either one," said Mrs. McParland, nodding forcefully. "I think it is poverty, poverty and drugs. You don't have higher crime rates in Oakland and Richmond than you have here, in Pacific Heights, because more black people live across the bay."

"You think, in other words, that the case is mainly economics?"

"Absolutely. You don't see rich people mugging other people on the street. You only see rich people stealing from their investors."

"You said that you had watched the defendant play, but that you don't know him personally. Do you know any black people personally? Let me be more specific. Do you have any black friends?"

"Close friends, as opposed to people I've known at work? Then, no, I'm afraid I don't."

I started to ask another question, but she raised her hand.

"You asked about friends; you did not ask about relatives. My husband, my second husband, is black."

She was perfect. She took every question head on and seemed determined to do the right thing, whatever the right thing might turn out to be. There was still one more question; three questions, really, all part of the same one. Sitting as straight as I could, I bent slightly toward her and smiled my encouragement.

"Do you believe that everyone should obey the law?"

"Yes, of course; everyone should obey the law."

"Even you?" I asked without any change of expression.

It took a moment before she realized I was serious.

"Yes, of course; even me," she replied, wondering how I could even think to ask.

"At the end of the trial, after the district attorney has made her closing argument and after I have made mine, Judge Silverman is going to instruct you on the law you have to follow. He is going to tell you that you may not find the defendant guilty unless the prosecution has proven his guilt beyond a reasonable doubt. My question is this: if after deliberating with all the other jurors, you believe the defendant probably did it, probably committed the crime, but that the prosecution has not proven it beyond a reasonable doubt, will you follow Judge Silverman's instruction—will you follow the law—and return a verdict of not guilty?"

Mary Ann McParland did not have to think about it. She would do what the law required.

Samantha Longstreet acted as if that question gave all the advantage to her.

"Let me ask you the question Mr. Antonelli just asked," she said to the next prospective juror, a young Asian man. "At the end of the trial, if you think that the prosecution has proven guilt beyond a reasonable doubt, will you follow Judge Silverman's instruction—will you follow the law—and return a verdict of guilty?"

The answer, of course, was yes.

I watched with growing fascination the way Longstreet went about her business. She could in less than two sentences make the kind of contact with a juror that made it seem they had always been good friends. Her questions might have seemed trivial, and almost irrelevant, to someone who had not spent their lives in a courtroom. What difference did it make if she had once spent a few days in the same state in which a prospective juror had been raised, or that she had once had an office just around the corner from where another juror now worked? What difference if she mentioned to a die-hard Giants baseball fan that she had played softball in college but had not been very good? No difference at all, if you have never tried a case, or have no understanding of the scope and reach of human sympathy. She could object all she wanted when I was asking the same kind of questions, but she knew how important it was that the jury liked her, that the jury trusted that she would never tell them anything she did not honestly believe. I could only marvel at the hypocrisy.

Voir dire went on forever, a contest which of us could ask more questions, which of us could take more time. What should have taken ten minutes took hours, and, strangely enough, no one seemed to mind. The questions might have been the same, but the answers seldom were. The jurors were different people of different ages and different backgrounds, some of them born in San Francisco, others only recently arrived. Most trial court judges would have hurried us along, letting us know with growing impatience we were only wasting time. Leonard Silverman seemed quite prepared to let us talk ourselves to death, if not from exhaustion, then old age. Finally, a week after we started, we were finished and the jury was sworn.

After the jury had been excused and Judge Silverman had left the bench, T. J. Allen leaned back and stretched his arms.

"Jesus, man, you do this all the time? I got worn out just listening." There was a shrewd glint in his eyes. "You talk like someone in a book, one of those novels I used to read with Matthew." His eyes grew softer and became introspective. "Must be something to be able to do that, talk that way."

His expression changed with everything he said. His eyes would widen with surprise or approval, and then, an instant later, close halfway in search of the doubtful meaning in something he had just heard. He had more different looks than words.

"I see what you mean, though," he said, shaking his head. "About a suit and tie. How it makes things seem more serious. I saw that right away, the way the jury looks at you."

There was not much that Thaddeus John Allen did not notice.

Four

Sitting in the wingback chair in front of my desk, Albert Craven tugged gently on his starched shirt cuffs, crossed his right leg over his left, and stared at me with as serious a look as he had ever given me.

"You want to know about the Stantons? The only thing I can tell you is that whatever anyone thinks they know, they're wrong. San Francisco holds half the secrets in the world, and, one way or the other, most of them involve that one family. Remember when people used to say there was a fine line between genius and insanity? That line disappeared among the Stantons. Matthew's father, Emmett Douglas Stanton, was certifiable; his mother..."

Craven's aging eyes rolled up toward the ceiling. With a rhythmic motion that seemed to confirm a doubt, he turned up the palms of his fragile, blue-veined hands and began to balance an imaginary weight, the burden of his confusion.

"There isn't any way to measure what went on with her. None of it was normal. She was, years ago, the best-looking woman in the city. She was also the least contented, and the least stable, woman I have ever known. It was extraordinary what she would do. You might have dinner with her one night along with a few other people, and then, the next day, if you ran into her somewhere, she might walk right past you. Your best friend one day, a perfect stranger the next. Maybe she was the reason Emmett became so erratic. He really was in love with her. He was never the same after she left him."

"Left him? Divorced him? When?"

"Five or six years ago; I'm not really sure."

"How long after that did he marry his second wife?"

"Not long; a year, maybe two."

"Even though, as you just said, he was certifiable?"

"Probably because he was certifiable," remarked Craven with a droll expression. "Of course, if that was the reason, I should have been committed years ago, given how often I have made that same fatal mistake. Well, never mind. It isn't that he got married; it is who he married. But he was certifiable. Whether it was simply his condition—some flaw, some defect that would inevitably have taken control of his mind—or whether he was driven to it by Victoria..."

Craven pulled himself up out of the chair and walked across the enormous room, with its thick oriental carpets scattered over the gleaming mahogany floor, past the bookcases that lined the length of one of the walls, past the gray marble fireplace that had not been used, if it had ever been used, since sometime before the Second World War. He stood at the window and looked out. It was my office, but it was his building, purchased when the firm he had started nearly half a century ago became one of the most successful in the city.

"Did I ever tell you this used to be my office?" he asked, staring at the sun-streaked sky of an autumn afternoon. "I wanted you to have it," he went on, his voice becoming stronger and more vibrant as he spoke. "I thought we should do everything possible to make the fact that one of the great criminal defense attorneys had joined the firm seem almost respectable. Most of our clients —what you might call the financial backbone of the city—are among the biggest scoundrels and thieves around, but they have too much money to think themselves criminals. I used to tell some of them that we brought you in because of how often they talked about killing off the competition. The strange thing—well, not too strange: some of them are really quite stupid—is how often they thought I was serious."

He turned to me, his eyes lit like candles.

"Now, of course, after everything you have done, everyone thinks this is Joseph Antonelli's firm. Instead of dull conversations about trusts and estates and corporate governance, my clients want to know what murder case you're going to take next." He looked down at the tips of his black shined shoes. "They all want to know whether there is really a chance you can win the Stanton murder trial."

I could only shake my head at the idle curiosity of the uninformed.

"You can tell them that I don't have any chance at all. Now, tell me more about the father. What you started to tell me. He's dead, isn't he? But you knew him?"

I wondered why I bothered to ask. I had not needed Leonard Silverman to remind me that Albert Craven knew everyone in San Francisco, and that everyone, at least among the relatively small number who thought themselves the only people worth knowing, knew him. Albert could trace to three, or even four generations the lineage of every prominent family in the city; not from some antiquarian interest in the origins of things, but because he had been personally acquainted with all of them. He knew things about people they did not know themselves.

"Emmett died just last year, while mountain climbing in the Alps. It was reported as an accident, but there were rumors that instead of falling to his death, he simply let go of the rope because, in his madness, he thought he could fly. Whatever the truth, whatever the cause of his death, there was very little doubt, among those who knew him best, that for a number of years Emmett Stanton had been completely insane."

An unexpected look of cheerful cynicism cut across Albert Craven's soft, pear-shaped mouth.

"This, you understand, isn't at all inconsistent with the general, and widespread, belief that Emmett Douglas Stanton was a financial genius. It was precisely his success with numbers—those abstractions by which we conceal, and, having concealed, eventually forget the real world—that caused him, gradually at first, then with increasing speed, to withdraw into a world of his own numerical construction. He became, in other words, what nearly everyone else wants to be. That, at least, is what Matthew Stanton told me shortly after his father's unfortunate death."

The light outside had grown dim, and it had begun to rain. Albert, who noticed everything, noticed this. Reacting the way he nearly always did when the sun went missing and the weather turned cold, he shoved his hands into his suit coat pockets and bent his shoulders as if he were bracing for a storm. He had become, with advancing age, his own barometer.

"I knew him, of course. I did not know him well, however, and I was a little surprised when he called and asked me to lunch at the Fairmont. He lived there, or rather, just across the street, in an apartment at the top of Nob Hill. He had a house—a house! A twenty-thousand-square-foot chateau down in Hillsborough, the kind of place where a thousand people go to party on long, endless weekends, but, from what I have been told, there were seldom any guests. He moved to the Nob Hill apartment when his father remarried. Emmett and his new wife lived a few miles away in Woodside. Matthew did not want to be that close to them. That, by the way, is all he said about that: that he did not want to be that close. He did not give any reason."

Craven tried to remember exactly what had been said. He wanted to repeat as accurately as possible the important conversation he had had with Matthew Stanton.

"You have seen the photographs they use in the papers and on television. They're not even close. He was astonishingly good looking. He had this marvelous boyish quality, brownish blond hair, and the bluest eyes I think I have ever seen. Medium height, slight of built, with as gentle a smile as you could imagine. If I had to choose just one word to describe him, that would be it: gentle, gentle in everything he did, the soft way he spoke, the easy, casual way he moved, the way he made you feel there was not anything he would not do for you and that he would be disappointed if you did not ask. Like most first impressions, it was impossible, or almost impossible, to free yourself from it, even when, as you learned later, he was as single-minded, as ruthless, if you will, as anyone you had encountered. The world thought him a wealthy, reclusive young man with charming good manners and not a thought in his head. The world was wrong.

"He had invited me to lunch, he explained, because he wanted to talk to me about his father. I just told you how Emmett Stanton had become progressively more erratic. It was almost the first thing Matthew mentioned, though not in the way I would have expected.

"'He had to have been insane,' he said, shaking his head.

"This was not said with regret, or the slightest sympathy. No, it was as if he was simply stating an established fact. It was almost clinical, the detachment of an analyst, a trained observer whose only interest is in the cause, or the question of whether there is any cause at all.

"'He was completely honest; he never cheated anyone. What better proof of insanity could you have?'

"He said this with a grin that, I have to confess, completely disarmed me. He understood my reaction. He became quite serious.

"'He ran a hedge fund; there was not anyone who did not want to invest with him. Imagine a Bernie Madoff who was not a fraud. He had this ability—God knows where he got it; my father could never explain it—to see how things were going to change before anyone else even suspected a change was going to happen. He had a gift. Isn't that the word we use when we don't have any idea why someone is able to do something we can't? He told me once that a lot of what he did, a lot of what he knew, just came to him. He would be sitting at his desk, watching the stock market report of that day's trading, and suddenly knew, just knew, what to do next. Sometimes, he told me—and this is just incredible—it would come to him at night, when he was sound asleep. That's right, he would have a dream, and the dream would tell him, would show him, what he was going to do. He said it was like watching a movie about what was going to happen the next day, the next week, the next month. Does that sound like a normal person?

"'That was not all he dreamed about. He often dreamed he could fly. It was always the same dream. He wasn't flying off a building, he wasn't flying over the Golden Gate Bridge. It was much more prosaic, much more achievable, if I can put it like that. He would be standing still, and then, like someone standing waist deep in a pool, just stretch out and, using his arms the way you do in the breaststroke, glide through the air; not very far off the ground, just a few feet, and not very fast, no faster than if he were swimming.'

"And then, right after he said this, Matthew leaned toward me, and with a piercing glance that seemed somehow at odds with the tight, derisive smile at the corners of his mouth, remarked, 'I'll bet you even money that's what he was doing when he let go of the rope and stepped out into the air up on that mountain in the

Alps.' There was a long pause. His eyes turned cold and bitter. 'If it really was an accident; if he really died the way they said he did.'

"Matthew's eyes were really quite remarkable. They seemed to tell a dozen different stories, suggest a dozen different possibilities, interpreting, as it were, what he was saying, an interpretation that made you wonder how much he actually believed of what he was telling you. Speech, with him, became a kind of challenge, a dare to see if you could follow in all its various, sometimes sinister, implications what he seemed to be saying. His father had been insane, but then, so he made it sound, it was a cynic's joke. Emmett had not been insane at all, only an honest man in a world of charlatans and thieves. An honest, brilliant man whose brilliance depended on voices and visions in his head; all his instructions given to him in dreams! Dreams in which he learned to fly; not, however, with any grace and speed, none of what a normal crazy person would find irresistible in the bird-like fantasy of soaring high above the crowd. Nothing like it, only flight in slow motion, flight so close to the ground that if flight failed, neither injury nor death could possibly result. That, you have to admit—I swear this is the very thought I had, the thought I read in Matthew Stanton's story teller eyes—is as prudent a form of insanity as it is possible to imagine. There is also this: it was a dream; a frequently recurring dream, it is true, but, for all that, still a dream. Emmett Stanton had never thought, never suggested, he could really do it."

The longer Albert Craven talked, the more intrigued he became with what Matthew Stanton had told him. Part of the interest, of course, lie in the fact that Stanton had been murdered. Was there some connection, something about the reason Stanton had wanted to see him that might explain why Stanton had been killed?

"Yes, you're right," agreed Albert when I asked. "Nothing definite; a feeling only. It was clear he did not think his father had been insane. He thought his father's attempt to explain his success, his ability to see things a little earlier than everyone else, as good a description of intuition as you were likely to get."

Albert gave me a significant look, and then remarked, "You do it in court all the time, have an immediate sense of what a witness is going to say, and have the next question ready without any conscious thought of what that question is going to be. That is what Emmett had. And Matthew was right, what he said about someone having a gift. It's the word we use to cover our ignorance about how someone can have the ability to do things other people cannot."

There was a long silence. Albert Craven sat still as night, staring into the distance, pondering, as it seemed, the vast, unbridgeable gulf between the working assumptions of our everyday lives and what we ever actually know about anything.

"This was all by way of preparation, a way of drawing me in. He wanted me to feel that what he suspected—more than suspected, what he knew—had to be true; that it did not matter that there was no proof, no evidence, to support it, it was the only possible explanation for what had happened, and what, he was certain, was going to happen next."

"What was going to happen next?" I asked. "I'm afraid I'm not following."

"His father's death was not an accident; Emmett Stanton did not think he could fly; he didn't jump to his death on purpose. His father had been murdered, and he was going to be murdered as well."

Folding his arms across his narrow chest, Albert Craven bent his small round head to the side. He looked at me, waiting for my reaction. I did not have one. I had spent too many years in courtrooms to be very much surprised by anything. Albert, who had never tried a case, thought even talk of murder something like an irresistible sin. He could barely pronounce the word without lowering his voice. His eyes darted from side to side as if, though we were alone, we might be overheard.

"His father was murdered, and he knew who did it. His stepmother had killed him, or had him killed, and because he knew what they had done, he was going to—"

"He knew what 'they' had done?"

"His stepmother and the man she married, Michael Kensington."

"But why was Matthew Stanton telling you this? You said you did not know him all that well. Why would he confide in you? What did he really want?"

"To tell him everything I could about Kensington. He had discovered that Kensington and his stepmother had been having an affair. He believed they decided to get rid of his father so that, instead of what she might get in a divorce, they could get everything his father had; and, remember, Emmett Stanton was one of the richest men in the country. Matthew wanted to know everything he could about Kensington, because, as he explained, there did not seem to be anything to know. He was right about that: there wasn't anything to know."

The look in Albert's eyes told me there was a great deal more to it than that, and that Michael Kensington was far more interesting than what the absence of knowledge seemed to suggest.

"If you met Kensington at a cocktail party, you would remember him, even if you could not remember anything else, but you would not remember much, if anything, about him, only that he was there. He is one of those people everyone knows, but think that everyone else knows better. You are never surprised to see him, and you would not really notice if you did not. Try to imagine someone who, even when he is on center stage, is still, somehow, behind the scenes. It is when you don't see him that he seems to exercise an almost magnetic pull.

"There really wasn't much I could tell Matthew that he did

not already know. I ended up learning more from him than he did from me. Everything about Kensington is fragmentary, unfinished. He was born here, in San Francisco, into a wealthy family. His grandfather owned a shipping line and made a fortune when the government needed his ships in the Second World War. Kensington must have been a very good student. He went to Princeton, but left school in his junior year. He was in Los Angeles for a while, had something to do with the movies, but then, a few years ago, came back to San Francisco. There is no end to the rumors as to how much money he has or how he got it, but you won't find anyone who thinks he earned it."

"Or anyone who avoids his company because of their suspicions," I ventured.

"It's San Francisco. Honesty, sobriety, self-discipline, hard work—what kind of place do you think this is?" He laughed as he got to his feet. "'All the adventurers in the world, blown here by the winds of heaven.' Isn't that the way Robert Louis Stevenson described it a hundred years ago? Times change, people come and go, but San Francisco will always be what it has always been: a sinner's paradise. Although, much as I hate to admit it, the sins have become small time. Even worse, we seem to have lost the ability, or the willingness, to be proud of the crimes we commit. Everyone is too afraid of saying the wrong thing, offending someone by not agreeing with what everyone else thinks they want to hear."

As quickly as he had gotten up, he sat down again. A look of gleeful astonishment spread across his whitish pink face.

"That's the problem, isn't it? No one can break the rules anymore because all the old rules have disappeared. Divorce used to be not just difficult, but scandalous, which made adultery adventurous. Even murder was more serious. It was not random; kids did not get killed because other kids had guns and had watched too many violent movies and video games. Everything now lacks depth. There are no great love affairs; there is no great longing, one person for another. Sex is as common, and means even less, than a good-night kiss meant when I was young enough to lay awake nights wondering if the girl I was in love with would let me hold her hand, when I had to have a pocketful of quarters to call long distance a girl I did not want to lose while I was away at college. It is one of the reasons I was drawn to Matthew Stanton: he was not a prisoner of the present; he still had what they used to call the tragic sense. He wanted to go back to the beginning to understand what had happened, and then do something about it: seek justice, take revenge, the same way someone would have done as far back in history as you want to go. It is classic, when you think about it. Shakespearian, the stuff of Greek drama: a woman betrays her husband for her lover, a father dies and a son finds his stepmother to blame."

"But all we really know," I reminded him, "is that Matthew Stanton was murdered. We don't know anything about his father's death, other than that it was ruled an accident and that Matthew Stanton thought otherwise. As far as his stepmother and Michael Kensington, all we know is that they got married. Everything else..."

"Is what Matthew Stanton insisted was true; what, when I was with him, I believed."

"Believed he believed, or believed it was true?"

"Both. He had no evidence in the usual sense, but he had something perhaps more convincing: the gift, like his father had, an intuition about what happened and what was going to happen. It is what I told you before. Matthew Stanton was not what the world thought he was. He had far more depth than what everyone believed. If he had lived, who knows what he might have done, what he might have become."

Night comes early in November. The lights of the city had already started dancing in the darkness on the streets outside. I was in no hurry to leave, and neither was he. There was no place we had to be for another hour when, together, we would drive to his house in the Marina where a dozen or so of his innumerable good friends were waiting to surprise him on his birthday, a secret he had known for weeks.

"The good news, I suppose," he mused as he stretched his legs out in front of him, "is they won't be able to find enough candles to put on the cake, and even if they could, they would not know how many to use. No one really knows how old I am, and I've damn near forgotten. But I'm not that much younger than Willie Brown, our one-time mayor. I wish he still held the job. He brought a kind of classy flamboyance to it that the city needs. I can't remember if he was ever married—yes, I'm sure he was. But he was always dating good-looking women who kept getting younger, and people began to talk. So Willie explained that he was only following a law of mathematics: always date a woman whose age, combined with his own, did not exceed one hundred. I think he was in his sixties when he said that. He isn't doing that anymore. She would not be old enough to walk. You can get arrested for that kind of thing."

The memory of Willie Brown and what San Francisco had been brought a look of nostalgia into his eyes. There had been magic here, the city more a dream than a reality, like a woman you kept seeing in the distance, the one who would change your life forever if only you could, just this once, get close enough to lose yourself in her eyes. She was there, waiting, waiting for you, until, just before you got there, when you were just steps away, she decided you were not coming and, turning on her heel, she vanished into the night.

"If I were starting over, I would not live here, in the city. I would live where you do, the other side of the bridge, on a hillside in Sausalito where you can watch the city change with the lights and the weather and remember life the way it used to be. On the other hand," he remarked, breaking into a huge smile, "if I had ever met anyone like Tangerine, I would not much care where I lived."

It was true. Tangerine made you forget everything but her. She was that woman, the one you kept seeing in the distance, the one who would change your life forever, if only you could get close enough to meet. The difference was that when I got close enough, only steps away, she waited and did not leave. She was waiting, along with Albert Craven's wife and a dozen other people, as I arrived at Albert Craven's home, waiting as I stood there watching how easily he pretended surprise that anyone would ever think his birthday important enough to remember.

Five

I have never really understood why anyone would want to be a coroner. A physician was supposed to save lives, not study dead bodies. I knew that finding the cause of someone's death helped us learn how to treat what might otherwise kill us, but that did not explain why this particular field of medicine has been chosen by those who practiced it. The real reason, I thought, was that they simply liked mysteries. You cannot heal the dead. The first rule of medicine—do no harm—obviously had no relevance. The question for the coroner was not how to make the patient better; the question was how he died, which meant, in a homicide case, how he had been murdered. It was the question that had made the prosecution's first witness, Elizabeth Burroughs, the best-known author in America, a fact I brought up at the beginning of my cross-examination.

"Dr. Burroughs, when you were asked by the district attorney to list your educational background and your professional accomplishments, you left something out, didn't you?"

I was standing at the far end of the jury box, my hand resting on the wooden railing. Elizabeth Burroughs looked straight at me. She wore thick glasses and spoke with slow, measured words in a way that might have reminded you of a school librarian had it not been for a wide, rapacious mouth that kept twitching at the corners. She did not answer my question; she wanted me to make it more specific. She did not want to appear immodest.

"You are the author of nearly a dozen best-selling novels, novels in which the central character is a pathologist, a county coroner in San Francisco, are you not?"

The nervous twitching stopped. She smiled at me as if I had asked her to autograph one of her books. Elizabeth Burroughs had made millions writing barely readable fiction. It was common knowledge, or at least a common belief, that she continued as coroner only because it was her best source of new material.

"Yes," she replied, "I have been lucky enough to have written a few things the public seems to like."

"The cause of death plays a major role in the novels you write, doesn't it? In fact, it is always the central mystery."

With more than an author's normal vanity, she refused to admit that her novels could be described in such narrow, conventional terms. She doubted I had read them, or understood them if I had.

"The cause of death is of great importance. That's true; but it isn't just a question of how the victim was killed, it is the question of why someone wanted them dead. Without that, without the question of motivation, I'm afraid you wouldn't have much of a novel."

"And part of the motivation, I take it, is the question of how someone decides to commit murder in a particular way. Isn't that what your readers find particularly appealing? How a murder is committed, the sometimes complicated way it is done to avoid detection? If I remember correctly, you often have the killer inject a lethal substance just beneath the tongue, where detection is almost impossible, but where, of course, in your novels, the coroner always finds it."

She did not like the suggestion that her novels might in some way be repetitive, that the plot line seldom varied.

"There have been a whole variety of techniques by which the killer tries to conceal the cause of death. That is what makes a good mystery: the puzzle that has to be solved."

She said this with evident pride. It was there in bold letters on the jacket of every book she had written, the promise that this, her latest thriller, had more surprises than anything she had written before.

"I haven't read all your novels, Dr. Burroughs. Have you written one in which the coroner had nothing more to say about the cause of death than what you said here today: the victim died from a single gunshot to the head?"

The lines in her forehead deepened, her lips pressed tightly together.

"Well, I've certainly had murders in which the victim was killed by a gunshot, but a single shot to the head... No, I don't think so."

"Have you written one in which the murder weapon, the gun, was just dropped on the floor?"

Her eyes lit up. She was eager to answer.

"Yes, I did that once; in my second novel, the one in which—"

"How much did Matthew Stanton weigh?" I asked before she could finish.

"How much did...?"

"How much did Matthew Stanton weigh? You did weigh him, didn't you, as part of your autopsy, and measure his height?"

"Yes, of course."

She started to glance at a small black notebook she held in her lap.

"A hundred sixty-two pounds, isn't that correct?" I asked.

"Yes. I mean, I believe that is correct. I would have to check my—"

"He was five feet ten inches, isn't that correct?"

"Yes," she replied, closing her notebook.

I turned to T. J. Allen, sitting next to me, and asked him to stand up.

"How tall do you think Mr. Allen is?"

Elizabeth Burroughs bent forward, measuring him with her eyes.

"Six foot five, or six foot six.

"Six feet eight inches. And what would you guess is his weight?"

She shook her head. She was not sure.

"Two hundred forty-five pounds. My question, Dr. Burroughs, is this: if you were writing a novel, would you have someone six foot eight, two hundred forty-five pounds, murder someone ten inches shorter and eighty-five pounds lighter with a gun?" I asked incredulously. "Wouldn't you have him strangle him or kill him with a blow to the head?"

Samantha Longstreet was on her feet.

"Dr. Burroughs may write crime novels, but she at least knows the difference between fiction and reality. The issue isn't what some made-up character might do; the issue is how the victim, the real victim, Matthew Stanton, died!"

Judge Silverman looked at me to see if I wanted to respond.

"The witness testified that Matthew Stanton died from a gunshot wound. Imagine that this was a case in which the victim died of a physical beating. It would certainly be a legitimate question whether the defendant was capable of doing this if she were an eighty-year-old woman in a wheelchair. Mr. Allen is an extremely large and extremely strong human being. It is therefore equally legitimate to ask the coroner—who has made a career writing about the probabilities involved in murder—whether the defendant, had he wanted to kill Matthew Stanton, needed a gun to do it."

"We're not talking about probabilities, Your Honor," argued Longstreet. "This is testimony about the cause of death, not all the other ways the victim might have been murdered!"

She was right, and Silverman knew I knew it.

"Mr. Antonelli?"

"I'll withdraw the question, Your Honor." As I started to turn back to the witness, I glanced at the jury. "The answer isn't important, only the question."

Thinking I was through with her, Elizabeth Burroughs started to get up.

"You always have a surprise ending in your stories, don't you?"

She was halfway out of the witness stand. With one hand on the arm of the chair, she looked to see if this was really a question.

"I try to keep the reader guessing."

Though she tried not to show it, she could not conceal her irritation. She was there to testify about what she had found as the coroner, not answer questions about the way she constructed the mysteries that had made her rich and famous. Her eyes, never very friendly, were filled with malice. I was trying to make a fool of her, and she wanted me to know that she did not like it, did not like it one bit.

"It's never the most obvious suspect, is it? Never the one that all the evidence seems to say it is, is it, Dr. Burroughs?"

"Yes, but that's fiction, Mr. Antonelli, and as Ms. Longstreet just pointed out, fiction is not reality."

"No, it isn't," I agreed, tapping my fingers hard on the jury box railing for emphasis. "Life is stranger than fiction, isn't it? Or is that just something I read in some novel? One last question. The only thing you know for certain, the only evidence you have, is that Matthew Stanton was killed by a bullet to the head, isn't that correct?"

"That is the cause of death."

"Which is all you can testify to with respect to the question of causation, correct?"

There was a slight doubt, a moment's hesitation. My words meant one thing, but something in my voice seemed to suggest something else.

"As I said, I can testify—I have testified—to the cause of death."

"But that isn't your only connection to the case, is it, Dr. Burroughs?"

You could feel the change of mood, the sense of anticipation, as everyone—the spectators in the courtroom, the members of the jury—waited to see what this mysterious new connection might be. Burroughs did not answer, and I wondered why. There was nothing particularly sinister in what I knew. I walked the few short steps to the counsel table, reached inside my briefcase, and took out a newspaper clipping. I handed it to the witness.

"Do you remember this, a dinner three years ago to honor you after your most recent novel had won a national award? Do you remember who you were sitting next to at the head table? It's right there, in the photograph you're holding in your hand."

She looked at the newspaper photograph and glanced at her name in the headline.

"Emmett Stanton," she reported. She did not seem to understand the significance of this, what bearing it could have on the case.

"He's sitting on one side, but who is sitting on the other? Matthew Stanton, isn't it?"

She looked again, just to be sure.

"Yes, but—"

"You weren't just sitting there, at the head table, because you had won a literary prize, were you?"

"I don't know what you mean. That was the reason for the dinner. You said so yourself."

"I mean that you would have been sitting there had the dinner been for some completely different purpose, something that had nothing to do with you. I mean, Dr. Burroughs, that you had a close, continuing connection with the Stanton family. Among other things, you were on the board of directors of the Stanton Foundation, weren't you?"

"Yes, I was—I mean, I am, but—"

"But that didn't affect what you did as coroner in this case. Is that what you were going to say?"

"Before you interrupted me, yes, that is exactly what—"

"When you perform an autopsy, in addition to the specific cause of death, do you not also determine whether there are any other wounds, any broken bones, abrasions, any other injuries?"

"That's right."

"And, in addition, whether the deceased was suffering from any disease?"

"That's correct."

I stared at her with disbelief as I went to the counsel table and for the second time reached inside my briefcase.

"This is your report, the official coroner's report. I've read it," I said as I held it up for her, and the jury, to see. "There is nothing in it about any injuries or any illness."

"Are you questioning the validity of my report?" she demanded with a withering, hostile glance.

"I'm questioning a lot of things, Dr. Burroughs. You were close to the Stantons," I said forcefully. "You often spent time with Mrs. Stanton socially, isn't that correct?"

"I see her from time to time," she replied cautiously. "We

sometimes had lunch. She was part of a book club where I would—"

"Sometimes give lectures for some of Mrs. Stanton's other wealthy friends. What do you lecture about, the workings of the coroner's office, the procedures you follow when you conduct an autopsy? Is that what they pay you—they do pay you, don't they? —to lecture about?"

She was glaring at me. What right did I have to ask her what she did? She refused to answer. She just sat there, daring me to do something about it.

"You're wrong, Dr. Burroughs," I insisted, to her obvious confusion. "Wrong to think that none of this matters; and you, more than most people, should know it. All the books you have written, all the paid for lectures, are crime stories, stories in which one of the most crucial elements is the connection, the sometimes secret connection, among the different characters. What is curious about this case is that everyone seems to have known everyone else. Among others, as it turns out, you knew them all."

I started to turn away, finished with my cross-examination. Then I stopped.

"One last thing, or perhaps I should say, one last chance. Dr. Burroughs, you did not find in that thorough, professional autopsy you performed on Matthew Stanton any sign of injury or any sign of illness?"

"You read the report," she repeated with a lethal stare.

"And did not find a word in it about how Matthew Stanton was dying of AIDS," I said, staring right back. "Which raises the question, doesn't it, Dr. Burroughs, of why someone would murder a dying man."

As soon as I sat down, T. J. Allen was whispering in my ear that he did not believe it.

"Are you sure? He never said anything. Maybe he just found out; maybe that's why he was so angry and depressed."

Allen could not be sure, and I was not sure of much of anything. I certainly was not sure of the question I had just asked. It may have seemed dramatic, asking why anyone would want to murder a dying man, but it assumed that whoever murdered Stanton, or had him murdered, knew he was dying. The only thing I was sure about was that Burroughs had not included the fact of Stanton's illness in her official report. This was more than negligence; it was a conscious attempt to conceal evidence. There seemed to be only one reason why she would have done it.

"She was doing the family a favor," suggested Albert Craven with a shrug of his shoulders. "What other reason could she have? You can call what she did concealing evidence, but she would not have seen it that way. It didn't have anything to do with the cause of death, did it? Matthew Stanton was shot to death, the way she said. What difference if he would have eventually died of something else?"

"What difference? Maybe all the difference in the world. How do we know it did not have something to do with the motive? How do we know he had not given someone else the disease, and, if he had, how that person might have reacted? How do we know—how would our great mystery-writing coroner know—how a jury might react to the possibility that someone Matthew Stanton infected might have taken revenge? It might be enough to give a jury at least a reason to doubt that T. J. Allen is guilty."

We were sitting in my office. I had just come back from court. Perhaps because Craven had never tried a case, he seemed to like nothing more than to hear all about any trial of mine. It was more interesting, more exciting, when, instead of dealing with all the dull technicalities, the endless questions of procedure, the mind-numbing repetitive legal arguments, he only had to hear about what had happened that might make a difference in what the jury might decide.

"Burroughs put in jeopardy not just her career, but her reputation. It doesn't make sense. Did she really think I wouldn't bother to get Stanton's medical records?"

Craven was sitting in his ageless dignity, his small, manicured hands folded in his lap, his pale blue eyes shining with a schoolboy's eager curiosity. I started to laugh.

"I just realized why you have so many friends. They all know they can tell you anything, things they would never tell anyone else. They probably never stop to ask themselves why they trust you the way they do. It's because you are too honest ever to tell anyone the truth."

His round shoulders lurched forward, his smooth, unlined face turned a deeper shade of pink.

"Too honest to tell the truth, not too honest not to lie. I catch your meaning." Amused, but with what was still a puzzled expression, he scratched the side of his forehead. "I would never tell anyone what someone told me. Yes, but that is a simple enough rule of conduct. I'm an attorney, not some tabloid journalist. Of course I keep in confidence what someone tells me. You do the same thing."

"I don't have the same temptations," I reminded him, tilting my head to study him from a different angle. "I don't have lunch with different people eight days a week; I'm not invited to every dinner in town that has more than four invited guests. My name isn't mentioned in the Sunday paper when they list the prominent people who attended that week's most important, and most exclusive, social event."

Albert Craven bubbled with mirth. He could barely sit still, he was so eager to get in his own, unanswerable retort.

"But your name is the first one mentioned every time there is a murder. Think of it this way: if it weren't for dead bodies, both you and Elizabeth Burroughs would be out of work."

"That would be difficult," I admitted. "She would have to

start writing about the living instead of the dead. Is there a market for lesbian romance?"

"You're asking me? Probably; I don't know why there wouldn't be. Have you ever read anything she has written?"

"Just enough to get ready to cross-examine her: a few pages from three or four of her novels; enough to get a sense of what she writes about. Her characters all seem pretty much the same. They're almost mechanical. You never have to stop and think about anything she says. I found them boring, predictable, heavy on graphic descriptions of sex and violence, nothing left to the imagination, especially when she is describing an autopsy. It is like reading a clinician's handbook; all you want to do is get to the end of it."

"And every same-sounding book she writes ends up on the bestseller list," said Craven, throwing up his hands. "The only book worth reading," he went on, becoming more serious, "is one that, when you finish it, you want to read again. No one would ever want to do that, read a second time, anything Elizabeth Burroughs has ever written. But that isn't why she is so successful. Everyone now is addicted to crime; watching movies about it, reading books about it, newspapers, magazines, the internet. It is the great escape, that and sports, a way to forget the boredom of their lives.

"Remember *Brave New World*, the novel by Aldous Huxley that shocked everyone in the 1950s by the way it showed what the future, organized by science and pharmaceuticals, would be like? Remember what they called 'the feelies,' movies you watched while you clutched the arms of chairs that sent shock waves through your body to stimulate the emotions that were consistent with what you were seeing on the screen? It isn't a bad description of what you see when you watch the reaction of the crowd in a stadium, or what you see on the faces of an audience in the darkness of a movie theater. They write novels like that now. Everyone wants to feel what it would be like to live a life of daring and danger, something, anything, that isn't as safe and comfortable and meaningless as the life they have. We used to talk about lives led in quiet desperation; what we have now are lives of vicarious brutality in which all anyone seems to care about is victory or defeat, my team or yours."

It was true; almost everything was measured in terms of winning and losing. It did not matter how you won, only that you did. It was the reason everyone loved T. J. Allen when he was playing: he won championships and, for a while at least, made it seem that he could never lose.

"Everything has become a form of entertainment," Craven went on. "That is why this trial is so interesting. I told you about my conversation with Matthew Stanton. I kept trying to think of who he reminded me of. I could not quite put my finger on it. I told you he seemed to have what used to be called the tragic sense of life. What could be more antithetical to the way we live now than the belief, the knowledge, that when you scratch the surface of what our present-day pleasure seekers seek, you will find just the opposite of what any decent man or woman of intelligence would want to have? That is the sense I got with him, someone too serious to believe in the importance of winning at games; someone too serious to think that what other people think important has any importance at all."

Craven stared past me to the window and the changing light of a winter afternoon, trying to remember who Matthew Stanton had reminded him of. The name was there, just on the tip of his tongue.

"Someone," he mumbled, "someone famous, I think." His gaze came back to me. There was something he remembered. "Burroughs. What are you going to do about her?"

It was a good question. I did not really know.

"As she was leaving the stand, I told Silverman that I reserved the right to recall her as a witness for the defense. That got her attention. She stopped and gave me a sharp, questioning look. Everyone now knows, or thinks they know, that she left out the fact that Stanton had AIDS from her report. There is no excuse. It was either incompetence or deception. Either way, she could lose her license. Why would she have done it? Why take that kind of chance?"

Craven still thought it obvious.

"To do the Stanton family a favor."

"But there isn't any Stanton family, only the stepmother, Victoria Stanton. Why would she care whether it became public knowledge that her stepson—her murdered stepson—had AIDS? How many people, thousands of people, have had that awful disease? How many deaths have there been in San Francisco alone? Having AIDS is not what anyone would consider a blot on the family name. Having AIDS would make everyone, or nearly everyone, immensely sympathetic. That isn't the reason Burroughs tried to cover it up."

"Which would raise the question of why she thought Victoria Stanton would want her to cover it up," said Craven.

"Yes, exactly. Victoria Stanton, the stepmother of the victim in a murder case and she has refused every request I have made to talk to her about her stepson. The first time I will see her is when, finally, she walks into the courtroom."

"She wasn't in court today? She hasn't been there before?"

"She wasn't even at Matthew Stanton's funeral."

Six

"The prosecution calls Detective Owen Chang," announced Samantha Longstreet in a rapid-fire voice as she rose from her chair. Like an actress under the eyes of an audience, she stood there, waiting, until her next witness was sworn in by the clerk.

Owen Chang looked more like a lawyer in an upscale commercial firm than a police detective. Wearing a dark blue suit, cream-colored shirt, and an understated silk tie, everything about him was measured, meticulous, and precise. The moment he took the stand, he looked at the jury and nodded once, a single slight movement to show he understood the gravity of the testimony he was about to give. Longstreet asked him to describe what happened the night Matthew Stanton was murdered. Chang leaned forward. He spoke with the brevity of a clear, well-ordered mind.

"We had a call. Someone in the building where Mr. Stanton lived heard what they thought was some kind of fight, loud voices, things being broken. The two officers who responded discovered

Mr. Stanton dead from a gunshot. The defendant, Mr. Allen, was standing there, the gun still in his hand."

Longstreet's jade-colored eyes flashed with triumph. Allen was there, the gun still in his hand, and Matthew Stanton was dead.

"The gun was still in his hand?" she asked, as if, more than significant, this was unexpected.

Chang pulled back his shoulders and sat straight. He wanted to make sure she was finished, that there was not anything she wanted to add.

"Yes," he replied simply.

"The victim, Matthew Stanton, was on the floor, dead?"

"Yes, that's correct."

"And the defendant, Thaddeus John Allen, was still standing there?"

"Objection, Your Honor!" I complained, rising with a half smile of confusion. "The witness had already testified to this; which means either the district attorney did not understand what the witness said, or doesn't believe it."

Longstreet's eyes went wild. She turned on me with a vengeance.

"I object to the objection! No, more than that, I ask—I demand—that the court instruct the jury that defense counsel's remarks, his bizarre characterization, are not just improper, but inexcusable!"

Leonard Silverman took out his handkerchief and blew his nose. He smiled an apology to the jury and then, but only then, turned his attention to Longstreet.

"The objection is sustained. The question has been asked and answered."

Longstreet started to object again, to explain why she was right and Silverman was wrong, but she was too quick, her lawyer's mind too agile, to give him a second chance to correct her in front of the jury. She turned back to the detective as if what had just happened had been nothing important.

"Detective Chang, were you able to determine whether the gun had been fired by the defendant?"

"Yes. There was gunshot residue on his hand and on his clothing."

"Were his fingerprints on the gun?"

"Yes, they were."

"Finally, Detective Chang, is there any question whether the bullet that killed Matthew Stanton came from the gun owned and fired by the defendant, Thaddeus John Allen?"

Chang looked directly at the jury.

"No question; no question at all."

Allen grabbed my arm.

"I didn't! I told you about the gun; I told you what happened; I told you—"

With the jury watching, I nodded my agreement and then got to my feet. I took two steps toward Chang, then stopped and stared down at the floor as if something had just occurred to me. I raised my eyes just far enough to see him.

"How many shots were fired, Detective Chang?"

He looked at me with a puzzled expression; he was not sure what I was asking him.

"As I testified, the victim was killed by a single gunshot to the head."

"That isn't what I asked. How many shots were fired from the gun, the one you claim was owned by the defendant?"

"The one I claim...? It was registered in his name."

"We'll come back to that. Again, how many shots were fired? It's a simple question, Detective Chang. Or is it your testimony that only one was fired because it only took one shot to kill Matthew Stanton?"

"If you're suggesting that more than—"

"I'm not suggesting anything; I'm asking you a question. For the last time," I said, a warning in my eyes, "how many shots were fired?"

He had not considered the possibility that more than a single lethal shot had been fired, and, now that he had to, he was cautious in his reply.

"There was no evidence of a second shot."

My hands held behind my back, I had been watching him from beneath my lowered brow. Now I looked away and began to pace back and forth, measuring each step as if it were part of a strict, logical sequence from a premise to a conclusion.

"If there was only the one shot that killed Matthew Stanton," I said, as if I were talking to myself, "the defendant must have killed him because there was gunshot residue on his hand, correct?" I asked, stopping still.

Chang agreed, but the agreement was tentative, a conditional response that, depending on what I asked next, might be subject to change. I started pacing again.

"But if more than one shot was fired, then that gunshot residue doesn't prove anything, does it?"

"I'm not sure I follow," he admitted. "I'm not sure I see the difference it makes if he fired once or more than once."

With a look of astonishment, I stopped pacing and stared at him.

"What difference it makes? The killer—the real killer—fires the bullet that kills Matthew Stanton. The defendant comes in, picks up the gun, and fires at the killer as the killer gets away. And you don't think that makes a difference?"

Owen Chang's thin black eyebrows shot straight up.

"But that is—"

"Far-fetched? Do you really think so? It's completely consistent with the evidence you presented. The defendant walks into the apartment, just after the first, fatal, shot is fired, picks up the gun from the floor, where the killer has dropped it, and fires at the killer as the killer gets away."

"You forget, counselor, it was his gun!" he insisted, jabbing his finger in the air.

Spinning away from Chang, I faced the jury, smiling in a way that told them there was something they did not yet know.

"You testified that the gun, the murder weapon, was registered in the defendant's name, correct?" I asked, my gaze still fastened on the jury.

"That's right; it was his gun. It was—"

"Stolen! Two weeks before the murder," I remarked, slowly turning toward him.

He was too smart to deny something he could not be sure about, but he came as close to calling me a liar as he could.

"No one has suggested that before," he replied with a skepticism it was impossible to miss.

"Really? It is surprising you would say that, Detective Chang. Mr. Allen reported the theft to the police when it happened. Here," I said as I went to the counsel table and got the police report. "Read this. What does it say about the gun, the gun no one has ever suggested had been stolen?"

Forced to read it out loud, forced to recite the date and time that T. J. Allen had reported the gun stolen, Owen Chang, with the help of the district attorney, tried to dismiss it as an attempt at misdirection.

"Detective Chang," asked Longstreet on re-direct, "other than the defendant's own claim that his gun was stolen, was there any confirmation of this so-called theft? Any independent witnesses, any evidence at all?"

"No," he replied, "just the fact that it was reported stolen."

"To your knowledge, was an investigation made into this reported theft?"

"No, there was not."

"If you were going to kill someone, can you think of a better way to hide the fact that the murder weapon belonged to you? No, never mind," said Longstreet quickly as she saw me rise to object. "No need to answer. The question answers itself."

"Actually, it doesn't answer itself at all," I observed as soon as Silverman asked if I wanted to re-cross the witness. "You, the police, get a report of a stolen gun and do nothing about it. Isn't that what you just said?"

"Yes," he started to explain, "but we have—"

"A lot to do; yes, I'm sure we all understand. Of course, if you just dismiss every report as the made-up story of someone planning a murder, that should reduce your workload considerably. Look at that report again. The defendant not only reported that the gun had been stolen, he reported the precise location where it had been taken. He reported it stolen from his locker, didn't he, Detective Chang? The locker in the facility where he played. Isn't that correct, Detective Chang? Isn't that what the report says?"

"That is what he claimed, yes."

"What he claimed? Very good. He claimed that a gun registered in his name—notice that he made sure that the murder weapon was registered in his name because that way," I remarked, turning to the jury with laughter in my eyes, "there would not be any difficulty getting it back from the police if he dropped it on the floor after murdering Matthew Stanton! Now, Detective Chang," I said, wheeling back around, "no one went to the arena to check on the reported theft, correct?"

"As I said, there wasn't any—"

"Investigation. Which just proves how remarkably prescient the defendant was. He reports the gun missing, because that way he can shoot Matthew Stanton and no one will think it was him, because the murder weapon, his gun, was stolen. This is very smart. You have to be a kind of genius to understand that you can report a theft that never happened because the police will never do anything more than take down what you tell them. It's perfect! What better alibi than telling the police that the gun you are going to use in a murder has been taken by someone else?"

"Is there a question Mr. Antonelli would like to ask?" protested Longstreet with undisguised disdain. "Because for the life of me I haven't heard one."

"I'll ask it," I shot back before Silverman could rule. "You have no evidence, do you, Detective Chang, that the defendant's report of a stolen gone was untruthful?"

"You mean, other than the fact that he used it to murder Matthew Stanton?"

"You don't find that odd, Detective Chang? That instead of getting a gun that was not registered to anyone, he uses a gun registered to himself? That instead of a gun that could not be traced to him, he goes to all the trouble of inventing a theft; a theft that, again, he would have known could easily have been disproved by a routine police investigation? Can you give me, can you give the jury, one good reason why anyone would do this, or anything like it?"

Owen Chang was undisturbed. My question did not faze him in the least.

"It's sometimes hard to know why anyone does anything. All I know is that Matthew Stanton was murdered, that the murder weapon belonged to the defendant, and that there is no question that he fired it. His fingerprints were on the gun, he had gunshot residue on his hand, and he was there, in the room, holding the gun when the police arrived."

My hands shoved down deep in my pockets, I stared down at the dull wooden floor. There were strange connections in this trial, connections I did not fully understand; connections that, as each new one appeared, reminded me of the line Leonard Silverman had used, the line so close to the one he had read, years ago, in a Joseph Conrad novel, "All of America contributed to the making of Matthew Stanton."

Silverman was looking at me now, peering down from the bench; wondering, perhaps, how much I had started to learn about what had happened and all the things that had made it happen the way it had.

"When the police arrived," I said, repeating Chang's last remark, "that wasn't the first time you had been there, was it, Detective Chang; not the first time you had been in the building where Matthew Stanton had his apartment?"

"I'm not sure I know what you mean. I think it is the first time there has been a homicide in that building."

"It's one of the most exclusive addresses in the city, isn't it? One of the most prestigious buildings on Nob Hill; one of the most expensive places to live in San Francisco."

"I'm sure that must be right, but—"

"People own their apartments, don't they?"

"Yes, I believe that is correct."

"But a company manages the building: takes care of maintenance, provides housekeeping services, parking. There is even a chef on call, correct?"

"That's my understanding."

"Your understanding?" I asked with a look of surprise. "You make it sound as if your knowledge is second-hand. What is the name of the person who runs the company that manages the building, the building where Matthew Stanton lived and died? Isn't it Marilyn Chang? And isn't Marilyn Chang your wife?"

Everyone on the jury looked at Owen Chang with a new set of eyes. He was no longer a police detective with meticulous taste who dressed at perhaps unusual expense for someone in his position; he was dressed how a man from an extremely wealthy family was expected to look. He was still a detective, an obviously intelligent one, but police work no longer defined him; it was not something he had to do. The jury did not suddenly distrust him; it was just that they were not quite as prepared to take him as seriously as they had before. There was also, though they may not have been conscious of it, a question, a doubt, about what he must have thought when he walked into the most expensive apartment in one of the most expensive buildings in San Francisco and found a dead white man and a black man in custody.

Owen Chang did not bat an eyelash. My question had no more importance than when Samantha Longstreet had asked him to state his name for the record.

"Yes, my wife's company manages the building," he replied in a relaxed, laconic voice. He seemed to think that this was such a well-known fact it was a wonder I thought it necessary to ask.

There was something marvelously duplicitous in that studied blank expression, a complete indifference to what you thought, whether you believed what he was telling you, or discovered behind that mask of smooth good manners an inveterate liar. He knew that, at the end, he could never be caught in an inconsistency, much less a contradiction. That made me ask my next question as if the answer were as obvious and unimportant as he had tried to make my last one seem.

"Not only does your wife's company manage the building, but you and your wife were good friends with Matthew Stanton, weren't you?"

He started to open his mouth, but then realized what the question meant. He hesitated, not very long, only a second or two, but enough time to betray an indecision.

"We knew Mr. Stanton, of course—"

"Of course! Because he lived in a building managed by your wife's company. But you knew him better than that. Isn't it true that you socialized with him? Isn't it true that you often attended the same events, the same dinners, the same gatherings of some of the city's most prominent people?"

He became, not evasive, exactly, but defensive, as if there might be some suspicion that he and his wife's social connections might have affected his investigation. He turned and faced the jury.

"My wife is a very successful business woman. She knows a great many people and has a great many friends. She is involved in a number of charitable causes, and we attend a great many social events. Yes, we knew Matthew Stanton. We knew him socially; well enough that we would exchange a few words with him if we ran into him at one of those social affairs. It would go too far, however, to say we were good friends. I had never been in his apartment before the night he was murdered."

"You and your wife have a great many friends; you attend a great many social events. You knew Matthew Stanton, you would exchange a few words with him at the innumerable events you attended. Among all these friends of yours, among all the social events you attended, did you ever encounter the defendant?"

"No, I don't believe so."

"But you knew who he was, didn't you? The night you found him in Matthew Stanton's apartment wasn't the first time you had seen him, was it?"

This was not what Chang had expected. He learned forward, searching my eyes, wondering where I was going with this.

"No, I knew who he was."

"It was not the first time you had seen him?" I asked, repeating the question to make sure that both he and the jury understood that this was, for some reason, important.

"If you mean, had I seen him play basketball, then, yes, I had seen him."

"On television?"

"Yes, on television."

"I take it you mean the televisions sets they have in the luxury boxes that companies like the one your wife controls pay millions of dollars to have. That is where you used to watch the defendant play, in a private suite with all the food you could ever want, and anything you might want to drink. Isn't that correct, Detective Chang?"

He had not taken his eyes off me. His gaze was more steely and his voice a little sharper, but those were the only visible signs of his growing irritation.

"As I said earlier, my wife has built a very successful company."

I stared hard at him, and then, once again, began to pace back and forth.

"When you arrived at the building, you went directly to Stanton's apartment?"

"Yes."

"Because the police received a phone call?"

"Yes, that's right," he replied, settling back in the chair as my questions became more of what he had expected; more of what, through long years of experience, he had learned how to answer.

"The phone call, however, did not report a gunshot, did it?"

"No. As I testified earlier, it was a report of a loud, violent argument. The caller, who lived in the apartment below, heard a crashing, breaking noise, like someone throwing things, a chair, a lamp, that kind of thing."

"You didn't respond to the call yourself, did you?"

"No. As I said, two patrolmen responded. They were just a couple blocks away. And, as you just pointed out, no shots had been fired. They thought they were responding to a domestic disturbance."

"After they arrived and discovered Matthew Stanton had been murdered, then you came, is that correct?"

"Yes. I'm a homicide detective, and—"

I stopped in my tracks.

"And you were already there, weren't you? You weren't on duty that night; you were home, with your wife, in the apartment you own on the second floor of the same building. Isn't that the reason you were called, because you were just an elevator ride away?" I did not wait for him to answer. "Tell us, Detective Chang, what was your first thought, your first reaction, when you walked inside and saw the defendant? Why did you think he was there?"

"He was under arrest," he replied, shifting his weight in the chair. "He was handcuffed. I didn't have time to wonder—"

"You didn't wonder why he was there, why he had murdered your friend, Matthew Stanton?"

"If you mean, why did I think he had... Would you please stop doing that!" he shouted suddenly. "Stop that damn pacing, stop going first one way then the other! It's making me...!"

I stopped and stood there, pondering his request.

"No, I don't think I will," I said finally, and started pacing again. "It helps me think. Now, where were we? Yes, the question was what your first reaction was when you saw T. J. Allen. You got a call telling you that Matthew Stanton had been murdered in the same building where you live—the most exclusive building in the city—and you walk in and there he is, the famous T. J. Allen. You weren't surprised?"

He seemed to hesitate, not sure what he should say.

"You weren't surprised, then. Why was that; why weren't you surprised to see T. J. Allen in Matthew Stanton's apartment, handcuffed, in custody for murder?"

"I had heard some things," said Chang vaguely.

"Heard some things?"

"Allen had been in the building, had been at Stanton's place, before. Quite a few times, from what I had heard."

I kept moving, but only long enough to get to the edge of the counsel table, where I stood, tapping the fingers of my left hand just hard enough to make a soft echo in the silence of the courtroom.

"You thought they were friends, is that it, Detective Chang?" I asked, raising my eyebrows in a way that suggested I knew more than he thought I did.

"Friends? Well, yes, I suppose..."

"More than friends, is that what you are trying to say; that they were lovers? Is that the reason you were not surprised, because you thought they had had a lovers' quarrel?" I threw up my hands in a show of frustration. "With a gun? He's six eight, Stanton five nine or five ten; he could have killed him with his bare hands, but instead he shoots him with a gun, a gun he reported stolen two weeks earlier! But never mind; he's there with a gun, the gun used to murder Matthew Stanton, and you were not surprised because, why, exactly, Detective Chang? Because you thought they were gay lovers, or because the defendant, T. J. Allen, is black?"

"Objection!" screamed Longstreet as she jumped straight up from her chair. "The defendant's race has—"

"Everything to do with it!" I insisted, to her vast annoyance.

"Nothing to do with it! Does Mr. Antonelli really believe the defendant was singled out because of his race, arrested because of his race; that the decision to prosecute him was because of his race? He knows better than that. He wants the jury to believe there is somehow a racial bias at work, that the playing field is tilted against him. He wants the jury to sympathize with the defendant, to give him the benefit of the doubt every chance they get!"

Leonard Silverman slipped his wire-rimmed glasses down to the end of his nose, and for a long, silent moment peered over them at Samantha Longstreet. Her lips drawn tight as a bowstring, she waited impatiently for his response.

"First, what you suggested the jury should not do is what, as you know as well as anyone, the jury in a criminal case must always do. Whenever there is a doubt, a reasonable doubt, the jury is not just permitted, the jury is required to give the benefit of the doubt to the defendant. Second, with regard to race. If you are suggesting that defense counsel should not be allowed to inquire whether the police investigation was affected by racial bias, I'm afraid I would have to overrule your objection. You will, of course, have an opportunity to remove any such suspicion on re-direct, if you think it necessary to do so."

Silverman started to push his glasses back into place, when suddenly, he decided to question the witness himself.

"Detective Chang, the San Francisco police department has a large number of black officers and patrolmen, both male and female. Have you ever been cited, or otherwise disciplined, for any biased act?"

"No, never, Your Honor."

"Have you ever been cited, or otherwise disciplined, for acting in an inappropriate way with a black suspect you have either questioned or taken into custody?"

"Never," he swore with an emphatic shake of his head.

"Mr. Antonelli, you may continue your cross-examination."

When Chang's eyes came back to me, I started a completely different line of questioning.

"When you watched T. J. Allen play, when you sat there with some of your socially connected friends—including, once in a while, members of the Stanton family, who owned the team—what did you think of him then?"

"What did I...?" He waited to see if I was serious, and then shrugged his shoulders and smiled. "He was a great player. They probably wouldn't have won the championship without him."

"Yes, I know he was a great player. But what kind of player

was he? Was he a great scorer, someone who put up twenty, thirty points a night?"

He still was not sure what I was after. Everyone knew what kind of player Allen had been. Why was I asking?

"He was a great defensive player; great rebounder, great passer. He made everyone around him play better, and everyone on the other team play worse."

You could almost feel it, the agreement, the common opinion, of the courtroom crowd, the shared memory of what the great T. J. Allen had been able to do, the way he could almost will his team to victory.

"And sometimes he became so intent on doing everything he could to help his team, he would argue with the officials, or have I been misinformed?" I asked as innocently as I could.

"No, you haven't been misinformed," replied Chang, while nearly everyone laughed. "He would go crazy when he got called for a foul, jumping up and down, screaming his outrage at what he thought was a bad call. I don't know how many games he got thrown out of, but it must have been a record."

"He did not mind that, getting thrown out of a game? It didn't stop him from getting more fouls the next time he played?"

"Stop him? That was his strength—the way he played as if the rules did not matter, only who was stronger, faster, better."

"And that is the reason, one of the reasons, you admired him as much as you did, because he would do anything to win, whatever rules might get broken?"

Chang was nodding his head, eager to agree.

"It was not, then, because you thought he and Matthew Stanton were lovers, and it was not because he was black; it was because you knew that T. J. Allen never let the rules—never let the law—get in his way, that you thought he must have murdered Matthew Stanton. After all, why obey the law in life when he never did it on the court?

You're wrong, by the way," I said as I turned and started back to my chair at the counsel table. Neither Matthew Stanton nor T. J. Allen were gay. They were not lovers; they were instead very good friends. They read books together. And they never read books about sports. Matthew Stanton and T. J. Allen were both too serious for that."

Seven

Tangerine had been insistent. Trial or no trial, we were going to have a dinner party.

"We were just at one a few weeks ago, the birthday party for Albert."

Her bare feet up on the sofa, she leaned back against the pillow at the other end and with a look of truly monumental despair, the look of a teacher who has tried, and failed, to help an unusually dull student, she reminded me of what should have been obvious.

"When you're invited to someone's home, it is usually expected that you will invite them to yours."

I had her now. She did not understand the nature of my relationship with Albert Craven.

"He only invites me when he needs an additional guest, someone to fill in one last place at the table. He only invites me because he knows I'll never have a dinner of my own. He only invites me because—"

"You are not having a dinner of your own. I'm having a dinner party for Albert and his wife and a few other people. I'll let you know if I need someone to fill the last place at the table. But I wouldn't count on it, if I were you," she remarked as she swept her legs off the sofa and was suddenly, magnificently, on her feet, breezing past me on her way to the kitchen. "If I need anyone, I'm sure I can find someone else."

It was the way she moved, the elegant, effortless, slow-motion dance; the mesmerizing, can't take my eyes off her, smooth, slinking shuffle; her eyes, her nose, her mouth, her chin all glowing with the utter certainty that nothing, nothing important, would ever change, that made her so damn irresistible. By the time she came back, carrying a bottle of wine and an empty glass, I was ready to beg to be included in any party she cared to throw. She sat down on the sofa, her feet this time on the floor, and gave me one of her blazing black-eyed stares.

"It will be interesting. I promise. I'm inviting a few people you don't know."

"That should not be difficult; I don't know anyone. I spend all my days with strangers in court."

"And all your nights in bed with me."

"And on weekends, sometimes even days."

"Are you getting tired of that?"

"The days in court?"

"They give you almost two hours for lunch. We could rent a room." Her eyes lit up with mischief. "Or use one of those small rooms where lawyers meet with their clients."

"And then I would not be able to remember where I was, or what I was supposed to be doing, when court reconvened."

"Yes, but you could give such a wonderful explanation, a three-word tabloid title, that would say all anyone would need to know about why you did not win and your client, your innocent client, went to prison: 'Laid Lawyer Lost!'"

It was almost too tempting.

"We better play it safe. Let's just have your dinner party. They won't stay late."

But they did, every last one of them, all twelve of Tangerine's invited guests; stayed as if instead of dinner, they had been asked to stay the weekend; stayed until the moon had disappeared and the rising sun was not more than an hour away. A dozen guests for dinner, and if not all of them were well-known distinguished names, they each had their own eccentricities, which was another way of saying that none of them were quite normal. I had seldom seen Tangerine more excited. Like a child with her first chemistry set, she could not wait to see what combinations might cause an explosion. It started before we sat down at the table; it started the moment Susan 'Suzy' Fairchild walked in the door.

"What a nice, cozy little house," she remarked, looking around the living room with the measured glance of an appraiser.

For a second, I thought she was going to ask for the exact square footage. I took her coat and shook hands with her husband, Roger, who seemed slightly embarrassed by his wife's condescension. He was a physician, a surgeon; one of the best, from what I had been told. Like most men truly gifted, he was modest about his own achievements. His wife, who had more reason for modesty, seldom stopped talking about herself. The comment about the house contained within it everything she thought important. One of the most successful real estate agents in the city, she knew, or thought she knew, everything about who you were by where you lived. In her eyes, I was not a criminal defense attorney; I was just a guy who lived in a small house on a hillside in Sausalito.

"I had a place in the city," I said as casually as I could. "On Nob Hill, but I like it better here. It has a better view."

She seemed to take it under advisement, but only for a moment.

"It's very nice; and you're right about the view," she said as she glanced out the sliding glass doors to the black waters of the bay and the city on the other side. "I just could not imagine living anywhere except San Francisco."

Her eyes, which, once they left me, had never come back, suddenly brightened. Tangerine was coming toward us. It was as if, great good friends, they had not seen each other in years. She threw her arms around Tangerine, kissed her on the side of her face, and told her, what was nothing but the truth, that she was still the most beautiful woman she had ever seen.

"I love what you have done with this place," she insisted eagerly. Her lying eyes were filled with such admiration I almost believed she meant it.

And she did, in that moment, talking to a woman whose friendship she wanted to keep. Suzy Fairchild always meant what she said, until there was something to be gained by a new opinion.

"But don't you miss being in the city?" she asked, as if instead of just the other side of the Golden Gate Bridge, Tangerine had been banished to some rural hamlet that could not be found on the map.

Two by two, the other guests arrived. Harry Caulfield, the publisher of the *Chronicle*, came with his wife, Beatrice, the editor of the arts section of the paper, which included everything from movies, television, and book reviews, to music and the fine arts. She had written a book about the post-impressionist movement in the United States which received a favorable review in the *Chronicle* and passed unnoticed in the other papers. She was talkative, cheerful, always eager to meet new people. Her husband, Harry, was cautious, reserved, and if he liked you, tried hard not to show it. Whether this was because he was afraid you might not think as highly of him if you thought him a friend, or that, having covered so much cruelty and duplicity in his long career in journalism, he thought he might not like you so much if he knew you better, it was difficult to say. The only real enthusiasm I saw from him was when Tangerine came up to greet him and he started to laugh at his own tongue-tied incoherence as he tried to find the words to return her warm, affectionate welcome.

Douglas Loescher, an interior decorator who had worked for some of Suzy Fairchild's wealthiest clients, and had helped Tangerine decorate our house, slipped in almost unnoticed. In his early forties, slight of build and with bashful eyes, he had a habit of standing with his hands held in front of him in the respectful pose of someone trying hard to make up his mind whether what you had just suggested might be the best color for the room was really best after all. It never was, but he made you feel that your taste, if not perfect, was really quite good, and certainly better than that of most of the other clients with whom he had to work.

Suzy Fairchild looked at the measurement of things; Douglas Loescher studied the small detail, the way a color changed with the light, the way a fabric yielded to the touch. Let loose in an art museum, she would have gazed at the height of the ceiling and the thickness of the walls; he would have been found standing, mesmerized by the countless brush strokes in a painting by Matisse. I did not like Suzy Fairchild, but I liked him. There was nothing essentially dishonest about who he was and what he did. It did not bother me in the least when Tangerine told me later that she thought he had a crush on me. I felt flattered.

A few minutes later, Albert and his wife Isabel arrived along with James J. Drexel and Anna Mangini. Drexel, a retired judge, had known Albert since they were in law school together, sometime, as he liked to insist, a year or so after the earthquake of 1906. Anna Mangini was an old friend of his who, when she was much younger, had been arrested for riding naked on horseback one Sunday afternoon in Golden Gate Park.

"That's how I first met her," explained Drexel. "I was practicing law. I got a call from someone at the jail. First time I saw her, she was in a jail cell wearing a police officer's coat."

He said this in the same quiet, but authoritative voice with which he had for thirty years instructed juries and admonished lawyers. For her part, Anna Mangini stood there in a long black dress, her bright, almost incandescent eyes shining with the remembered glory of what she had once dared to do.

"If you're wondering why I did it," she said, as everyone who had come in before her turned to watch, "it's very simple. It was a warm September afternoon and, quite frankly, I looked rather good naked. I might have done it even if my boyfriend at the time hadn't dared me to do it."

"And what did he do when the police arrived?" I could not help asking.

She was somewhere in her fifties, but there was not so much as a strand of gray in her jet-black hair. There were lines, deep ones, across her forehead and crow's feet at the corner of her eyes, but this only added to the impression of an eager intelligence. You knew immediately that she was someone who could get to the point as quickly as anyone you had ever met.

"What did he do?" she laughed. "He ran off to take care of the horse!"

Tangerine was everywhere at once, greeting people when they arrived, making sure they had something to drink, introducing those who had not met before and doing it in a way that made them almost think they had. I marveled at how easy it all seemed to her, the instinct for what made someone feel comfortable, the way she anticipated every, even the smallest, need. I was so caught up in watching her that I forgot there were still a few more guests yet to arrive. When two women in their late thirties were suddenly standing right in front of me, introducing themselves, it took me a second to realize what they were doing.

"Paula Goddard," said the first one with a smile so brief that had I blinked at the wrong time, I might have missed it. "And this is my husband, Georgina."

Did she notice a slight sense of surprise, a moment's doubt whether I had heard her right? She was ready to challenge me on the spot. She was a married woman, as married as any woman had ever been, and no one would be allowed to question it.

"It's good to meet you both," I replied, my gaze as steady and determined as her own; one that, like her own, preserved, or perhaps established, a distance.

The distance had originated with her. It had been there, in her eyes, when she first began to introduce herself. It was not that she thought, or had any reason to think, that I was in some way biased against her and her same sex marriage; it was more basic than that. I was a man and I was not gay, which meant, for her, that I could never really understand, and could never really appreciate, her struggle for equality. I had not met her before, but everyone in San Francisco knew who she was, a dominant voice in city government who was forever offering resolutions that, if only the world would listen, would solve all the problems of human existence.

Her partner—her husband—had what seemed at first gentle brown eyes, but, on closer examination, seemed full of calculation. She might be quiet and withdrawn, shy of conversation in public; but at home, in private, it was not hard to imagine the two of them critiquing everything that had happened and how to gain whatever advantage they could from whatever the situation now demanded. I watched them, a double-bodied politician, shaking every hand as they worked the room. They only seemed lost when everyone was asked to take their places at the table and they discovered that they would not be sitting next to each other.

"Is the table set for fourteen," I asked Tangerine, "because you think thirteen an unlucky number?"

A strange smile, the kind that promises a secret, a secret you could not guess in a thousand years, darted across her mouth. It was just killing her, knowing what she knew; knowing what, when I finally found out, was going to produce a reaction that—

and this was the fun of it—was going to be beyond anything she could anticipate.

"What? What are you...?"

The front door suddenly flew open. If anyone had knocked, I had not heard it. Standing in the middle of the living room with a look of what I can only describe as eager astonishment in his eyes, eyes that started out of his large, ungainly head like two bulging globes, my former client, Alan Boe, was grinning from ear to ear, as surprised, as it seemed, as the rest of us that he was there. He was holding a bottle of wine in one hand and, a gift for Tangerine, a dozen red roses in the other. Tangerine ran up to him, kissed him on the cheek, and thanked him. It was like watching the ugliest kid in school whose first ever date was with the homecoming queen. He laughed —at himself. He was the only one who had worn a coat and tie.

"I'm sorry I'm late," he said as Tangerine walked him to the table and the waiting empty chair. "The ferry was not on time."

"The ferry wasn't...? You didn't drive?"

The question seemed to amuse him. He nodded politely toward the other dinner guests as he sat down.

"I live in Berkeley," he explained, taking in everyone with his gaze. "I teach there, in the philosophy department. I don't own a car; I don't really need one. The truth is I don't often leave Berkeley or the campus. As a matter of fact," he added with an enormous grin, "I think this is the first time I've gone anywhere since Mr. Antonelli somehow managed to convince the jury that, even if I had murdered the university chancellor, the prosecution had not been able to prove it."

While nearly everyone else now looked at Alan Boe with something like alarm, Albert Craven laughed at their bewildered expressions.

"Yes, everyone, Alan Boe, Professor Alan Boe, is a cold-blooded killer who should be on death row having his last meal before his execution. But thanks to my friend and partner, the great Joseph Antonelli, he is again a free man who can come and have dinner with us."

"He wasn't really guilty, though, was he?" asked Suzy Fairchild, who could barely bring herself to look at Alan Boe, sitting directly across the table.

"Because I have known all of you for years, I can tell you with some assurance that most of you have done more criminal things than Alan Boe has ever dreamed of doing."

"I thought about killing him," said Boe. "I told the police I had thought about it. They seemed to think that was a kind of confession until I asked them whether they had ever thought it might not be a bad idea to kill their police chief."

"You took the ferry?" asked Tangerine, still shaking her head in disbelief. "From...?"

"From the Ferry Building. I took the train, BART, from Berkeley to the city, and then walked the few short blocks to the ferry, but it was running late, and then, when I got here, to Sausalito, it took longer than I thought to walk up the hill."

"You should have called."

"I don't have a phone."

"You don't...?" laughed Suzy Fairchild. "Everyone has a phone."

"That, obviously, isn't true," he replied, looking straight at her.

It took her a moment to realize he was serious. She had, of course, never met anyone like him, but she did not yet know how unusual, how different, Alan Boe really was.

"No, I meant..."

"That everyone with even a modicum of intelligence has a phone. Let me assure you, Ms. Fairchild, no one knows better than I how absurdly ignorant I am."

I glanced down the table to where the retired judge James J. Drexel was sitting.

"Do you know how I won that case? I put him on the stand and asked only one question."

Drexel nodded, and waited for me to tell him. Sitting several places away, Anna Mangini leaned forward.

"Only one question? Really? What was it?"

The intensity about her was electric. She could ask you anything, even something as simple as this, and you felt it was as profound a question as anyone could possibly ask. I forgot about Judge Drexel, Albert's old friend, and looked at her.

"I asked him to state his name."

She almost jumped out of her chair with excitement.

"That was it? That was all it took? But he didn't just state his name." She turned to Boe.

"That isn't what you did, is it? You didn't just tell the jury that your name is Alan Boe."

The dark, shining eyes of Anna Mangini grew even brighter with the certainty that she was right, that something had happened in that courtroom that had not happened before. Just looking at him told her that whatever he had said or done had been not just unprecedented, but unique.

The bulging eyes of Alan Boe seemed to go everywhere at once, not just around the confines of the room and the people in it, but back through time, back two years to the day he was on the witness stand, watching that jury of twelve men and women watching him.

"Mr. Antonelli asked me to state my name, and I did so; and then, if I remember correctly, he looked up at the judge and announced that this was the end of the case for the defense."

I was trying hard not to laugh. What Boe had just said was literally correct, and about as far from the truth as it was possible to go. My question, his answer, had nothing to do with what happened. It was not anything Alan Boe had said under oath; it was who Alan Boe was that made it impossible for the jury to think there was even the slightest chance he could have committed murder or any other crime.

"I was there; I saw what happened."

Harry Caulfield laid down his fork and shoved his plate to the side. A knowing smile cut the corners of his jagged mouth. He shook his head at what he had witnessed.

"I had not covered a jury trial, a criminal case, in years, and I decided I should get back into it, remind myself of what it is like to be a reporter. That trial, the murder of the chancellor, with a philosophy professor charged with the crime, and Antonelli the defense attorney—everyone wanted to follow that story. And forgive me, professor, but you had a reputation for what a lot of people thought outrageous behavior: leading protests against the administration, calling for the chancellor's resignation because the university was—"

"Becoming a commercial enterprise," Boe interjected. "Which, for a university, is worse than a criminal enterprise, because some things that are unlawful are not always unjust. Turning an institution that is supposed to help liberate the mind into a place that gives instruction on marketable skills, what is that, if it isn't the organized murder of human intelligence?"

"Yes, precisely!" cried Caulfield. "That is what I mean. You were controversial, and then, the first day in court, when the judge asked if anyone on the jury knew either of the attorneys or the defendant—the most routine question that gets asked—you stand up, introduce yourself to the jury, and start talking about all the things you would like to say. You took over the courtroom. No one had seen anything like it. The jury—I watched them—could not take their eyes off you. You came into court charged with murder, and when you left, there wasn't anyone who did not think you were the most honest, trustworthy person they had ever met."

Caulfield paused. He had just thought of something.

"I notice you never call him Joseph; it is always Mr. Antonelli."

"Yes, of course. Mr. Antonelli never called me by my first name. You wonder why. It is because we both believe that formality is important. Formality makes it easier to remember that what you are doing should be taken seriously. I never call a student by his or her first name, and all my students call me Mr. Boe, not Professor Boe or Dr. Boe, because everyone in a university, teacher and student alike, are equally engaged, or should be equally engaged, in the pursuit of the truth."

"The truth?" inquired Beatrice Caulfield with a thin smile of nervous irritation. She had a critic's inveterate dissatisfaction with anything of which she did not immediately approve. "Doesn't everyone have their own truth? Isn't everyone the judge of what they see and how they feel? In the arts, at least, the only sound criterion, the only appropriate way to measure things, is the degree of creativity they involve."

With surgical precision, Alan Boe cut the chicken breast on his plate and took a long drink from his wine glass. He pushed back from the table, as if that was all he was going to have, and gave her a glance so piercing that it seemed to question everything about her.

"Creativity, which means, in the way we understand things today, the ability to do something, to make something, no one has done before. But exactly how does that come about? How does anyone create anything?"

It struck her as just this side of idiotic. She did not understand how he could ask such an obviously foolish question. She became impatient.

"Creativity isn't something you can teach, professor; it is

something that you have, something you are born with: the ability to see things in a way no one has seem them before."

"Wouldn't that be a fair description of insanity? To see things in a way no one has seen them before."

"No, that—"

"Someone hallucinates, has visions, sees things no one else can see. Would that not cover both insanity and modern art? You wrote a book, a very good book, about post-impressionism. Am I wrong in thinking that the whole basis of this movement is the insistence that the meaning of a work of art is what the spectator, rather than what the artist, thinks? That it is the person viewing a painting who decides what the painting means? That there is no standard, no objective standard, by which to decide whether the painting in question has any serious meaning at all? Because, as you pointed out, the truth of anything is whatever each of us happens to think it is."

"That's right: each of us has to make our own judgment."

"And each of our judgements is as good, as valid, as any other?"

"Yes, absolutely."

"Whether we are reasonably intelligent and well-educated or completely insane?"

"I don't think you can say that someone who can't tell the difference between fantasy and reality could make the same kind of judgments."

"What would you call someone who thought a Rembrandt painting inferior to one of those post-impressionist creations that consist of nothing more than a paint-spattered canvas, something any three-year-old could have done?"

"You are still missing the point!" she exclaimed, frustrated that he could not see it. "The issue is creativity, what the artist has done that no one else has done the same way!"

"So you would not make a distinction between a Rembrandt

and a paint-spattered canvas? They're equally deserving of praise?"

"That suggests the kind of objective standard the modern world rejects," she replied dismissively.

"Because the arts are the creative arts. Yes, I understand. Until a few hundred years ago, no one spoke of the creative arts; they spoke of the imitative arts. Painting, sculpture, literature, all the arts were measured against what they were meant to represent. Picasso might paint his three-dimensional figures without any resemblance to what a human being actually looks like; Rembrandt tried to capture a woman in all her beauty. He tried to capture the eternal, that is to say, the essential female." The luminous eyes of Alan Boe seemed to grow larger and become, if that were possible, more penetrating. "There was madness in this as well; not in how they saw things, but in their astonishing devotion to the task at hand. The really great ones were driven by an inner necessity they could not have resisted even had they tried."

Beatrice Caulfield became more and more agitated. Everything Boe was saying was wrong, but she could not find the words, she could not fashion the argument, that would make this as obvious to the others as it was to her. Her hands, clenched into small fists, pressed hard on the table. She was about to say something in anger, when Albert's wife, Isabel, asked a question of her own.

"Your trial, Allen; it was all that Albert, all that anyone, could talk about. No one, certainly not Albert, thought you were guilty, but it must have been awful, knowing you were innocent, to go through something like that, on trial for your life for something you did not do."

There was genuine sympathy in Isabel Craven's quiet, cultured voice, and the kind of fearlessness in her eyes that told you that once she believed in you and trusted you as a friend, nothing in the world could stop her from coming to your defense, especially if no one else was willing to help you. Boe recognized this at once. He had pushed back from the table when he talked to Beatrice Caulfield; he put his elbows on the table and leaned forward when he spoke with Isabel.

"It was not awful at all; it was the best time I ever had. I never felt more alive. I had spent much of my life studying Plato, and I had the chance to learn what it must have been like for Socrates when he was put on trial in Athens."

"But Socrates was not charged with murder," said Judge Drexel from his place two chairs down from where I sat. Unlike most judges, and most lawyers, he had always had an interest in the classics.

"He was charged with something much more serious."

"More serious than murder?" asked Paula Goddard, startled by the suggestion.

"Instead of the death of an individual, he was charged with the attempted death of the city. He was charged with impiety—not believing in the city's gods—and with corrupting the young. The two charges together converge in the accusation that he was undermining the very foundation, the basis, of Athens' way of life; and that would be murder, murder of what Athens was."

James J. Drexel was still thinking about what Alan Boe had said about being on trial. He wondered whether he had felt that way at the time, or only after the trial was over and he could put things in perspective.

"I was on the bench a long time, and I don't remember anyone, any defendant, who ever said they enjoyed the experience. Didn't you understand what could happen? Joseph must have explained that you might go to prison for life if, in fact, you weren't sentenced to death."

Alan Boe looked down the table at me, a knowing smile on his thick, heavy lips. Isabel Craven, and not just her, all the women at the table, could not stop looking at him. I had seen the same thing during the trial. His ugliness was mesmerizing, compelling, but combined with an intelligence so astonishing that it suggested a need for that almost grotesque appearance to shield the eyes from something too bright, too dazzling, to see. Those go blind who look too long at the sun.

"There was no reason for me to be afraid. I was innocent."

"Innocent people sometimes get convicted," Drexel reminded him.

Alan Boe could only laugh.

"Better to be convicted if you are innocent than if you are guilty, don't you think?"

Drexel was not sure he understood, but then, a moment later, he thought he did. Running his hand over his short gray hair, he tried to remember something he had once read.

"Better because you did not do anything wrong." He was sure that was it. "Because it is better to suffer an injustice than to commit an injustice. Correct?"

Alan Boe agreed. "You know your Plato."

Drexel looked like he had just been awarded the top prize at school.

Paula Goddard dismissed it as a school teacher's trick, a way to make a point with impressionable college students.

"You would really rather spend a lifetime in prison than commit some injustice of your own?"

She expected Boe to reply, but he just stared at her, as if, for his part, he could not believe she was serious, or that far lost to all reason.

"If I knew my only alternative was to go to prison for something I did not do, or break the law, I would not hesitate; and I'm not sure many other people would, either."

"Breaking the law is not always unjust," I reminded her. "The situation you describe isn't the choice between committing murder and being convicted of a murder you did not commit.

You're describing a situation in which, for example, someone on trial for a murder they did not commit gets someone to give them an alibi by lying on the stand. Perjury is against the law, but in this instance, it would lead to a just result."

"Is that what you're going to do in the trial you're in now?" asked Goddard. "Get someone to commit perjury to save your client, the famous basketball player who murdered my friend, Matthew Stanton?"

"Stanton was a friend of yours?" I asked as I casually lifted my glass to take another drink. I did not want her to think the question anything more than polite curiosity.

"We moved in some of the same circles," she replied with what I thought deliberate ambiguity. She seemed to want me to think there was something secret and mysterious about Stanton that I did not know. She nodded toward Douglas Loescher. "Douglas knew him better, of course."

It was the way she said "of course," the dramatic finality of it, that made it sound like it had been common knowledge that Matthew Stanton had not been the straight white male others thought he was. Loescher understood immediately.

"I knew Matthew," he said. "I knew him rather well, but not in that way. Matthew was not gay. I confess that was always a disappointment. He was really great looking, and utterly fascinating as a person."

Was there anyone in the city, anyone among those who made things happen, who had not known Matthew Stanton?

"His father, Emmett Stanton, handled all our investments," offered Suzy Fairchild. "Everyone wanted to invest with him, even if he was a little crazy."

"He wasn't crazy!" objected Albert.

"Really? How do you explain his divorce, his remarriage, the way he died? How do you explain this fascination he had with owning a professional basketball team? Emmett had a brilliant mind, he knew how to make money better than anyone I ever knew, and yet, with all that money, all that power, all he wanted to do was spend his time with a basketball team!"

"That shouldn't be too difficult to understand," suggested Alan Boe unexpectedly. "Isn't that what children do, spend their time playing games?"

"He wasn't a child!" insisted Paula Goddard, with some heat. "He was a man in his fifties. And Suzy is right: he was brilliant, as brilliant as anyone I ever met."

"He had a gift for making money?" asked Boe.

"Yes, of course; everyone knew what he could do."

"But he did not have a happy life?"

"He had more money than anyone in town; of course he had a—"

"He had more, then, than he needed?"

"A lot more than he—"

"What he did not need, then, cost him time?"

"Yes, I suppose you could say—"

"So he wasted much of his life, and when he was not making money, he had a basketball team—a game for children. He never had, in other words, a grown-up life. Is that what you would now say?"

Paula Goddard did not have an answer to that; no one had an answer to that. No one seemed to think it needed one. Everyone started talking to the person next to them. Alan Boe did not seem the least disconcerted. He was used to asking questions no one knew how to answer.

I drank a little more while our guests were enjoying each other's private wit. Tangerine watched over everyone with all the eagerness to please of a young mother with children just learning to talk. That was how it suddenly struck me: everyone, or almost everyone, a child; only Alan Boe with a sure grip on reality, only Alan Boe with a clear understanding of what a serious human being is serious about. I could not resist. I asked the only question that made any sense.

"Does anyone know anything about Matthew Stanton that might help discover who his real killer really is?"

All the conversations stopped, all the tinkling glasses went silent. Everyone stared at me with blank faces and baffled eyes.

"Let me rephrase the question," I said with a respectful glance at the only judge there. "Is there anyone here who can tell us who Matthew Stanton really was?"

"I may be able to tell you something about him," replied someone I was certain had never even met him.

Eight

Alan Boe looked straight at me.

"I have been following the trial in the newspapers, not because of any interest in Matthew Stanton, but because you are the attorney for the defense. I don't think I need to explain why that fact alone was enough to interest me in the trial. Certain things about Matthew Stanton and the circumstances surrounding his death made me become more and more intrigued. His murder was not some isolated event. It was connected to the great changes that have taken place in the way we think about things, the abandonment of tradition; the way everyone now sees themselves as part, a small part, of the crowd. It seems to me that Matthew Stanton understood that he was living in the time of the barbarians, and that he wanted to find something better."

Alan Boe was speaking like an actor on a well-lit stage in front of a faceless audience in a darkened theater. Every eye was on him, every voice gone silent, everyone listening intently to every bell-like word.

"His father, by all accounts a financial genius, was divorced from his mother. That would have been difficult enough, but there was more involved, as all of you must know. Emmett Stanton did not leave his wife because he had fallen in love with a younger woman; Matthew Stanton's mother left her husband because she had fallen in love with a woman."

"That's right," said Beatrice Caulfield. "I remember when it happened."

She looked at Alan Boe, wondering how he happened to know what had once been something of a scandal, but had by now been long forgotten. I did not wonder at anything he knew. A few words, a half-finished sentence, a few stray remarks, and he could tell you more about something that had happened than a full-time historian.

"Matthew Stanton's mother left his father for a woman, and then his father married again and he found himself with a stepmother who seems to have embodied all the worst instincts of the present age: an endless desire for fame and money, a lunatic carnival in which immorality has become the trademark of success, the only worthwhile ambition to become the object of other people's attention; and everyone too busy to realize that everyone they admire and think important only empty-headed fools whose only thought is how to think like everyone else, public opinion the only god still left.

"Matthew Stanton did not have to dream about one day becoming rich and famous; he did not have to sit at home and watch on television the actors, the athletes, the entertainers who have become the only kind of people we look up to. He had seen, close up, what these people, who everyone so much likes to talk about, really were. He understood, he had to have understood, that there was nothing there, that these were people with empty minds and twisted souls. He understood, he had to have understood, that the lynchpin of our existence is gone, that there is nothing that holds us all together, no common belief, nothing we think worthy of sacrifice; nothing, except our own addiction to self-indulgence. He saw it all around him; he was, by all accounts, too intelligent not to have seen it.

"Think what it would be like to spend every day of your life surrounded by people who talk about nothing except how much money they have and how they are going to get more. It is more than greed, more than wanting to have more than what others have; it is the sign, the proof, of your own great intelligence. You have more money than people, you must be smarter than everyone else. Your success could not possibly be just a matter of chance. Matthew Stanton was too intelligent not to know that that was precisely what it was. Chance. He had not worked for anything, and he noticed, he had to have noticed, that it did not matter. No one cared how he had become wealthy, only that he was. No one cared about Matthew Stanton because of what he had accomplished; no one cared about him because of the kind of man he was. Everyone cared about Matthew Stanton because he had money.

"His father marries his stepmother, and then, just a few years later, his father dies. Emmett Stanton died while on a mountain climbing expedition with, among others, his young wife. It is ruled an accident, but no one seems to know quite how it happened; which leads to the suspicion—and Matthew Stanton was too intelligent not to have that suspicion—that his father had been murdered, murdered by the stepmother he had already learned to loathe; murdered with the complicity of Michael Kensington who had become her lover. His father dead, his mother gone, Matthew Stanton is the sole heir of his father's estate. Or almost the sole heir, because, if I understand this right, everything is in a trust, the control of which would pass from Matthew Stanton to his father's widow if he were to die. So there he is, convinced his stepmother murdered his father, and that she and her new husband, the mysterious

Michael Kensington, now have a powerful motive to murder him."

"Hamlet!" cried Albert Craven, turning to me. "I just remembered. The other day, when I told you that Matthew Stanton reminded me of someone. Hamlet. It's the same situation, the same characters, the same sense of the vanity of things! What Alan was just describing—Stanton, a young man of power and position, who sees the futility of ambition, the insignificance of what others think so important. Ambition, power, murder, fame; contempt for all the moral hypocrisy, all the bastard sayings of what the world thinks wise. When Hamlet kills Polonius, his death is just as accidental as the chance that Polonius would ever say anything profound."

Struck by this last remark, Alan Boe looked at Craven as if he were seeing him for the first time.

"I've never thought of that. You're right: Polonius is the spokesman for all the conventional wisdom of his time."

Not to be outdone, Beatrice Caulfield turned her critic's mind to what she thought Hamlet meant.

"It is the classic study of indecision, the problem of weighing anything in the balance: the failure, the inability, to come to a decision and then act on what you decide."

Alan Boe was quick to correct her, and quicker still to make her think he was only reminding her of what she really thought.

"But he knows what he should do, what has to be done, doesn't he?"

"Yes, of course. He knows what his mother and stepfather have done, and what has to be done about it."

"His only doubt is whether, in the end, anything will make a difference. Isn't that what makes Hamlet timeless, his constant questioning about what happens in the larger scheme of things? That is what Matthew Stanton must have felt. Nothing was going to change the past; nothing could bring his father back to life.

There is always something hollow in revenge. Like Hamlet, Matthew Stanton must have felt, more than hatred, resentment, for what had been done to him, forced to live with this new necessity, the need, the requirement that he do something about what someone else had done. Murder someone's father, you also murder him—not his body, but his soul—because instead of living how he wishes, he now has to find the remedy, the punishment, for what you have done. Murder the father, you make the son a slave, and like any slave who remembers freedom, he will, soon enough, be driven to rebellion."

"And what act of rebellion was Matthew Stanton driven to commit?" asked Anna Mangini, making it seem more a challenge than a question.

"It would not have been anything as stupid as murder," replied Boe. "That would not have been his idea of revenge. He would have thought of something that would prevent his stepmother and her new husband from getting what they wanted."

"A way to keep them from getting the money that he controlled," remarked James J. Drexel, who had been listening with the close attention of a courtroom judge.

"But all he had to do to do that was stay alive," Anna Mangini reminded him. "He had to do something that would take away the money they already had."

Alan Boe thought there had to be more to it than that.

"More than their money; what people thought about them: their reputation, their ability to attract attention, whatever made other people think them important."

Everyone seemed to have an idea of what that might have been, though no one could know for sure what Matthew Stanton might have done had he lived, had he not been murdered.

Roger Fairchild had spent most of the evening exchanging an occasional remark with those who sat on either side of him, but otherwise apparently content to listen to what others had to say. I was not sure if this was because, as a surgeon, he did not have any interest in a criminal case, or that he was too self-conscious to venture an opinion on anything that was not in his field. I rather liked him for this. Ignorance seldom stopped anyone else from expressing an opinion on things they knew nothing about.

"One thing you can be reasonably certain about," he said in a voice that, perhaps not surprising in a surgeon, carried a clear sense of authority, "his stepmother did not kill him."

His wife, Suzy, seemed surprised he had actually spoken.

"How do you know that?" she asked.

"Women don't shoot people in the face," he explained. With a brief smile, he turned back to what was still left on his plate.

"Why would you think anything like that?" demanded Paula Goddard, visibly agitated. "You think only a man—?"

"Don't be ridiculous!" cried Douglas Loescher from across the table. "Why do you always have to insist that there aren't any differences between men and women, that there aren't—"

"The only differences are the ones we have invented, the ones we don't have the courage, or the intelligence, to eliminate."

Roger Fairchild put down his fork and smiled at her.

"You must not have studied anatomy in school."

The look Goddard gave him could have melted steel.

"Do you really think the presence of a penis makes it easier to fire a gun?"

Fairchild had to stop himself from laughing. Whether because of what he was about to say, or the reaction he knew it would produce, I could not have said.

"Yes, absolutely."

"Yes, absolutely? Are you—?"

"A surgeon who has operated on I don't know how many gunshot victims, almost none of whom have been shot by a woman; except, occasionally, by accident. And not so much as even once by a woman of the sort we have been talking about: an educated woman with more money than half the population put together. I didn't say she didn't have him killed, and I did not say women were less capable of murder. They're probable more capable, if you want my honest opinion. Women have more self-control; they think ahead. A woman who wants you dead isn't going to shoot you; she's going to use poison, or perhaps, in her case, if she was responsible for the death of Emmett Stanton, make it seem an accident. Call me sexist if you want, but if I don't think men and women are equal, it is because, on the whole, women are better at calculating their own advantage, better at taking the longer view, of seeing how each thing leads to another. So, yes, absolutely: the presence of a penis makes it easier for men to fire a gun. Men are more impulsive, more violent, less able to control themselves when they think they have to react."

I had spent too many years in courtrooms to resist the sudden impulse to ask a question I knew would throw everything into confusion.

"Isn't that the reason why women have always been needed—to civilize men?"

Paula Goddard almost jumped out of her chair. She stared at me in horrified disbelief.

"It's just a question," I insisted in all innocence. "Why do you find it so offensive?"

"Because when you talk about women civilizing men, what you are really talking about is a patriarchal society in which men are in charge of everything and women are oppressed, forced into roles men think they should occupy; a society in which men are free to live however they want and women are expected to know their place!"

Alan Boe slapped his hand on the table so loudly that everyone, including Goddard, turned to look.

"You just put your finger on it!"

"My finger on it?" she asked, completely confused.

"What you just said: that women know their place. That is what is missing, what explains, or helps to explain, the discontent, the uncertainty, the doubt Matthew Stanton must have felt."

"That women did not know their place?" she demanded angrily.

"It isn't that women don't know their place; it is that no one, man or woman, knows their place. Everything is chaos; there is no sense of order. No one knows what they should want and so everyone wants everything. It is the problem, the unique problem, of the modern age: we do not know what we are supposed to be."

"That's even worse!" Goddard sat bolt upright, her mouth pinched tight. "You think everyone should know their place! This is supposed to be a democracy; everyone decides for themself who they are and how they want to live!"

Alan Boe was pure benevolence. The angrier, the more outraged, Goddard became, the more tolerant, the more understanding, he appeared to be. It had an effect no one who had not spent time with him could have anticipated. Goddard began to relent, to draw back from what, in any other setting, might have ended, if not in violence, then in insulting, hateful words. Her gaze lost its intensity; she became curious.

"You're right, Ms. Goddard; this is a democracy. Everyone has the right to decide how they want to live. More than that, everyone is considered to be a unique individual, fully capable of being whatever they want to be. But without any standard, without a clear sense of human excellence, to guide us, everyone, or almost everyone, becomes what everyone else thinks they should be. It is what I was trying to say earlier: the world is a lunatic carnival in which, among all the colorful, shifting scenes, we become so absorbed in what we are seeing that we forget it is all a made-up fiction in which no one has to play the same character twice, a fantasy in which everything, including the difference between the sexes, is confused. Men become women, women become men, while children are thought to have an equal right with their parents to make all important decisions. Yes, I know," he added with a friendly, modest shrug, "you think I am a hopeless reactionary who believes homosexuality a sin against God."

"If you don't have a bias against gays and lesbians," she said, all the anger gone, "then I don't understand why you would say what you just said. What does someone's sexual orientation have to do with anything? How is it anyone's business what two people do, how they decide to live their lives?"

Through the sliding glass doors, I could see far away, on the other side of the bay, the lights of San Francisco sparkling like a million lit candles, the burnished dream of an endless promise, the promise that every night would bring a new enchantment, and that the city would remain changeless through all the changes time might bring. It was the only place where Alan Boe was even possible.

"I don't think Alan is questioning the right of people to do what they like in private," said Albert Craven. "He was describing how Matthew Stanton must have seen the world. I knew him, Matthew Stanton, not very well, but well enough to know that Alan is exactly right. Matthew saw things as an outsider. He was as detached, or perhaps I should say isolated, as alone, as anyone I ever knew. They say that Emmett Stanton could see what the market was going to do before anyone else even suspected the market was going to change. Matthew could see things as well. He could see through the surface of what other people did. Alan is absolutely right about this. Matthew really did believe we were all part of a lunatic carnival. I suppose that is the reason he and T. J. Allen became such good friends."

Anna Mangini had finished dinner, and along with the others had started to drink. You did not notice at first that she was doing it all the time, sipping constantly from her glass, slowly, methodically, stopping only when her glass was empty and then only while she waited it for it to be filled. It had no visible effect. Her demeanor, her attitude, her temperament, never changed; she was always ready with a comment on anything she heard. She might be an alcoholic; she was never a drunk.

"His good friend, who is now on trial for his life. Are you certain he did not do it?" she asked, turning to me with her remarkable, incandescent eyes. "Or are you not allowed to tell us what you really think? Could you really tell us if you knew he was guilty? You must have defended people who were. What was that like? Can you tell us that?"

Judge Drexel was quick to stop her before she went any further.

"No, he can't. A lawyer for the defense... Well, never mind; just leave it at that. The defense lawyer has only one job: make sure his client gets a fair trial. The only issue is the evidence; the only question is what the evidence does or does not prove."

"But here, just among us," said Harry Caulfield, "if I promise we won't publish anything in the paper, tell us, did Allen kill Matthew Stanton, or was it someone else?"

"Someone else," I replied honestly. "But who that someone else is, I'm afraid... The thing about this trial that is so different is how everyone involved in it, from the coroner to the lead detective, was in some way involved with the Stantons."

Suzy Fairchild wondered why I thought it strange.

"Everyone knows the Stanton. There isn't anyone who didn't know—"

"Everyone? Or just everyone you know?"

It was not clear she thought there was a difference.

"Everyone in the city," she said with a stiff, distant glance.

"Yes, I understand. You know the Stantons, everyone knows the Stantons; and yet the only one here who does not know the Stantons is the only one who could tell me anything about who Matthew Stanton really was!"

Everyone took a second look, as it were, at Alan Boe. They seemed to agree with what I had said, but no one quite understood how it was possible. Anna Mangini hazarded a guess.

"I think it must be because Alan and Matthew Stanton have something important in common: contempt for what everyone else seems to want. Matthew Stanton had too much money to think it the answer for everything; our new friend, Alan Boe, has never needed money, nor, I imagine, much of anything else."

Harry Caulfield was not interested in who Matthew Stanton had been, or what had made him what he was. As often as any newspaper publisher, he had quoted that wonderfully self-serving line that journalism is the first draft of history, but that did not mean he had any desire to read the final draft, or even to know whether one had been written. He was not interested in the past; he wanted to know what was going to happen. He wanted to know more about the trial.

"If you're convinced Allen did not do it, but you don't know who did, what are you going to do? Are there any witnesses you can call?"

My elbow on the table, I held my thumb under my chin and stretched my index finger across my mouth. I did not say anything.

"Really," he persisted. "Off the record. Do you have a trial strategy, a plan, a list of witnesses?"

I took another drink, a long, slow one, and then, putting down the glass, looked, not at Harry Caulfield, but at his wife.

"You know the coroner, Elizabeth Burroughs, I assume. You've read her novels?"

Beatrice Caulfield was not unwilling to take credit for Burrough's early success.

"After we reviewed her first book, it became an instant best-seller. We have reviewed all of them, including the one coming out next month. She's famous now, so it will be the lead review in the Sunday paper."

"Is it any good?" I asked, as if, for some reason, I was seriously interested.

"She's enormously successful. She's always on the *New York Times* bestseller list. She's—"

"Is it any good?" I repeated. "Is she a good writer? When you get to the end of one of her novels, do you want to read it again?"

"She's a mystery writer. She doesn't write literary fiction. She writes what the public likes to read."

Her husband leaned in.

"I don't see what this has to do with what you are going to do in the trial."

"Everything. In addition to being a witness for the prosecution, a witness who destroyed her own credibility when she had to admit that she had concealed the fact that Matthew Stanton had a terminal disease, Burroughs not only knew, but is a close friend of the Stantons. She served on the Stanton Foundation board of directors. She is rich and famous, like nearly everyone else involved in this case, and, like everyone else, part of the same, incestuous circle that thinks they control everything that happens in San Francisco.

"But you're wondering what this has to do with the fact that she became rich and famous as a writer. Simply this: she knows, probably far in advance, when she starts a new story, what is going to happen. A trial isn't like that. A murder trial is not a murder mystery. I'm not talking about the fact that real people are involved, or that real lives are at risk, in a murder trial. I'm talking about the fact that you never know what is going to happen in a trial until it does. A trial strategy, a detailed plan? I did not know what I was going to ask Burroughs on cross-examination until I heard the first question come out of my mouth. Trying cases isn't a science; it is an art, like writing a novel, but a novel of the kind a serious reader would want to read more than once. A good writer doesn't know what he is going to write before he starts writing. A great writer—one of those we used to read years ago—hears the story tell itself in his head, and while he listens, scribbles down what he has heard. That is what I do in a trial: listen, and try to make sense of what I have heard. You want to know what I am going to do with the next witness the prosecution decides to call? I haven't got the faintest idea."

NINE

Samantha Longstreet's voice echoed off the walls.

"The prosecution calls Victoria Stanton."

The widow of Emmett Stanton, the stepmother of his now dead son, Victoria Stanton might have stepped straight from the pages of *Vogue*. With a thin, straight nose and high cheekbones, sharp square shoulders and long lacquered blonde hair cut straight across her forehead, she had the provocative look that men, especially older men of wealth and position, found irresistible. Her long-lashed eyes, blue, cold and dismissive, never moved, never noticed anything that was not directly in front of her. She could talk to you for hours, and then, if she lost interest, not remember your name.

The court clerk, though short and overweight with deep set sullen eyes, had an impish grin and a laugh so deep throated that each time you heard it, you started laughing yourself. When she finished giving the oath, she walked away, shaking her head. Victoria Stanton, like other rich people, was a fool. Victoria Stanton did not notice. The district attorney, on the other hand, treated her less like a witness whose presence was required than a visiting dignitary who had graciously agreed to appear. She sympathized with what must have been a tragic loss.

"It must have been extremely difficult," said Samantha Longstreet, "to go through what you have: losing your husband in a tragic accident, and now your stepson in a vicious murder."

In a voice trained to mirror exactly the emotion she wished to convey, Victoria Stanton agreed.

"First Emmett, the great love of my life, then Matthew, whom I could not have loved more had he been my own child."

Standing next to the counsel table, Longstreet listened in an attitude of profound respect.

"I know this must be difficult as well, but I'm sure that, more than anyone, you want to make sure justice is done, and that the murder of your stepson does not go unpunished. And so I have to ask—"

"Objection, Your Honor," I said calmly. "The prosecution is suggesting that a verdict of not guilty would mean that justice had not been done, and that the murder of Matthew Stanton would go unpunished."

"I never said that!" insisted Longstreet, turning on me with an angry glance. "That isn't what I said at all."

"So a not guilty verdict would not mean that justice had not been done?" I asked, lifting an eyebrow.

"Your Honor!" she cried, throwing up her hands.

Leonard Silverman just looked at her.

"He's twisting my words. He knows perfectly well what I meant."

But Silverman was not there to save her from her own mistakes.

"Mr. Antonelli raised an objection to what you said. You insisted that it was not what you meant. He asked whether, in that case, you meant that... Well, I don't think I need to repeat what he said. In any event, I am sustaining his objection. The suggestion you made, the necessary implication in what you said, is inadmissible."

She started to turn to the jury with a smile of contemptuous indifference, but Silverman fixed her with a stare of such icy coldness that she looked back.

"The jury isn't here to decide whether they agree with the rulings of the court. Don't waste their time or mine trying to appeal to them on a ruling you don't like!"

Her face turned pale. She dug her fingernails into her hands to keep from saying something that would only get her into more trouble.

"I apologize, Your Honor. I did not choose my words as carefully as I should have. It won't happen again," she promised, and then turned back to the witness.

"In addition to being Matthew Stanton's stepmother, did you also have a business relationship?"

"Yes, the family owns a professional basketball team."

"The team on which the defendant was a player?"

"Yes, that's correct. T. J. Allen was one of the best players we had; an all-star, before he was injured, before he hurt his knee."

She belonged in New York or Los Angeles, the way she dressed in elegant, fashionable clothes, so used to having whatever she wanted that she could never think of herself as spoiled, or selfish, or utterly superficial. But far from an empty-headed mannequin, she could rattle off a former player's statistics like a gambler on a lucky streak calculating the odds. It was not just what Allen, or anyone else who had played the game, had done on the court; she knew to the penny all the millions they had been paid. It was stunning, a dizzying account of the revenues and expenditures of a multi-billion-dollar enterprise, a sport turned entertainment business that, in the age of television and celebrity, had turned athletes into the only people anyone wanted to know.

The testimony of Victoria Stanton went on for hours, dozens, hundreds of questions, each one building on the one before, as Samantha Longstreet went about the task of showing how enormously successful the Stantons had been. The question was: why was she doing it? It became clear only at the end, when she asked about Allen's connection to the business the Stantons had built.

"The defendant stopped playing for the team a year ago. Was there a reason for this, a reason he retired? You said earlier the he hurt his knee, but..."

In a slow, graceful change of position, a slight adjustment of the angle at which she held her perfect, oval-shaped head, a movement so slight it made it seem that she had not moved at all, Victoria Stanton looked at the jury.

"The injury to his knee ended his season; his exorbitant financial demands ended his career."

Longstreet expected her to continue, but she seemed unwilling to detail the demands that had ended the career of the player she had earlier said was one of the best they had. I wondered how much of this was deliberate, a way to appear reluctant to give testimony against the accused; a way to avoid suspicion that she herself might have something to hide.

"Could you be more specific?" asked Longstreet. "What financial demands did the defendant make, and how did they end his career?"

Standing next to the jury box railing, Longstreet stroked the sleeve of her dark blue jacket, a jacket that would have looked custom made had anyone but Victoria Stanton been on the witness stand. Now, by comparison, it looked like something bought off the rack.

"T. J. wanted what is called a max contract, and he wanted it for five years."

"A max contract? Would you explain exactly what that is?"

"To make sure every team has the same amount of money to spend on player salaries, the league has a salary structure in which, among other things, a maximum is set. Only the very best players can be paid this amount, and it would be difficult, if not impossible, for a team to pay it to more than two of its players."

"But the defendant had been an all-star, one of the best players in the league."

"He was, or rather, he had been. He was already thirty-three years old. In five years, he would be thirty-eight. He had just been injured, had missed most of the year. We were willing to pay him close to the maximum for another year, perhaps even two, but he would not hear of it. He would not listen to anything except what he insisted he was owed."

Staring down at the floor, Longstreet repeated the last words, "What he was owed." She looked up, a question in her eyes. "What did you think he meant by that?"

Leaning forward to emphasize the importance of what she was about to say, Victoria Stanton explained.

"T. J. thought he had made a great financial sacrifice by staying with us instead of becoming a free agent and going to another team. He told everyone that he didn't care about the money, that he only wanted to win championships. In fairness, I think he believed it when he said it. He was always a great competitor. I never knew anyone who wanted to win more than he did. But that didn't mean that he didn't want to get paid what he thought he was worth. He thought we had an understanding; that because he did not become a free agent, if he took less than he could have made elsewhere, we would make it up to him the next time around. That's what I meant when I said he insisted he was owed a long-term contract for that kind of money."

Her arms folded in front of her, Longstreet leaned against the edge of the counsel table.

"When you say 'that kind of money,' how much are we talking about?"

"Between forty and forty-five million a year."

The courtroom became, more than quiet, perfectly still. It was as if everyone had stopped breathing. Professional athletes made a lot of money. Everyone knew that; their salaries were often mentioned in the newspapers and discussed on television in terms of the relative worth of a player. But now, suddenly, in a courtroom where everything was supposed to be about fairness and justice, it seemed like the wretched excess of a world gone completely mad. Even the district attorney, who must have known what her own witness was going to say, looked genuinely shocked.

"Forty, forty-five…? And what was he offered instead?"

"Our final offer was for twenty-two million a year."

"Only twenty-two million!" exclaimed Longstreet with a grim, sarcastic smile. "Easy to see how he might feel underpaid! Sorry," she added before I could object. "Twenty-two million, and he turned it down?"

"He said he wouldn't consider it." With an easy, effortless movement, she turned again to the jury. "It seems like a lot of money, forty or forty-five million a year, and it is. Twenty-two million is a lot of money. What no one seems to understand is that it really isn't about the money at all; it is about what the money means. Imagine two players on the same team. One of them is making twenty or thirty million and the other is making just a hundred thousand more. What is the difference? Everything, in the mind of the player. It tells him that the organization thinks the other player is better. It wouldn't matter if players were getting paid hundreds of thousands instead of tens of millions. The issue is always going to be who gets more—who the team thinks is worth more, who the team thinks is better. That is what made T. J. go crazy: the thought that we did not think he was worth as much as some of the other players."

"But you tried to do something about that, didn't you?

Didn't you, the team ownership, offer him something more than the contract you mentioned?"

"T. J. was more than just another player, more than one of the best the game has ever seen; T. J. was family. We didn't want to lose him; we wanted him to become a permanent part of the organization. We wanted him to become, in a way, the face of the organization, the way Magic Johnson has been for the Lakers, someone who, the moment you saw him, would remind you of how good, how great we were. We told him that at the end of the contract, when his playing days were over, we wanted him to become vice president of the team; to become, as I said, the public face of the organization and involved in everything we did."

"What was his reaction? Did he understand that you were offering him what was, in effect, a lifetime position?"

"He could not let go of the feeling that he was being cheated. So far as he was concerned, the offer of a vice presidency was the equivalent of being given a gold watch at retirement. It made him even angrier than he had been before. Next thing I know, he bought a gun, a gun he kept in his locker, and he started making threats, telling everyone how sorry we were going to be, that we were going to regret treating him with such disrespect. That was the word he kept using—disrespect. We had disrespected him, and no one could do that to him. And then there was this thing he had for Matthew. That is what really scared me, though it turns out it should have scared me even more than it did. I should have seen it coming, knowing what I did about him, what he was capable of, how brutally violent he could be," she said, a look of horror on her face.

Full of sympathy and understanding, Samantha Longstreet asked if she would like a moment to compose herself. It was picture perfect, as well orchestrated as any courtroom scene I had seen acted: the witness suddenly overcome with emotion at the realization she might have prevented an awful tragedy; the aggressive, tough-minded prosecutor revealing, if for just an instant, a human side. I was ready to start clapping, but the show was not quite finished. With a brave smile, Victoria Stanton insisted she could go on; but then, before Longstreet could ask the next question, she reached inside her purse for a handkerchief and wiped away the tears no one was close enough to see.

"You were saying that the defendant had 'this thing' for your stepson, and that it really scared you. What did you mean by that?"

Victoria Stanton shook her head; she did not want to answer. It was too painful.

"Please; I know this is difficult," coaxed Longstreet, moving closer. "Whatever it is, it will be better once it is all out."

"Matthew was very thoughtful," she began, nodding her acknowledgement that the district attorney was right. "He tried to help people; he tried to help T. J. They seemed to get along. I don't mean they were close friends or anything like that. Matthew usually kept to himself. Everyone knew he was wealthy, which meant everyone wanted to get close to him. Maybe that was the reason he spent time with T. J.—he was rich and famous on his own. But Matthew, as I said, was thoughtful. He read a lot, and I guess he must have tried to talk to him about what he read, because what T. J. did, what he started saying about Matthew... It was hard to believe that anyone these days could have said anything like it. I can't even bring myself to repeat it, even after what he ..."

"I understand, it's painful; but, please, just tell us, tell the jury what the defendant said that made you so scared about what he might do."

For the first and only time, Victoria Stanton looked at T. J. Allen, sitting in the chair next to me.

"He told people, friends of his, that Matthew was treating him like some ignorant fool who did not even know how to read.

He said he was— and this is what I could never forget—treating him like the house nigger, and no one could treat him like that!"

Allen shot out of the chair. I grabbed him by the arm and pulled him back as hard as I could to stop him from shouting out an obscenity-laced denial.

"That miserable, lying..." he whispered as he sank back down in the chair. "I never said that; I never use that word. Never, not even when it is just me and some of the brothers. It's the last thing I ever would have said about Matthew!"

I was too busy trying to gauge the reaction of the jury to listen. They had seen Allen's vigorous, immediate response; the outrage on his face, the way I grabbed him by the arm. Longstreet seemed to think it showed how angry he could become, but the jury was looking at him with what I thought was the hope that his denial was true.

"In basketball it is the difference, isn't it, between a set and an unscripted play?" I whispered to Allen.

He stared at me with his huge, dark eyes, wondering what I meant. Then, suddenly, he understood.

"Damn right," he agreed, rolling his eyes at Victoria Stanton's studied fraud.

With one long, last look at the jury, Samantha Longstreet announced that she was finished with the witness. Leonard Silverman peered down at me and in a laconic voice that shielded his eager curiosity of how Vitoria Stanton would stand up under what he, and everyone else in the courtroom, expected would be a withering cross-examination, asked if I wished to cross-examine the witness.

My elbows on the table, I tapped my fingers together as if I were taking the question under advisement. Dropping my left hand, I grasped my chin with my right, lifted my eyebrows, and shook my head.

"I don't know."

Silverman started to laugh.

"You don't know?"

"I can't decide."

"You can't decide?" The grin on his mouth, furtive at first, was furtive no longer.

"It isn't a question of whether to do it, Your Honor; but where to begin. The problem," I said as I got up slowly and, as it were, reluctantly from my chair, "is that when I call as a witness someone I am representing, Mr. Allen, for example, I usually ask, as the very first question, whether they did what they are accused of doing, whether they are guilty or innocent of the crime. Mrs. Stanton is not my client, she has not been charged with anything, and yet, for some reason, I can't decide whether I should not ask her that same question."

Silverman did not know where I was going with this, but he was reasonably certain that I was not in the slightest doubt about what I was going to do.

"It seems to me, Mr. Antonelli, that you have made your decision and, instead of wondering whether you should cross-examine the witness, you have already started. Ask your question."

Lowering my head, I began to walk back and forth, looking for all the world as if I still had not decided what to do. I stopped, put my hand on the jury box railing, looked up, caught the eye of Victoria Stanton, rubbed the back of my neck, started to speak, and then, changing my mind, let go of the railing, took two more steps, stopped abruptly, and with a piercing stare, tried to look right through her.

"Tell me, Mrs. Stanton, when did you first decide to have your stepson murdered—before or after you killed his father?"

She almost bolted out of the witness chair. Longstreet was not far behind her. I help up my hand.

"My apologies! I should have known better than that," I admitted with a chastened look of contrition. Longstreet settled back into her chair. Victoria Stanton started to relax. "I've asked you two questions instead of one. The first question is: when did you decide to have Matthew Stanton killed? The second question is: was this before or after you killed your late husband?"

Longstreet was screaming her objection. Silverman was banging his gavel to silence the crowd.

"You wish to make an objection, Ms. Longstreet?" he asked in a calm, civil tone.

"Of course I wish to make an objection! Defense counsel is accusing the witness of murder!"

"I understand that," replied Silverman with a pleasant smile. "I have not yet understood the grounds for your objection."

"He's accusing..." she sputtered. "He can't do that, Your Honor. There has not been any evidence introduced that would support an accusation of the sort he's making, nothing that would suggest—!"

"She's your witness, counselor. You asked her what the defendant had done to make her think he was responsible for Matthew Stanton's death. She said she had been scared of what he might do, and that she feels in some sense responsible, knowing what she claims she knew, for not stopping the murder from happening. All that Mr. Antonelli did was ask the witness directly whether she herself is guilty of the crime. If defense counsel is allowed to ask the defendant, under oath, if he is guilty, it is difficult to see why he cannot ask the same question of a witness for the prosecution. So, I'll allow it. The witness may answer," he said as he turned to Victoria Stanton. But then he remembered something. "The form of the question, that needs to be changed," he instructed me, shaking his head. "You can't ask someone when they decided to do something before you ask them whether they did it. But you know that."

"No, I didn't arrange to have Matthew murdered," shouted Victoria Stanton, before I could start to ask. "And I certainly did not kill my husband, Emmett, whom I loved very much. I resent what you are doing, Mr. Antonelli," she added, raking me with her long-lashed eyes. "It's outrageous, a disgrace that you, that anyone, should be able—"

"You're in a court of law, Mrs. Stanton," I reminded her in a cold, measured voice. "This is a murder trial, not some dinner party with a few dozen of your rich, useless friends."

"My rich, useless... Where do you get the nerve to talk to me like that; who do you—?"

"Where do I get the nerve? From watching people who think they can get away with anything; people with so little conscience they would let someone else go to prison, or the gas chamber, for something they themselves have done. Now, Mrs. Stanton, let's begin at the beginning. Your husband, your late husband, Emmett Stanton, died in a mountain climbing accident, correct?"

"Yes, that's correct; we were—"

"He died in a mountain climbing accident somewhere in the French Alps, correct?"

"Yes. We were on holiday and—"

"There were two people with him when he fell, correct?"

"Yes, I was there and—"

"Michael Kensington was there as well, correct?"

"Yes. As I was about to say, Michael—"

"Was there, and no one else. Just the three of you, correct?"

"Yes, that is what I was about to explain. You see—"

"You had been having an affair with Michael Kensington, isn't that correct?"

"No! Well, I mean..." She looked past me to Samantha Longstreet, hoping she could do something, but Longstreet glanced down at some papers on the table in front of her.

"A year, slightly less than a year, after your husband, Emmett Stanton, died, you remarried, correct?"

She had been perched on the front edge of the witness chair, but now she sank back.

"Yes, I remarried."

"Who did you marry?"

She looked out at the courtroom crowd, wondering, as it seemed, how she might get lost in it, hide somewhere where there were no questions to be answered and no one could judge her.

"You married Michael Kensington, isn't that correct?" I did not wait for an answer. "Your husband's death, that accidental death to which only you and your future husband were witnesses, proved rather convenient, didn't it?"

Lifting her chin, she threw me a dismissive glance, as if she had no idea what I was talking about and neither did I.

"Convenient, not just because it allowed you to marry Michael Kensington, but because, except for Matthew Stanton, you now had control of everything Emmett Stanton had owned, including the basketball team whose finances you so expertly described in your testimony earlier. Tell us, Mrs. Stanton, how much did your husband, Emmett Stanton, pay when he bought the team twelve years ago—several hundred million, wasn't it?"

"Something like that," she replied with a shrug. Whatever he paid, it had been an affordable price.

"And isn't it true that the *Wall Street Journal* has recently estimated it to now be worth approximately four billion?"

"It is hard to know what anything is worth until you put it up for sale."

"Yes, but when you put something up for sale, you usually put a price on it first. Do you disagree with the estimate I just gave you, that the team is now worth six or seven times what was paid for it?"

"No, I don't disagree; but I can't really see what that has to do with—"

"With the murder of your stepson? If the team were sold, who would get the four billion it is now worth?"

My arms folded across my chest, I stood in front of the counsel table, leaning back against it. Every time her gaze drifted away, every time she looked at the jury or glanced at the courtroom crowd, my eyes were there, waiting, when she looked back.

"The Stanton Trust owns the team."

"The trust is divided into shares, isn't it? Emmett Stanton had fifty-one percent, a controlling interest; his son, Matthew, thirty percent; and you, as Emmett Stanton's wife, had the remaining nineteen. Emmett Stanton's shares passed to Matthew Stanton when Emmett Stanton died. That left Matthew Stanton with eighty-one percent. You had what you had before, nineteen percent. But now that Matthew Stanton is dead, what happens to his eighty-one percent? It all goes to you, doesn't it? Which means that in the event of a sale, you would get the entire four billion, isn't that right, Mrs. Stanton?"

Her eyes hot with rage, she gripped the arms of the witness chair so tight her knuckles lost all color.

"The money doesn't matter. Four billion, ten billion; nineteen percent, a hundred percent: we were never going to sell. What for? To buy something else?"

I looked at her to see if she really meant it. Suddenly, I realized that she was not lying, and I realized something else as well, why she would never sell: owning the team gave her something money alone could never give her.

"Your husband, Emmett Stanton, bought the team, but neither he nor his son Matthew were involved in the day-to-day operations, were they?"

"No. There was—there is—a general manager, a whole management team."

"But you were the one who had the last word. Whenever a major decision had to be made, you were the one who made it.

Isn't that what the sports writers always said?" I asked with a smile for the frequent failure of the newspapers to get things right.

"I wouldn't say I had the final word. As I said, Emmett wasn't involved in day-to-day things, but he was always involved, always consulted, when something important—"

"Always asked whether he agreed with what you thought should be done—is that a fair way of putting it?"

I asked this in the accommodating voice of someone who did not underestimate the extent of her achievement. Her only response was to smile back. It was not a friendly smile, just an acknowledgement that what I said was true.

"You were, in fact, the public face of the franchise. Everyone wanted to talk to the players and coaches, but when it came to the business side of things—which players would be offered new contracts, which players might be pursued in free agency—every reporter wanted to see you, not Emmett Stanton, but Victoria Stanton. None of the stories about what was going to happen next, none of the stories about whether T. J. Allen was going to be re-signed to a five-year contract ever said 'Victoria Stanton, who has a nineteen percent interest.' They said Victoria Stanton, owner. Isn't that the title you go by?"

"Reporters write what they want to write."

"Reporters write what no one tells them to correct. Matthew Stanton did not have the same feeling about owning a professional sports team, did he?"

She dismissed it out of hand. I obviously did not know anything about what her stepson had really been like.

"Matthew was quite serious about everything he did, and that included the team. He knew as much as anyone about how the organization functioned. He took a real interest in the players." Pausing, suddenly caught up in the emotion of something she had just remembered, she stared down at her hand. "He took a real interest in T. J. Allen. He tried to show him how to take care of his money, how to invest it, so he would never have to worry about money so long as he lived." Her voice turned cold; her eyes turned lethal. "And look what it got him! Instead of gratitude, death!"

I ignored her, and I did it quickly. The next question was out of my mouth before her words could leave an echo.

"How many people are on the board of directors of the Stanton Foundation? Nearly two dozen, correct?"

Her mouth had not closed. The question startled her.

"What?"

"How many people on the board, two dozen?"

"Yes, that's right."

I went around the table and picked up a single typewritten page, a list of twenty-four names.

"Twenty-four very prominent and, most of them, very wealthy people. Would that be a fair description?"

"They're successful people, if that is what you mean. All of them are dedicated to making San Francisco an even better place to live."

"The Stanton Foundation has tax-exempt status as a charitable organization, correct?"

"Yes."

"The purpose of this charitable organization, according to your own official description, is to support the arts. The foundation gives grants, provides scholarships for artists, musicians, that sort of thing, is that correct?"

"Yes. As I said, the foundation is dedicated to improving the life, the cultural life, of the city."

"The money for this comes from individual contributions, including from members of the board?"

"We also have a number of corporate sponsors."

"In fact, nearly every major company that does business in San Francisco has contributed, haven't they?"

"Yes, I'm proud to say they have."

"And part of the reason they do this is because nearly everyone on your board, including yourself, contribute to the causes these individuals and companies have as their major charitable efforts. Isn't that how these interlocking interests work together?"

"Everyone does whatever they can to help."

"By everyone, you don't actually mean everyone, do you? You mean the few dozen, a hundred at most, of the rich and famous, the movers and shakers, the people who get things done. Isn't that what you mean: this small world of social and political insiders in which everyone knows everyone else?"

"I don't think I would put it quite like that," she replied with a polite smile and a steely gaze. "It would be more accurate to say that these are people who have done well enough to give something back; people willing to give their time and money for the kind of things that will help everyone, and I mean everyone, have a better life. There is nothing wrong with that."

"Nothing wrong at all," I agreed as I looked again at the list of twenty-four names. "Unless they think it more important to help one another than helping those who need it; unless it becomes more important to keep in the good graces of those with more money, and more power, than meet their obligations under the law."

She started to object, complain that I was taking things out of context, that I did not understand. I cut her off with a warning glance.

"Elizabeth Burroughs, the county coroner, is on the board of the Stanton Foundation, and she is not the only one connected to this case. Marilyn Chang, the wife of the lead detective, is another member." I studied her for a moment and then asked point blank: "Were you aware that Elizabeth Burroughs was going to testify in this trial?"

She began to equivocate, stumbling over her words as she first denied, then admitted that she had known.

"I knew it only in a general way. I mean, she's the coroner, so it would make sense that... But if you're suggesting—!"

"Did you at any time discuss with her what her testimony was going to be?"

"No, of course not."

"Why do you say 'of course not'? She's on your board, and, unless I'm wrong, you are rather good friends, are you not? You spent time together, attended some of the same social events, but you never, not even once, talked to her about what she was going to say about the cause of your stepson's death?"

"No, I didn't. I—"

"You're involved with everyone in this case, aren't you, Mrs. Stanton?"

I looked across at Samantha Longstreet. I kept looking at her until the silence became a kind of interrogation. She stared back, her eyes dark and impenetrable, determined not to show the least concern for what she knew was coming.

"Even the district attorney is on the board of the Stanton Foundation. Isn't that true, Mrs. Stanton?"

"Yes, she is; but so are a lot of other—"

"Prominent, powerful people. Is that what you were about to say? The kind of people who help each other any way they can?"

She started to argue, to insist that it was not true. I dismissed it with a wave of my hand.

"Never mind, Mrs. Stanton." I stopped, as if I had just realized the mistake I had been making. "It isn't Mrs. Kensington?"

"It's Stanton. I kept the name."

"The Stanton name. Yes, I can see where that might be important—the Stanton Foundation, the Stanton Trust," I remarked, nodding to myself, as I went back to the counsel table and opened a file folder. I read a few lines from a document and then closed the folder. "Because you were, for all practical purposes, in charge of the business operations of the basketball team, you knew about all the security measures that had been taken, didn't you? No one could just walk into the player's locker room, could they?"

"No, there was always security personnel to prevent anyone who wasn't authorized from entering."

"Every player has his own locker, with his own key or access code, correct?"

"Yes, that's right."

"You told the district attorney that you became 'really scared'—I think that is the phrase you used—when the defendant bought a gun. Isn't it true that at least half the players on your team are registered owners of handguns?"

"Some of the players make a lot of money, drive expensive cars, have a lot of—"

"They have guns. But when T. J. Allen got one, you were suddenly 'really scared.' Because T. J. Allen was a violent person, a danger to be around?" I turned and faced the jury. "He got called for a lot of fouls when he played," I said as an aside. I turned back to the witness. "Unlike at least half the players on your team, T. J. Allen had never been in trouble with law, had he?"

"No, he—"

"Had no record of domestic violence, no record of assault. You knew that; it was your business as the chief executive officer of the Stanton organization to know that, correct?"

"Just because someone has not been charged with a crime, doesn't mean—!"

"Yes, we're aware of that, Mrs. Stanton!" I shot back with a significant glance. "We're also aware, very much aware, that just because someone has been charged with a crime doesn't mean they're guilty. Now, the gun, the one that had you so scared. You knew he had it?"

"Of course I knew—"

"Because he kept it in his locker, in a place only authorized personnel could enter?"

"Yes, that's right; he—"

"Reported it stolen from his locker, where only someone who had access could have taken it!"

"Unless he took it himself and reported it missing so the police would think someone else had used it to murder Matthew!"

"So now you're suggesting," I remarked, moving toward her until I was less than an arm's length away, "that the defendant planned weeks in advance to murder Matthew Stanton, pretended his gun had been stolen, instead of getting one that could not be traced back to him, and then made sure to have it in his hand while he waits for the police to arrive so that he could, what, exactly? Claim that he must be innocent because no one guilty of murder could ever have come up with a story that stupid?"

I was through with her. I started back to the counsel table, but just before I got there, I stopped and turned around.

"Have you ever read *The Idiot*?"

"Have I ...?"

"The novel by Dostoevsky. It's about a young man, Prince Myshkin, who lives his life according to the moral principles of Christianity, with the result that he gets destroyed. You never read it?"

"No, I'm afraid I haven't," she admitted, though not with the embarrassment of having failed to do something she should have done, but with relief that she had not wasted her time.

"I ask because it was the last book your stepson and T. J. Allen read together. That's what they did: read the serious works of serious writers. You didn't know that, did you, Mrs. Stanton? But why would you? You didn't really know either of them very well."

Ten

"I never read that book, *The Idiot*, and I don't think Matthew did, either," said T. J. Allen when I went to see him after the trial was done for the day.

He had an excited expression on his face. He was sure there was a reason why I had said what I did about Dostoevsky's novel, and that this had to have some significance. I was not sure there was a reason. I had remembered that they had read *Crime and Punishment* together, but, in the heat of the moment, all the things I had been told, everything I thought I knew about Matthew Stanton, had somehow come together in the memory of a single, long-forgotten Russian novel.

"You should read it." I looked up at Allen, towering over me from the other side of the scratched metal table in that small, windowless room. "Everyone, everyone but Myshkin, is a fraud."

He was still waiting for an explanation, the reason I had brought it up.

"It just came out," I admitted. "You told me about reading *Crime and Punishment*. That was Dostoevsky's novel about guilt; *The Idiot* is his novel about innocence. Maybe that's what happened. Maybe I thought that if the jury thought anything, they might think about someone who had never done anything wrong. Why?" I laughed. "Did you think I always know what I am going to say before I say it?"

It was odd, really quite strange, but the only thing anyone wanted to talk about was Dostoevsky's unread novel. It was the first thing Albert Craven asked me when I got back to the office.

"You're probably responsible for a couple hundred copies being sold," he said as he settled, uninvited, into the wingback chair on the other side of my desk. "I was there today, in court; not all day, just this afternoon. I wanted to see Victoria Stanton and what she was going to do. You would think people would have more sense, wouldn't you?"

Loosening my tie, I sank back into my overstuffed chair. I was exhausted, exhausted and exhilarated at the same time; as tired as I had ever been physically, but emotionally and mentally still on the edge. Questions, answers, everything that had happened in court, were banging around my head like a drunkard's guilty conscience.

"Have more sense?"

"The way she dressed. She might as well have come wearing dollar bills." He immediately corrected himself, his eyes shining with a more vivid description. "Not dollar bills, stock certificates or bonds, something that would announce in terms no one could misunderstand that she has more money than God. It was like watching someone in a tuxedo walk into a bikers' convention. That was bad enough, but when you asked her if she had read *The Idiot*, the look she got, confusion and then indifference... No one left that courtroom thinking she was anything except what you said she was."

"Someone who had killed her husband, someone who had her stepson murdered?"

"No, not yet," he replied, becoming serious. "But not someone who could never have done it. When you asked that question, asked if she had read...was it to draw the contrast between someone who tried to live a decent life and the kind of life she leads?"

"Hell, Albert, I don't know," I replied, throwing my hands up. "It just came out. It was a lie. Matthew Stanton never read it with Allen. They read *Crime and Punishment*. But there was something I remembered about Myshkin... I can't even tell you what it was, but something that made me think of Stanton. It isn't the same. Stanton was not trying to live a Christian life. I don't know what he believed, or if he believed in anything at all. I don't know if he was religious. But there was something. I'm just not sure what."

"Everyone who can get a copy will start reading it, trying to figure out what you meant, when you don't even know yourself! Well," he said as he got up, "it's always good to encourage people to read."

He had not taken two steps when he remembered.

"How stupid of me. I came in to tell you that someone is waiting to see you and then managed to forget all about it. I assume she's still there. Let me go look."

It was nearly six o'clock and I was meeting Tangerine for dinner at seven. Even if I had the time, I did not want to see a new client.

"Don't bother. I'll tell whoever it is she'll have to make an appointment for some time after the trial is over."

I walked Albert to his office and then went out to the lobby. A rather striking woman in her thirties wearing a plain dark dress was reading a magazine. Her handbag and raincoat were in the empty chair next to her. She had long black hair and large, almond-shaped eyes, eyes that seemed to draw you closer the moment she looked at you, eyes that, with her straight, finely shaped nose, gave her the look of one of those elegant, timeless faces painted on Egyptian walls and vases thousands of years ago.

"Mr. Antonelli," she said as she rose from the chair and offered me her hand. "I'm Sheila Bergson. I know it's late, but I was there today, in court, and I had to see you. Matthew Stanton and I went to school together. There are things I think you should know."

She followed me like a curious tourist, careful not to miss anything, whether the pictures on the wall, the framed black-and-white photographs of Albert Craven's early partners when they were all just starting out, or the view out the windows we passed on the short journey down the thick padded carpet to my office. When I opened the door, she cast an admiring glance at the floor-to-ceiling bookshelves, but did not stop to get a closer look at the books they held. I had the feeling that she did not need to, that she knew what they were; not all of them, of course, but enough to have a sense of what I read, or at least what I thought important.

"You have a lovely place to work," she observed after she had taken the chair Albert Craven had left a few minutes earlier. "Though if it were my office, I would probably spend all my time staring out the window, watching the Bay Bridge change in the changing light."

She had a voice like music, jazz music, every word a new interpretation of what, until she spoke it, had been an unexamined thought. She had gone to school with Matthew Stanton; it was impossible to think he had not been in love with her.

"Matthew and I were close, very close; we were quite good friends." She smiled at the look of surprise in my eyes. "Friends, good friends. You're wondering why. We understood, we both understood, that it couldn't be anything more. I'm Jewish; Matthew was not. We had gone out a couple times for coffee, and I could tell what was happening; I knew what was happening to me. I was a sophomore, Matthew was in his junior year. Two kids in college, what better time, what better place, to fall in love, and so I told him one gorgeous day in October as we were walking across campus that I could not see him again, that my mother had always told me that if I ever brought home a boy who wasn't Jewish, I could not come home again. He thought I was making up an excuse and that I was not interested in him. It wasn't until a long time later that he finally believed me, that he understood that it was the only reason we could never be more than friends. I wonder now whether it would have changed anything if I had not been Jewish, or if it had not seemed so important to me."

"What might it have changed?" I asked. "Did something happen, something that had some connection to what happened to him, that he was killed?"

It seemed unlikely, too much time had passed since they had both been in college, but she seemed haunted by the idea. Her eyes were full of secrets.

"I was a French major. I read all the great French writers: Flaubert—not just *Madame Bovary*, but *A Sentimental Education*, *Salammbo*, *The Temptation of Saint Anthony*, *Bouvard and Pecuchet*—everything Flaubert wrote," she recited, glowing at the memory of what she had done. "I read Proust. And then I started reading twentieth-century French writers. I read Andre Gide. I read his novel, *The Counterfeiters*, and I told Matthew all about it."

She suddenly gave me a strange, quizzical look. There was more than a question in that look, more than a question about me. It was a double question, a doubt about the meaning of things, the way we are all prisoners of the past, of what we have done, what we have thought, before.

"In court today, what you said about Dostoevsky. Did you ever wonder how many people—how many young men—read *Crime and Punishment* and started thinking about what it would be like to kill someone, an old woman, someone no one cared about, to get the money they needed to do something important, something that would help them do something important, something that would help them leave their mark on the world? *The Counterfeiters* is a different kind of story. It doesn't deal with murder in the usual sense. It deals with suicide, but suicide that has been forced on someone, a fifteen-year-old boy who thinks he has to kill himself because he lost the game, a game he doesn't know has been fixed."

A sad, rueful smile passed over her mouth and her eyes filled with all the regret of nostalgia. She shuddered, literally shuddered, at what she had not been able to forget.

"A fifteen-year-old boy from a family where there was so much violence he often had to stay with neighbors, a boy who spent his time reading what Gide describes as works of 'pessimistic German philosophers.' He is, this boy, literary, precocious, and friendless. When a group of older boys ask him to join them in an adventure, a way to test their courage, he knows only that he will be thought a coward, and would think himself a coward, if he refuses. The rules are quite simple. Everyone agrees to draw lots to see which one of them will kill himself."

Her eyes became distant and remote, and I thought she was thinking about something else, something that somehow had a connection to the story she was telling me. She looked at me as if she was sure I knew already what it was.

"The boy loses, and now he has to do what he promised. The older boy who had arranged everything had a gun. Everyone except the boy knows the gun is not loaded, that it holds only blanks. They want to scare the boy, find out if he will really go through with it; whether he will pull the trigger and kill himself. The time is set when he has to do it. They're going to do it in the classroom of the school they attend, do it while the class is in session. The ringleader sits next to the boy, counting down the time he has left: ten minutes, nine minutes, eight...then the seconds, ten, nine, and then there is no time left. The boy takes the gun, stands up in the middle of the class, puts the gun to his temple, and pulls the trigger...and falls down dead! Everyone, everyone in that evil conspiracy, thought it was only a joke, that there weren't any real bullets. Everyone, that is, except the boy who started it, who hated the young boy because he thought he was weak."

For some reason, Sheila Bergson seemed almost frantic. She was talking about a character in a novel, a novel written a century ago, but it was as if she were reporting something that had just happened; happened, moreover, to someone she knew.

"The story was real. Gide used a newspaper account to construct his story around it, the story of how, because of their connections, no one was punished for what they had done. I suppose that is the reason I told Matthew: the evil of what had been done, and the corruption that allowed the older boy, the boy who had set everything in motion, to get away with what, by any definition, was cold-blooded murder. It's strange, isn't it, Mr. Antonelli? How something written in a novel, something written a long time ago, can change so many lives? If I hadn't read Andre Gide, if I hadn't told Matthew what I had read, if Matthew hadn't told... If Matthew had not been such a fool!" she cried with an anguish that only deepened the mystery of whatever it was she was trying to tell me.

"If Matthew hadn't...?" I asked when she began to stare into the distance. At first, I did not think she had heard me, but then she looked at me again, sorry that she had, if only for a moment, lost control of herself.

"Matthew told some friends of his, some of his fraternity brothers. Matthew was intelligent, extremely intelligent, but he was not a student, not then. He had already flunked out once, at the end of his sophomore year—I don't think he had opened a book all year. He did not know what he wanted; he did not know why he was in college, except that it was what you did, what was expected of someone like him—rich, privileged, and, at least with respect to money, his future guaranteed. There was not anything he had to do, and, because of that, nothing he looked forward to doing; nothing worth the kind of sacrifice someone without his advantages would think an opportunity and not a sacrifice at all. He did not have any interest in French literature, he just liked being with me, and so he listened when I would tell him with all my gushing enthusiasm what great new thing I had just discovered. And so he told his friends, proud, in a way, that he could talk about something serious, something he was sure they would not have known anything about.

"They were all the same, those rich kids who were always going to be rich. They were there to get a degree, and to learn as little as they could get away with. They were there to have a good time; their only worry whether they could find a different girl to sleep with every week. When they found out that one of the freshmen who had pledged their fraternity was gay, they decided to make his life as much a living hell as they could. And then Matthew, in all innocence, tells them this story, this hundred-year-old story from a novel they never heard of and could never have understood, and it seemed the perfect thing to do themselves, the perfect way to get their revenge, their ounce of flesh, from a sweet, harmless boy who only wanted to be their friend."

"They made him think they were all going to draw straws to see who would commit suicide. They told him that he could do it, too, become one of them, part of their group, if he had the courage?" I asked, hoping it was not true, and certain that it was.

The look in her eyes, that wounded look of injured innocence, taught me more about her than anything she could have said. The story, what she had read, what she had reported, what had, because of that, happened again, had changed her forever because it had changed Matthew Stanton forever. The story, both stories, had become, not just something from her remembered past, but, as she understood, part of everything that would ever happen, part of everything that would ever happen to her.

"They did exactly the same thing. They told him, this young boy who had only been on campus a short time, that they trusted him, that they knew he would keep his word, just as they would each keep theirs. They promised each other that they would not hesitate, that they would not change their minds. There were five of them. Matthew was one of them. He did not see any reason not be involved; no one was going to get hurt. There were no bullets; the gun was empty. They were not going to do it in a classroom in front of other people; it would be just the six of them, out on one of the athletic fields in the evening when no one else would be around. What Matthew did not know, what no one except Thomas Elkins knew, was that the gun was loaded. Elkins hated that boy, hated him because he was gay; hated him, I think, because he was afraid someone would find out and think that Elkins might be gay as well. Elkins put the bullets in the gun and then made sure—they all made sure—that the boy drew the short straw.

"They stood there, watching, wondering if he would really do it; wondering, if he did, whether he would feel angry or relieved when the gun did not fire and he realized it had all been a joke. And then, holding back their laughter, they watched as the boy, his hands shaking, tears running out of his eyes, more scared than anyone they had ever seen, but more scared of showing himself a coward, someone who could not be trusted, put the gun to his head. He held it there for what seemed an eternity, trembling with fear. Thomas Elkins shouted, 'Do it!' and he did. The others, who did not know what Elkins had done, looked on in horror as the boy they only meant to scare—no, that isn't right. They didn't want to scare him; they wanted to humiliate him, make him feel that he was nothing, nothing but an object of contempt. When the boy fell dead at their feet, they knew immediately what

Thomas Elkins had done. Elkins did not care. He justified it. He reminded them that it was a suicide, which is what they had all agreed to do, and that even if they had not meant it, the boy had not known that. He had committed suicide just like he said he would."

"What happened?" I asked, stunned by what she had described. "They did not get away with calling it a suicide. What happened to Elkins? What happened to Matthew?"

It was there again, that hopeless look, not of despair, exactly; despair may not last. No, it was something more final: the knowledge, the utter certainty, that what has happened can never be changed, that we are damned forever by what we have done, and damned forever by what we failed to do.

"Do you read much, Mr. Antonelli? I don't mean the kind of nonsense most people read today, if they read anything at all, but serious things, serious novels? You knew who I was talking about when I mentioned Gide. Have you ever read Jorge Borges, the Argentine writer? He could have written this story. In a way, he did write this story: the endless repetition of an evil deed; the infinite reflection of something you have done, or failed to do, in a double set of facing mirrors. That is what happened here, a repetition, the same thing happening that had happened before. Gide's story, the real reported event as the basis of it, told again by this murder made to look like suicide. In Gide's story, they get away with it. They came from wealthy, important, powerful families. Promises were made, financial arrangements were entered into; everything was kept out of the public eye, everyone who could have done something about it looked the other way.

"The same thing happened again. There really are not that many variations in the way things happen, are there, Mr. Antonelli? The children of the rich seldom become famous for self-discipline and a sense of responsibility. Everything was handled, everything was taken care of. The death was ruled an accident, the boy was blamed. He should have known better; he should have known there is no such thing as an empty gun. He should never have pointed it at himself; he should never have pretended to play Russian roulette. Thomas Elkins said he still could not believe what had happened. Only Matthew tried to tell the truth."

It was late, nearly seven. The night was everywhere. The shaded light from the lamp on my desk cast a soft, mystic glow, the memory of ancient things, on Sheila Bergson's marvelously intelligent face. Her steady, and at times relentless, gaze never left my eyes. It was like looking in a mirror, listening to my own confession, the way she held me, spellbound, her words becoming an echo of what I heard inside my mind.

"I've read Borges," I heard myself say. "His stories are unforgettable; you can't get rid of them, they follow you, take hold of you, when you are thinking of something completely different. They come to you, sometimes, years after you first read them. Do you remember the one about the race the gauchos used to have, where they would cut the throats of the bandits they lined up together, the bandits who knew they had only a few second left to live but ran anyway because they knew they were supposed to, and because they wanted to see who could go the farthest, who would win the race with death?"

"That is what happened to Matthew; that is what I am trying to tell you, what I am trying to explain," she said, her eyes wide with anticipation, determined to tell me what she knew. "He tried to tell the truth about what happened, tried to tell them that they had meant to play a joke, a cruel, unforgivable joke, as he now understood, but a joke. There were never any bullets in the gun. They all knew that. Then, when the gun was fired, when the boy was killed, they knew that Thomas Elkins had been lying all the time. No one believed Matthew; no one wanted to believe him. Elkins insisted the gun was not loaded when he last looked at it;

insisted that someone else must have done it. No one, no one at the university, wanted to pursue it any further; no one wanted a public scandal. No one wanted the police; no one wanted a trial."

"No one called the police?"

"Campus security took care of everything, the way they did with everything that happened there, whether it was some guy who got drunk at a party and raped the girl he was with, or someone on the football team who stole a stereo system out of a student dorm. They boy had shot himself, killed himself—a suicide. Everyone knew he had problems; everyone said so. Everyone but Matthew, who suddenly discovered a conscience.

"That is what I want you to understand, what may help you in this trial. Matthew had never cared very much for anything. He was careless in every sense of the word; careless about what happened to him, careless about what happened to other people. Then, suddenly, this careless world of his, this world of everyone doing whatever they felt like doing and the devil take the consequences, came crashing down. He had not just seen a young man killed, he had not just witnessed what he knew was murder; he had gone along with it! More than that, he had given Thomas Elkins the idea, told him the story I had told him.

"He came to me that night, right after it happened, and told me what he had done. He told me he was as guilty as Thomas Elkins because he could have stopped it, told them how wrong it was to make anyone, especially a boy like that, think the only way he could prove his own courage, prove that he was as good as they were, was to take his own life. He was distraught, beside himself with grief, and then, a few days later, when he realized that no one was going to do anything about it, that the only thing anyone was worried about was whether they could keep what happened secret, that everyone—the parents, the university—was in on it, he just walked away, quit school, and never came back.

"He changed in ways I would not have thought possible. He

had been charming, fun to be with, in that careless way he had; quick to laugh, always teasing me about how hard I was studying, insisting I should try to have a good time; and now, all the laughter gone, he began to study all the time."

"I thought you said he quit school."

She looked at me with a strangely defiant, and yet somehow gentle, smile.

"He had to quit school to become a serious student. He wanted to learn how to make sense of what had happened; he wanted to know how he was supposed to live. He understood that everything in his life had been a fraud. He wanted to do something, something with himself. He wanted to have the kind of courage that scared little young man had had. He told me that. He didn't mean just physical courage, but the courage to do something that would make everyone stand up and notice; something that would show everyone how selfish, how superficial, all these self-important people really were. He did not want anyone else to get hurt; he did not want anyone else thinking there was anything to look up to in the mindless lives of pampered, self-indulgent people who thought that because they had money, they were smarter, better, than other people. He did not want anyone to become like him. The others forgot what happened, what they had done, but Matthew never did. He wanted to remember. He could not change what had happened, but that did not mean he could not use it, a constant reminder of a debt he knew he could never pay and which, for that very reason, made more important the obligation to try.

"We have lost the tragic sense of life, the belief, the understanding, that it is the certainty of failure that makes the attempt worthwhile. I don't know why he was killed, Mr. Antonelli, but I know as well as I have ever known anything that your client did not do it. No one that Matthew had spent that much time with could ever have wished him harm. Whoever killed him—whether it was his stepmother, as you suggested in court—it had to be because there was something they wanted to protect, something Matthew threatened to take away."

Sheila Bergson smiled and sat back in the chair, relieved the she had finally unburdened herself, finally told someone about the Matthew Stanton she had known. Known and loved, if I was any judge of it.

"You would have married him if you hadn't been...?"

"It meant everything to my parents. It was what I had always been told, how important it was that I marry a Jewish boy. I understood the reasons; I don't understand them quite so well anymore. I wish I had married Matthew; I wish I had let us fall in love. We would have, I'm sure of it. If I'm completely honest, I did; I fell in love with Matthew Stanton, and you are the first person I ever told. I never told him. I wonder if it would have made a difference if I had."

"What happened to the others?" I asked as she prepared to leave. "Especially Thomas Elkins?"

"He became a lawyer. He has a civil practice—trusts, estates, things like that. He represents some of the wealthiest people in Los Angeles."

Eleven

I was nearly an hour late. There was not an empty table in the place, or even an empty chair, except the one waiting for me. The restaurant was full of noise, a hundred different conversations going on, but none of them so important that the room did not go silent the moment I put my hand on Tangerine's shoulder and bent down to kiss her. When she looked up with those dazzling eyes of hers, I thought everyone would burst into applause.

I sat down, stretched out my legs, crossed my arms over my chest, and teased her for the effect she had.

"Everyone came to have dinner with someone they wanted to be with, and they spent half their time looking at you. And you've been here for almost an hour, waiting for me, and you don't even notice. I tried to call, by the way."

She tilted her head just far enough to make an innocent smile seem seductive.

"I try not to notice when people are looking, so I sat here, nursing a drink, wondering if I would have to walk out of here the same way I walked in—all alone." She paused briefly, then added,

"I didn't really wonder. I knew you would come. I knew something must have happened, something about the trial. I know you must have tried to call."

"You didn't have your phone? All I got was your recording."

"I turned it off. I was getting too many calls. It's interesting, isn't it, Antonelli? How easily everyone talks about doing the right thing until the right thing comes with a cost."

I sat up and leaned across the table, searching her eyes.

"You're getting calls about the trial? Let me guess. Calls telling you I shouldn't be putting the Stantons on trial? Some of the people who came to dinner last week?"

"Suzy Fairchild, for starters, and half a dozen other supposed friends of mine. They didn't ask for anything, they just thought I should know that a lot of people were saying what a shame it would be if, in addition to losing her husband and her stepson, Victoria Stanton should have her name dragged through the mud. No one was asking that T. J. Allen not get the best possible defense, but was it really necessary to destroy someone's reputation? They could have been reading from the same script. Didn't we understand how much good the Stanton family had done for the city? Didn't we understand that there were always people trying to drag them down because they envied their success?"

"I'm sorry," I said, "sorry you had to deal with that."

"Don't be sorry. I'm not. It's always good to know who your friends are, and who they're not. It was actually kind of fun," she said with a quick, knowing grin. "I realized, especially about Suzy Fairchild, that I never really liked her very much. You know how it is. You get thrown together with people; they're part of the circle you're in, part of the life you're living. You always talk about the same things; everyone has the same opinions, even if some of them express them a little differently. You're not even aware of it, how predictable, how boring it all is; the same way that after you have been in the same room a hundred times you aren't aware of what color the walls are painted. And then you get a call and someone you thought you knew starts making complaints, complaints which are really veiled threats, about the only person you really care about, and you—at least it is what happened to me —start laughing!

"I really did that, Antonelli! You would have been proud of me. I laughed, and then I told her that you had never told a lie in your life, that everything you had ever said in a courtroom was true, and nothing you had ever said was more true than what you had said about Victoria Stanton." The smile on Tangerine's mouth kept getting bigger, the sparkle in her eyes kept getting brighter. "I told her—I really did!—that if she wanted to stay friends with a cold-hearted murderer, that was her business, but that I sure as hell—I said that, too—was not going to be friends with her. So, the hell with them, Antonelli; the hell with all of them. It's just you and me and no one else, and I'll love you forever, I swear I will, unless, of course, I change my mind next week or the week after that, and run off with a younger Italian. Now, let's order dinner before I drink too much on an empty stomach and you have to carry me out of here dead drunk. And while we wait, tell me what you were doing, why you were so abominably, unforgivably late."

During dinner I tried to tell her what Sheila Bergson had told me; I tried to tell her what I had thought, what I had felt, listening to the tragic story of a young boy's death. It was like trying to describe a portrait by Rembrandt or a landscape by Van Gogh to someone who had never seen them. Tangerine understood the difficulty.

"Do you remember what you told me when Leonard Silverman asked you to take the case, the line he quoted, 'All of Europe contributed to the making of Kurtz'? After you told me that, I read *Heart of Darkness*. If someone were to mention Kurtz to me now, I would know exactly what they were talking about. You know him as well as, or better than, anyone you have ever met. And if someone tells you that someone reminds them of Kurtz, doesn't that tell you more, doesn't that describe someone better, than a lot of words about how they look, how they speak, how they treat other people? You know Kurtz! He lives inside your mind. They all do," she added with a knowing, revelatory gaze, "all the great, unforgettable characters great writers wrote about. It's a mistake to call it fiction; it's the truth. The real fiction is the reader. All of us who try to become like the characters we read about. That is the difference—don't you think?—between one age and another: what people want to read, what they think is important to know. Our parents read Faulkner and Hemingway and Fitzgerald; we read James Patterson."

"Or Elizabeth Burroughs. But not all of us." I raised my glass and began to study it like a fortune teller's crystal ball. "You read *War and Peace* just last year. I think you fell a little in love with Pierre."

"Of course I did; he reminded me of you."

"Unable at the crucial moment to shoot Napoleon?"

"Willing to sacrifice everything because of his love for Natasha."

"That, too. When you read *Heart of Darkness*, you didn't fall in love with Kurtz."

"No one could fall in love with Kurtz."

"But someone did. The girl, the young woman, he had left behind; the woman he was engaged to marry, the woman who waited in London for his return; the woman Marlowe goes to see at the end. She still believes Kurtz was a very great man who had given his life in the service of his country, bringing civilization to a savage tribe; Kurtz, who taught the natives a savagery they had not known."

"And what is the connection with Matthew Stanton? What

do you now think Leonard Silverman meant when he said that all of America contributed to what happened here?"

"It's *Heart of Darkness* told backward. Kurtz turned his back on civilization; Matthew Stanton turned his back on the savagery, the absence of even the semblance of civilized life, in the way we live now. I've listened to all those descriptions of Stanton, standing there, separate and apart, watching the lunatic carnival, in Alan Boe's astonishing phrase, going on all around him. He understood that everything was a fraud; everyone he used to think were the adults he was supposed to admire—what he was supposed to, one day, be himself—nothing but grown-up children, the only thing they thought important whatever they had to have next. It must have made him crazy, knowing what he knew; knowing that none of it was ever going to change, or, if it did, only get worse."

"Is that what Albert meant that night at dinner when he said he reminded him of Hamlet? That nothing mattered; that nothing would make any difference?"

"I think so, but Hamlet had not done what Matthew had. Hamlet had not taken part in what was supposed to be a cruel joke that ended up a murder. Sheila Bergson keeps asking herself what would have happened had she never told Stanton about the story Andre Gide had written. Would anything have happened had she never read it? If she thinks like that, imagine what must have gone through his mind! If he had not told the story to anyone, or if he had spoken up, told those so-called friends of his that he would tell the boy they were going to humiliate him, make fun of him, nothing would have happened. He could have stopped it, and he didn't. The boy is dead, and he blames himself. He's filled with guilt, and because he's the only one who tried to tell the truth, he is the only one who believes he deserves to be punished. And then, like some Greek tragedy, punishment comes. Call it chance, call it fate, call it anything you like, but when his father died, he had to believe that it was all connected, that this was how he was being paid back. We all believe in gods, especially when we're convinced they don't exist."

With each word I became more certain that it was true. Her elbow on the table, Tangerine folded her fingers down toward her wrist and rested the side of her head against the back of her hand.

"Do you really think he thought everything was his fault? Wasn't he too intelligent for that?"

I stared past her at the faces of the anonymous crowd. Everyone lived in a world of their own creation, certain there was a reason why things happened the way they did, convinced, to some extent at least, that what happened depended on them. People with too much money thought everything could be controlled; people who lived blameless lives thought they had acquired the right to be left alone. I understood, I could feel, what Matthew Stanton must have felt.

"No, not that everything was his fault. I think it's quite possible that, deep down, he knew there was not any real connection between what he had done, or not done, and what happened later. That was the whole point: there was no causation, there was no reason, for anything. The world was irrational, and so was everyone in it. The more important people thought they were, the more ludicrous, the more idiotic, it was. What difference did it make whose basketball team won its games or lost them? What difference whether a championship was won, whether the crowd had something to cheer about? What conceivable importance whether the Stantons had their name on a sports arena, or if their name was known to anyone at all? All the difference in the world to everyone else. Which only proved what a fraud it all was. Maybe that's why I suddenly thought of *The Idiot*."

"The idiot? Who...?" asked Tangerine with a blank expression.

"In court today, at the end of my cross-examination of

Victoria Stanton. It had been going on for hours, all afternoon. I started it," I remarked, shaking my head at the sheer audacity of what I had done, "by asking when she had first decided to have her stepson murdered, before or after she had killed his father."

Tangerine's eyes shot wide open. She started to laugh.

"Did you really? No wonder I started getting all those calls. What did she—?"

"She denied everything, insisted it was an outrage—that was the word she used—not just that I had suggested it, but that I was even allowed to ask. You never used to see this, this sense of entitlement in a courtroom. No one thought they could decide what they could or could not be asked. But from the time she walked into the courtroom she acted as if she was doing everyone a favor. She practically held her nose when she took the oath. I did not think about it at the time, but she looks like a store window mannequin. The work she must have had done to have a face with skin that smooth, and—"

"And eyes that vacant, is that what you were going to say?" laughed Tangerine. "Everyone used to say she looked like a million dollars, and that it probably cost a lot more than that. Plastic surgery isn't cheap."

We finished dinner, but I did not want to leave. The restaurant was still crowded, and the crowd made time seem to stop. There were people everywhere, and the two of us were all alone. Tomorrow I would be back in trial, but tomorrow would not come until the night was over, and as long as we sat there, just the two of us, the night would not end. The trial, like every trial, was a story, a fiction in which I was both the author and the main character. It was the made-up invention of my life. Only Tangerine and what I felt when I was with her were real. We ordered more wine.

"When I was a young lawyer, just starting out, I used to read about the great lawyers of the past. One of them, Earl Rodgers, who, among other cases, defended Clarence Darrow when Darrow was charged with jury tampering in Los Angeles, which Darrow had clearly done, drank all the time; even, sometimes, in court. He'd pour liquor into the water pitcher on the counsel table and drink throughout the trial. A lot of them drank; a lot of them, like Earl Rodgers, were alcoholics. I sometimes think we might be better off if we still had a few lawyers who did that, drank more than they should. They might not be such mindless mechanics, the way most trial lawyers are now. They know the law, they know what is written on the printed page, but they don't know what anything means, and they have no flair. They are thorough, methodical, and dull, about as inspiring as a member of an accounting firm."

Tangerine wrinkled her nose. A smile like a fugitive raced across her mouth.

"Why not take a bottle to court with you tomorrow? Just put it on the counsel table and when the district attorney is questioning her next witness, pour yourself a glass."

I only wished I had the courage. The trial, like every trial, was an obsession. I could not forget it no matter how much I might drink. I put down the glass I was holding and started telling Tangerine more about what had happened when Victoria Stanton was on the stand.

"She admitted—or rather, she did not deny—that she had been having an affair with Michael Kensington and that they were there, in the French Alps, when Emmett Stanton had his accident. Longstreet isn't going to call Kensington; he isn't going to be a witness for the prosecution. I'm going to call him; he's going to be a witness for the defense. He is somehow at the center of this, and I still know hardly anything about him."

"He's a gambler," remarked Tangerine. "Cards, horses, stock market, real estate."

"And I know he's from a wealthy family; I know he went to

Princeton but that he did not finish. But beyond the bare outline of his biography, everything seems vague, uncertain. I did find out one thing, though. They did not meet after she married Emmett Stanton; they had known each other before, years earlier, when they were engaged."

Tangerine was surprised. "Victoria Stanton and Michael Kensington?" she asked, just to be sure. "Engaged?"

"I should have said almost engaged. They were waiting for the right occasion, a dinner party, at which both families would be told. It never happened. The night before she ran off with a boy she had known in college, a boy she was crazy about, a boy who was crazy about her. He did not come from a prominent family; he did not have any money. He was working his way through school. When he graduated, a year ahead of her, he got offered a position overseas and he wanted to go. They were in love, and she agreed she would follow him to Europe as soon as she graduated the next spring."

Her hands clasped together just below her chin, Tangerine knew what must have happened next.

"But the boy was gone, and Michael was there, and the families, the rich, prominent families, knew each other."

"And she fell in love, or thought she had, a second time. She wrote the boy and told him she was engaged to—"

"And he was on the next plane back," she said, shaking her head at how predictable it had all been.

"Exactly," I replied, but with a hint that there was more to it. "Victoria Stanton was a lovely young woman; not beautiful in the artificial way she is now. Lovely, winsome, with a smile that could break your heart. She was young; she did not care about money—why would she? She had always had whatever she needed. She loved Michael Kensington, but only, or mainly, because Michael Kensington was desperately in love with her. But when the boy walked in the night before her official engagement was to be announced, she forgot everything except what she had sworn she would never forget: how much in love she still was with the boy she had not seen in half a year. They drove to Reno that night and got married."

"Which is, in a way, just the beginning of the story, isn't it?" asked Tangerine, sure now that she was right.

"The beginning, and the end."

"Because she realized she had made a mistake, that she shouldn't have married a boy who didn't have anything, that she should have married Michael Kensington?"

"The other way around. He was the one who realized it was a mistake. I said she didn't care about money, but that was because she had always had it. I think she would have gone anywhere with her new husband, lived anywhere he liked, but she assumed that he wanted the same things that everyone else she knew had wanted, and that if he had never had them, it was because he had never had the money to get them. She assumed, the way they all assume, that everyone envies the rich.

"From everything I have been able to find out, he did not envy anyone anything. He was a free spirt, maybe one of the last; someone who wanted to wander the earth with her by his side. And she would have done it! I really believe that. Done it because she loved him and was willing to make that kind of sacrifice. That was what he could not abide! That she thought it a sacrifice, that she thought of herself as a victim; a willing victim, if you will, but still a victim of his strange determination to live a life that made no sense at all, an adventure that had no purpose, no final objective, nothing that once achieved would allow them to live the way everyone else she knew lived; an adventure that would always be an adventure, working when he had to, and never longer than he had to, moving from one place, one country, to another because he wanted, not just to see, but to learn about the world.

"He was in love with her, but he was more in love with what

he thought he owed it to himself to be. No matter how hard she tried, she could never be what he needed: she could never look forward to the next thing he wanted to do. They were married a little less than a year. He left her somewhere in Italy, a note on the dresser in some small hotel his last goodbye. He died trying to cross the desert in North Africa a year or so later."

Tangerine had a faraway look, nostalgia for a past she would have liked but never had.

"I would have done that, danced with someone across the world, danced right off the edge and fall forever into space." She searched my eyes to see if I remembered. "Not that long ago, when you were in the middle of another trial, we were going to buy a sailboat and just disappear, you and me, and never come back. I would, with you, go somewhere we've never been," she went on, growing more certain and excited, more determined, more intense, "go somewhere and just live, together, never, even for a moment, out of each other's sight, our only thought how much better everything was today than the day before, and how tomorrow would be even better yet. What else is there, Joseph Antonelli? How else spend the brief part of time chance has given us?"

"When the trial is over."

"Yes, when the trial is over, we'll just go. Yes. And it won't matter where we go, there will be just us. We'll be like those adventurers Robert Louis Stevenson wrote about, 'blown by the winds of heaven.'" Suddenly, she looked at me, a question in her bright, shining, moon-like eyes. "Do you mean it? Really mean it? Would you just quit, quit what you have been doing all these years, and just go off with me? And you wouldn't have any regrets?"

I felt like Gatsby, staring across the dark waters of the sound at the green light beckoning on the other side, the green light where Daisy lived with her husband; the green light that symbolized everything Gatsby had ever wanted, everything that would make his life have meaning.

"I wish I had green eyes," said Tangerine, her laughing eyes looking deep into mine. "Gatsby. I know that look; I know what it means. You told me, remember, you told me you have that feeling when we sit outside and look across the bay at the city all lit up; how you remember Gatsby and the green light and everything it meant, and how I have that same meaning now for you. And it isn't just the green light, but—do you remember?—you told me just after we first met that my voice reminded you of how Fitzgerald described Daisy's voice: 'a voice that sounded like money.' I didn't like that, not at first, and then, after I read *The Great Gatsby*, I liked it a lot that you thought that. I don't really know why. Maybe just the way it sounded: clean, clear, careless of cost."

Drawing her fingers slowly across the naked spiral of the crystal glass, a cunning smile, secretive and sensual, slipped sideways across her mouth.

"Now take me home and take me to bed and tell me you're going to love me always and dance with me forever, everywhere we go, blown by the winds of heaven. And I'll tell you every lie I've ever heard and why I am only telling the truth when I tell them to you."

We left the restaurant, and left the city, and drove across the Golden Gate and through the narrow, winding streets of Sausalito to the chocolate-colored shingle-sided house where we lived. We forgot about everything except each other and the world that, with each other's help, we had created for ourselves. I did not think about the trial, or anything else, until the next morning.

I was halfway across the bridge, driving back to the city, when I heard Tangerine's voice, playing in my mind like a song I could not forget, telling me how I had once told her that her voice sounded like money. I had forgotten that, but I remembered telling her about Gatsby's green light. I thought of her that way, as Daisy, waiting in the distance on the other side where money and privilege were everyone's realized dream. Daisy did not leave her husband, Tom Buchanan, for Gatsby, and she let Gatsby take the blame for the death she had caused. Tangerine had left her husband for me, and never thought to blame me for anything, but despite that difference, there was no difference at all. She was, and would always be, no matter if we never, as she said she wanted, spent a moment apart, a mystery, the great mystery of my life, the green light that flickered forever, out there, on the farther shore.

And then I wondered what green light there had ever been for Matthew Stanton. Albert Craven thought him like Hamlet, pondering the useless necessity of revenge. Leonard Silverman thought him somehow similar to Conrad's Kurtz, a product of what America had become. I had thought him, in a moment's intuition, like Prince Myshkin in Dostoevsky's *The Idiot*. Why had I thought of Myshkin? Stanton was not innocent of the world's corruption, not after what had happened while he was in college; not after what he was sure his stepmother had done. He was not an innocent, but neither had he been someone like Kurtz. He was neither Myshkin nor Kurtz, but he shared in what they had in common: the knowledge, the experience, of what the world likes to think of itself and what the world really is; the difference between the cant and hypocrisy of a world that insists it is the highest point civilization has ever reached and a world in which the only thing worth having is whatever might win the applause of people as ignorant as themselves. The question, the question to which I had yet to find an answer, was what, if anything, had Matthew Stanton wanted to do about it? What was the reason he had to be killed?

Twelve

"The prosecution calls Cynthia Washington," announced Samantha Longstreet in a quiet, supremely confident voice.

T. J. Allen tensed with something like physical fear. He stared straight ahead, his jaw clenched tight, his shoulders bent forward. He turned to me and started to ask a question, but the question, whatever it was, died on his lips. The look in his large, dark eyes seemed a helpless apology, a failed explanation, for what was about to happen.

Whoever Cynthia Washington was, she was gorgeous, a black woman in her late twenties with skin the color of a tropical beach. She was tall, nearly six feet, with amber-colored eyes and a slim, athletic body. Sitting alone at a sidewalk cafe, everyone who walked by would have slowed down to get a better look. Listening to her in a court of law, you had a rather different impression. Her voice was unfortunate. It was too high, with a tendency to break when she got angry or irritated, which, as it turned out, seemed most of the time. She took the oath, took the witness stand, and looked everywhere except at Allen.

"Are you acquainted with the defendant, Thaddeus John Allen?" asked Longstreet as she began with remote efficiency the methodical interrogation of a witness who has already been taught the questions.

"Yes," she replied with a brief, decisive nod.

"For about how long?"

Longstreet was standing in front of the jury box, but far enough away that the jury had to look from her to the witness and back again as they followed the exchange.

"Almost six years," she replied in that odd, scratchy voice of hers.

"You have a child together, do you not?"

"Yes. Alicia, she's five years old now."

"You lived with the defendant for nearly three years. When did you stop living with him?"

"Six months ago. That's when he beat me up, when he broke my arm, when I had to go to the hospital, when I thought he was going to kill me, when I...when I could not take it anymore, the violence, the abuse, the..."

A deathlike silence descended on the courtroom, broken only by a single, muffled cough as someone in the crowd tried to stifle their reaction. But Allen, strangely, began to relax. He became more confident, less apprehensive. The fear in his eye had vanished, all the tension gone. He crossed his long legs, folded his arms over his chest, leaned back in his chair, and fixed the mother of his daughter with a knowing and surprisingly sympathetic smile of gentle cynicism and doubt.

"You're lying!" he shouted with bizarre, full-throated glee.

"Your Honor!" Longstreet shouted back with a warning glance that froze the grin on Allen's face.

Judge Silverman was almost as quick to tell him that another outburst like that and he would be following the proceedings from the comfort of a jail cell.

"Sorry," Allen mumbled, half rising from his chair.

Longstreet played Allen's outburst as what you would expect from a man who mistreated women.

"Was this the first time he hit you?" she asked in a tone that left no doubt she thought it impossible that it could have been.

"No, he did it fairly often—whenever he got angry, whenever things weren't going the way he wanted them to."

Slowly, and, as it were, reluctantly, I got to my feet and objected to the district attorney's line of questioning. It was irrelevant to the issue the jury was there to decide.

"A witness comes in and tells the jury that the defendant hit her. For what purpose, except to make the jury believe that if he hit her, he must have murdered someone else? To say nothing of the fact that the prosecution has not even bothered to show a direct connection between what the witness says he did and the crime for which the defendant is now on trial, the prosecution has not introduced any evidence that the witness's allegations were ever reported to the police, much less made the subject of an investigation."

I paused, as if I wanted to add something, another objection to what Longstreet was doing, and then shook my head.

"On second thought, Your Honor, I withdraw my objection. On condition that the district attorney does not object when I bring in a witness to testify that the defendant never hit her, and then, following her logic, argue that this is all the proof needed to prove that the defendant did not murder Matthew Stanton!"

Longstreet stared at me as if I had lost all my senses. Silverman looked at her as if he could not understand why she was so upset.

"Does the witness have any evidence that pertains directly to the issue in this case? Does she have any evidence that can link the defendant to the murder of Matthew Stanton?" he asked in a calm, temperate, but quietly demanding voice.

"Yes, Your Honor, she most certainly does!"

"Then I suggest you get to it, and get to as quickly as you can," said Silverman with a severity that she was not expecting.

She turned on her heel and made it seem that she was only starting where she had left off.

"You stopped living together because of what he had been doing to you. But did you still see him from time to time?"

"Yes, of course; we have a daughter. He would come to visit her; sometimes he would take her for a few days."

Nodding that she understood, Longstreet clasped her hands behind her back and took a few slow, measured steps, building, as it seemed, to something crucial to her case. Suddenly, she stopped moving.

"Did the defendant, T. J. Allen, ever, in your presence, threaten to harm Matthew Stanton?"

"Yes, he did. He threatened to kill him just a few days before Matthew Stanton was murdered."

Longstreet looked at Cynthia Washington with a somber, penetrating gaze. She wanted her to understand that the question she was about to be asked would decide, once and for all, whether the defendant would walk out of the courtroom a free man or spend the rest of his life in prison.

"Are you sure? Are you absolutely sure that the defendant said he was going to kill—said he was going to murder—Matthew Stanton?"

"Am I sure? He screamed it in my face. Swore he would get even with him. Swore he would kill him with his bare hands!"

"But not with a gun, is that what you're saying?" I asked, and then, immediately, waved my hand in the air, acknowledging that I had spoken out of turn.

"Your Honor!" protested Longstreet. "Would you please tell counsel for the defense that he has to follow the rules, that he can't just interrupt whenever he happens to feel like it?"

Leonard Silverman would have ruled against himself if the law required it.

"You're not a witness, Mr. Antonelli; you are not under oath and you don't get to testify. I shouldn't have to tell you this, and, I assure you, I won't tell you again. Do we understand each other?"

"Yes, Your Honor," I replied, showing neither anger nor contrition.

I had broken the rules, and only cowards complained about the price they had to pay. Leonard Silverman was right, but so was I. He understood that; Samantha Longstreet did not. Her eyes flashed with eager malice as she stood stick straight in her high heel shoes.

"I ask that Mr. Antonelli's remarks be stricken from the record and that the jury be instructed to disregard them," she demanded.

If there was a better way to make someone remember something than ordering them to forget it, I had not discovered it. Neither had Silverman. He gave Longstreet a moment to think about it, but it was too late: she could not appear to be indecisive. Her gaze became more determined, more insistent.

"The jury will ignore Mr. Antonelli's last remark," Silverman instructed with a slight, impartial smile.

Holding my right hand with my left, I rubbed the back of my fingers with my thumb, smiling to myself as if things were going exactly as I had hoped. Had the jury been able to see the second smile, hidden behind the first, they would have seen an actor trying to play a part in a play he had not finished reading and did not yet know the ending.

Longstreet had more questions, all of them variations on the same theme: Allen was a violent man who had assaulted the woman with whom he had been living, the mother of his child, and had said he was going to murder Matthew Stanton. Cynthia Washington insisted, swore under oath, that Allen had beaten her and, just as he had promised, Matthew Stanton was dead. The jurors looked at Allen in a way they had not looked at him before. Instead of the popular athlete everyone admired, Allen had a record of domestic abuse, a man so unable to control himself that he had broken a woman's arm. When Silverman recessed court for lunch, I had ninety minutes to get ready for a cross-examination that might be the last chance I had to save T. J. Allen from a guilty verdict and prison.

"You never told me anything about this!" I almost shouted as soon as the door to the small conference room shut behind us. I was as angry as I had ever been. What he had done was inexcusable, holding back something this important, something this devastating. "I told you never to do that with me! Never! You don't decide what is important and what isn't! You hit her? You tell her you're going to kill Matthew Stanton? And you didn't think I should know about that?"

"Because it never happened!" Allen yelled back. "Not like she says it did. First, I never hit her. I pushed her, pushed her damn hard. I shoved her, shoved her away from me, when she started coming at me with a bottle, a bottle of vodka she had damn near emptied drinking herself into a stupor! She's supposed to be taking care of Alicia, and I come over and she's locked Alicia in her room so she can... And what I said—what she says I said—about getting even with Matthew, swearing I would kill him with my bare hands? Yeah, that's true. I said it; probably said it more than once. It's the way I talk when I get mad at myself. When you're playing and the guy you're guarding goes off, can't miss a shot: 'I'll get even, I'll murder the bastard!' All it means is that next time, I'll be all over him. I'll ruin his game. That's what I meant. Matthew and I played chess. Let's just say I didn't always win. Didn't always win?" He laughed as his head rocked back and forth at the memory of how outmatched he had been. "He beat me so bad it wasn't even funny. So, yeah, sometimes, though I was usually laughing when I said it, I'd say something like that: 'I'll get even; I'll kill him with my bare hands.' Words, man; just words."

I wanted to believe him, and I did, but there was something he had left out, something he was still holding back.

"When you first heard her name, when Longstreet called her as her next witness, you looked scared, as if you were afraid of what she was going to say. What was it? It wasn't what she said; you just explained that. It's something else. Whatever it is, you have to tell me. I can't—"

"It's my fault; everything that happened, everything that happened to her."

"What happened to her? You mean the drinking?"

"It was my fault," he insisted, disgusted with himself for what he thought he had done. "Cynthia got pregnant, but I wouldn't marry her. That's why we were living together: because we had a daughter. But that didn't mean I was going to settle down and sleep with only one woman. Do you have any idea what it is like to be a famous athlete, a professional basketball player?" He bent forward to share what he insisted was anything but a secret. "From the time you're in college, there are women everywhere. They all want to make it with whoever happens to be the big star. But that's nothing compared to what happens when you turn pro, because now you're not just famous, you're rich. You're not living in a dorm room or some crummy apartment, you live in a mansion in some exclusive gated community. You go to expensive restaurants, the best private clubs; you drive a Porsche or a Bentley, you own a dozen of them. Everywhere you go, any city you play in, you don't go looking for women, they come looking for you. So then some girl you slept with gets pregnant and has your kid. Marry her? You'd have to be crazy. Because," he went on with a glance of shrewd calculation, "while you have to pay child support, she isn't going to get half your money if things don't work out and you end up with a divorce.

"That's why I didn't marry Cynthia. Because I was too damn selfish, too convinced that there wasn't any reason to stop spending time with other women; too worried about what would happen if I married her and it didn't last. That's why she became the way she is, bitter and disappointed, drinking away what she thinks is the bad deal she got dealt. I know that now. If it hadn't been for Matthew, I might never have known it."

There it was, the question I had not been able to answer; the question that seemed to lie at the heart of everything involved in the case: what was it about Matthew Stanton that had made him so interesting, so important, in such different ways to so many people? How many lives had been changed, one way or the other, by what he had done?

"If it hadn't been for...? What did he do that made you think what happened was your responsibility?"

"He called me a fool. He said anyone was a fool who thought that playing a game in front of crowds of other people was important; that it didn't matter what other people thought of you, the only thing important was what you thought of yourself. The only important question was whether you lived an honorable life. Honorable, that was the word he used. He told me I was lucky; not because I was famous, but because I was a father and had someone to live for. And then he asked me, point blank, why I didn't think my daughter was worth getting married to her mother. Did I really think she would be better off being raised without her father in the house?"

Matthew Stanton's questions had achieved their desired effect: T. J. Allen had changed. The question was whether the change had come too late. The woman he now believed he should have married was not waiting for him to change his mind; she was on the witness stand doing everything she could to get the father of her daughter sent to prison.

"But not with a gun? Isn't that what you were saying?" I

asked as soon as court reconvened and I began my cross-examination. "Isn't that what you said when the district attorney asked you if the defendant had ever threatened Matthew Stanton? That he threatened to kill him with his bare hands?"

Cynthia Washington was not sure what she should say. Whatever her feelings of disappointment, she had not acquired the hard edge frequently seen in young women who had dreamed of romance and found themselves single parents instead. There was a fragile vulnerability in her doe-like eyes. She had trusted T. J. Allen, and he had betrayed her. She would have given anything if that had not happened.

I asked the question again, but this time it was less a question than an offer of understanding.

"When he said that, when he said he would get even with Matthew Stanton, when he said he would kill him with his bare hands, he wasn't screaming, his face full of rage, was he, Ms. Washington? He was laughing, wasn't he? Laughing because he had once again lost a game, a game of chess, a game he often played with Matthew Stanton, isn't that right? Isn't that what happened?"

She hesitated, trying to decide how she should answer.

"All anyone wants you to do is to tell the truth, Ms. Washington," I told her. I moved a step closer. "You weren't living with Mr. Allen at the time, were you?"

"No, we hadn't been living together for quite a while."

"But he came by, to visit his daughter, to visit you, fairly often, correct?"

"Yes, that's right; at least once a week."

"And when he came by, you said he screamed it into your face. Did you mean screamed or shouted? He shouted it, didn't he? Not the way someone shouts something in anger, but the way they shout when they're excited, happy, the way T. J. was after he had spent time with Matthew Stanton, isn't that the way it was?"

A thin smile, an image of infinite sadness, started across her mouth. She looked down at her hands, held together in her lap. Wearing a pale blue dress, she seemed younger, much younger, than her age; more like a young girl than a young woman.

"You said, when the district attorney was asking you questions, that T. J. had been physically violent, that he had broken your arm, and that you couldn't take it anymore. But you did not report any of this to the police, did you?"

"No, I—"

"You didn't tell anyone, did you?" I asked quietly.

"No, I didn't tell anyone."

"It isn't quite true—is it?—that physical violence, a broken arm, was the reason you stopped living together. He had moved out; you weren't living together when you broke your arm. Isn't that true?"

"No...I mean, yes. He had moved out, but he still came over; we still spent time together."

"Yes, I understand." My hand on the jury box railing, I waited each time she answered until I was sure she was finished. "I don't want to embarrass you, I don't want you to feel uncomfortable, but T. J. is on trial for his life and there are some questions I have to ask. Do you understand why I have to do this?"

"Yes, it's all right. I'll try to answer anything you need to ask me."

She said this with honest courage. She knew, she had to have known, what was coming, but she did not shy away. No matter how painful it was for her, I knew she would tell the truth.

"Months before he moved out, you started drinking, and drinking heavily, didn't you?"

A lost look in her eyes, she slowly nodded.

"You have to answer out loud," I reminded her as gently as I could.

"Yes. I was drinking, drinking way too much. I was upset, very upset. We had a child, a daughter, and T. J. acted like it didn't make any difference. He wasn't married, he was still single. He could do whatever he wanted, come and go as he pleased, see other women."

"And then one night, when you had been drinking, when you were upset because he had moved out, he came by to see his daughter and you took a bottle, an empty bottle, and you went after him, tried to hit him with it, and he grabbed you and shoved you away and you fell. That's how your arm was broken, when you fell on the floor. Isn't that what happened? Isn't that the truth of it?" I asked with a sympathy I did not have to invent.

She did not answer; she did not have to. Her eyes answered for her. With any other witness in any other trial, I would have stopped right there. She had, in effect, recanted, taken back each of the damning allegation she had made on direct. She had done nothing to help the prosecution make its case; I thought she might now help me make mine.

"Why are you here today, Ms. Washington? Did you call the police, did you call the district attorney's office when you heard that T. J. Allen was accused of murder to tell them what, in response to the district attorney's questions, you said today? Or did someone from the district attorney's office first contact you?"

"I didn't call anyone. The police came, told me T. J. had been arrested, told me he had murdered Matthew Stanton, and that they needed me to testify if T. J. had ever been violent, if he had ever said or done anything that would show he wanted to do harm to Matthew Stanton."

"Did you tell them that he had been violent, that he had physically abused you? Did you tell them that he had threatened to harm Matthew Stanton?"

"No, not really. I told them we had trouble, that we had fought, and that I had been hurt. But I said it was my fault," she explained, turning to the jury to make sure they understood. "I told them I had been drinking, that things got out of control, that he had not meant to hurt me. I was sure of that."

"What about the threat to Matthew Stanton's life? You said today that he had screamed in your face that he was going to kill him with his bare hands. Is that what you told them, the police and the district attorney's office, when you first talked to them?"

"I thought—I shouldn't have thought, but I did—that T. J. must have done it, killed Matthew Stanton. The police said he did, and when I asked the district attorney, Ms. Longstreet, she said there was no question about it. It was his gun and he was still holding it when the police came. There wasn't any question. All they wanted was for me to tell them if he had ever said anything, anything at all, about wanting to do so something like that. And he had—T. J., I mean—said what he said. And I was too scared, too confused to remember that he had not said it like he actually meant it."

"Too scared? Why were you too scared?"

"I was drinking, still drinking, when the police came to talk to me, and Alicia was in the other room, and I thought they must think I wasn't taking care of her the way I should. And then when I came to the district attorney's office, they started telling me that I had to be careful, that people who didn't meet their responsibilities could lose their children. I got scared, scared about what might happen."

I turned and looked across at Samantha Longstreet, sitting white-faced and rigid on the edge of her chair. I kept looking at her until, finally, when everyone understood what that awkward silence meant, I looked back at Cynthia Washington waiting on the witness stand.

"And so you told them what T. J. had said, but you didn't tell them what you thought—what you knew—he really meant. One last question. You lived with T. J. Allen, you're the mother of his child; you know him as well as, or better than, anyone else. Do you think he is capable of murder, capable of having killed Matthew Stanton?"

"Never! Not in a thousand years."

Longstreet was out of her chair before I reached mine.

"Tell us, Ms. Washington, tell the jury, did I ever ask you to do anything except tell the truth?"

Fragile, vulnerable, and almost certainly an alcoholic, Cynthia Washington was still a fairly shrewd judge of what people really wanted.

"You told me he was guilty, that there wasn't any question about it. You told me you wanted me to testify about what T. J. had done to me and what he threatened to do to Matthew Stanton; you didn't tell me you wanted me to testify that I was to blame for what happened or that he wasn't serious when he said what he said about Matthew Stanton!"

Longstreet smiled in disbelief.

"You never told me anything about that, did you?"

"I told you that it was my fault that my arm was broken."

"And I told you—didn't I?—that women in abusive relationship always think it's their fault. They always think that when someone beats them bloody, breaks their arm, or worse, that they provoked them into doing it. And that's what happened here, isn't it? He broke your arm and made you think it never would have happened if you had behaved the way he wanted you to. It's an old story, Ms. Washington; I'm only sorry you're still buying into it."

She spun on her heel and with all the sense of triumph she could pretend to feel announced that she was finished with the witness. And then she said one thing more.

"The jury can decide who was really at fault, who was to blame and who was the victim of the defendant's violent, murderous rage!"

THIRTEEN

Albert Craven sat at his modern chrome and glass rectangular desk, shaking his head as I described what had happened in court.

"They never learn, do they? They think they have a hold on someone, the fear they can take away her child! All these second-rate lawyers with their third-rate minds, telling everyone they only want to get at the truth, and then try to get a witness to tell only one side of the story!"

Slapping his hand on the glass-topped desk, he winced at the implications.

"How many lawyers who practice in the criminal courts would have known how to handle a witness like this young woman? You know what they would have done—gone after her, tried to make her seem like a bitter, angry woman who only wanted a way to revenge herself for what Allen had done to her. That's what they think they're supposed to do—prosecutors as well—be aggressive. These idiots think it is the key to everything: push everyone out of the way, show them who is in charge! That's what we have done with the law: made it a sporting event, a competition. Forget guilt or innocence, forget trying to understand where the real responsibility is; the only question, the only thing that matters is did you win or did you lose!"

"Settle down, Albert; I don't want you to have a stroke. I need you to stay healthy."

Touched by my concern for his well-being, he began to calm down. As traditional in his attitudes, and as generous in his gratitude for even the smallest gesture of goodwill, as anyone I had known, he started to thank me, but stopped when he heard my laughing.

"Why are you...?"

"You can't have a stroke. I'm calling you as my first witness."

"You're calling me...?" He tapped his forehead with the palm of his hand, briefly shut his eyes, and nodded. "What Matthew told me, that day we had lunch at the Fairmont."

"It'll be easy," I assured him. "All you have to do is tell the truth, what he told you, and how he said it."

"And then Samantha Longstreet will subject me to one of her ruthless cross-examinations and I'll probably have a stroke on the witness stand!"

"Don't worry about that," I said, grinning encouragement. "You will have already done your duty as a witness for the defense!"

"Yes, well, I'll keep that in mind. But, really, what kind of questions do you think she'll ask me?"

"She might ask you how many suits you own. Just tell her you can't count that high. Don't worry about it. You'll be fine."

Albert Craven had been in court twice in his life, and had thrown up both times. He reminded me of that. It was not because he was afraid it might happen again, but he thought it only fair to warn me of the possibility.

"Just pretend that instead of going to court to testify in front of a jury, you're going out to lunch with a dozen of your fashionable friends."

It was the easy banter with which we often began our conversations, the gentle teasing that helped break the tension, or the monotony, of whatever happened at the moment to be our central preoccupation, whether the urgent necessity of a trial or a difficult legal issue that had to be resolved. He had never tried a case, and I had never drafted a contract, but the differences in what we did were not as great as might be imagined. Criminal or civil, the law was all about obligation, whether those imposed upon all of us to refrain from violence, or those we agreed to voluntarily to achieve some mutual, but private, advantage. Albert Craven could spot a mistake in a contract, or the flaw in an argument, quicker than a second thought. I had heard him make changes in a document he had drafted while it was being read back to him.

"I've thought about what Matthew said, and I've thought about what I told you—that he didn't have any evidence, any proof, that his father didn't die in an accidental fall on a mountain climbing expedition, but was murdered instead. He had something more convincing than proof; he had the kind of certainty that, when you listened to him, convinced you he was right. He really was quite extraordinary. And the rumor, the story that something happened when he was in college, that he played Russian roulette, was true? I know: true, but not true; someone else, the young teenage boy, played a different version of that lethal game, drew lots to see who would kill himself, a rigged game that was not the game Matthew had thought it was. God, what that must have done to him!

"If I had known that before, when we had lunch, it would have painted things in different colors. The way he talked about his father, that he must have been insane because you had to be mad to be that honest; the way he explained, or tried to explain, how his father had been able to see things before anyone else, the sudden flash of intuition, the voices, the visions that came to him in his dreams! What was it but the insight of someone shattered by their own experience, someone who would never again believe that just below the surface, behind every friendly face, every promise of decent good behavior, there was not, more than hypocrisy, pure evil? That must have been the reason why he and T. J. Allen became such good friends."

"I've changed my mind. You're not going to be my first witness; you're going to be my last."

His first reaction was relief; he could wait a while before he had to start worrying about what might happen. His second reaction was curiosity. While a smile trembled on his mouth, he lifted his spare, wispy eyebrows like someone slightly offended.

"You don't think I would make a very good first impression?"

"It's the last impression that is important." The sequence I had been struggling with had finally fallen into place. "I'm calling some of the prosecution's own witnesses, and I'm calling Michael Kensington. They're not going to tell the truth; they're going to lie about Matthew Stanton. Then, after they do that, and after Allen testifies, I get to call the victim! Matthew Stanton gets the last word: what he said, what he told you. It will contradict what they said, prove they were lying. It will show that Allen was telling the truth. I just don't know if it will be enough.

"I still don't know the motive. What reason did his stepmother and her new husband have to kill him? To get everything Emmett Stanton had? Perhaps, but the money, as it turns out, isn't that important—not to take that kind of risk. She has what she wants; she does not want to sell the team. Four billion, ten billion, it doesn't matter. Matthew Stanton, through his father, had eighty-one percent of the ownership, but she's the one in charge. She runs everything."

"So long as Matthew let her do it," Albert reminded me. "He

could have forced her out. He could have sold the team and she would have been left with no team to run and less than a fifth of the money."

"But he never suggested anything like that when he talked to you, did he?"

"No, nothing like that came up. That doesn't mean he wasn't thinking about it. It would explain things, wouldn't it? Why Matthew was so certain his life was in danger, that Kensington and his stepmother were planning to kill him."

Albert's kind, curious eyes shot wide open. He looked at me as if he were sure I would understand, that I had somehow already understood, why what he was about to say was so important. But he did not say anything. He reached for the telephone and asked his secretary to get someone named Archibald Keeler on the line. He wasted no time.

"Six months ago, a year ago," he began, staring past me, "something happened. What was his name, the general counsel for the Stanton Trust?" He stopped and listened intently to the voice on the other end. "He was a senior partner in your firm and no one knows where he went?"

They spoke for several minutes, questions I could hear, answers I could not, and all the time Albert's gaze becoming more focused, more penetrating, as he concentrated on what was being said.

"Yes, I see; I understand. No one else will know. You have my word on it."

He hung up the phone, but instead of looking at me, his eyes remained fixed on a point in the middle distance as he debated with himself what he was going to do next. He might have been there all alone, for all he was aware of my presence. Finally, he picked up the phone for a second time and in a clear, decisive voice asked his secretary to "book Mr. Antonelli on the next flight to Hilo, Hawaii."

I almost fell out of my chair.

"Hilo? I'm not going to Hilo, or anywhere else. I'm in the middle of a trial, and—"

"This is Friday, and Monday is a holiday. You'll have three days to find him."

"Find who, Albert? Are you—?"

"Out of my mind? Probably. But it may be your only chance to win this case. Just listen. The fellow I was speaking to, Archie Keeler, is an old friend, the senior partner in the firm where Oscar Maddox was general counsel for the Stanton Trust. Maddox went missing a few months before Matthew Stanton was murdered. The story was that he had health problems and had gone somewhere in the south of France to convalesce. But it was all so sudden that there was a suspicion that he might have done something wrong—stolen money, that kind of thing—and that he had been forced to resign and had left the country to avoid having to answer questions about what had happened. It was not that big a story. He was a lawyer who handled the business affairs of the trust; he wasn't directly involved with the team. You never saw his name in the papers. He had health problems and had to quit. That was story enough.

"It was all a lie. Maddox didn't have any health problems. He just quit. He didn't even do that; he just left. Archie was the only person he told. He swore him to secrecy, made him promise that he would never tell anyone where he had gone or how to find him. Archie is an honorable man. He broke his promise and told me because he knows Maddox would want him to if Maddox knew what was at stake. He knows how to find him, but he doesn't have any way to contact him directly. All you have to do is get to Hilo, and then..."

"And then." Two words that began every adventure story I ever read in the novels I used to read when I was a boy. And then the masked man rode into town. And then, with one haunting, never to be forgotten look, she stole his heart and changed his life forever. And then, after I called Tangerine and told her to pack a bag and meet me at the airport, we were on our way to Honolulu where, two hours after we landed, we were on another, smaller plane for the forty-five-minute flight to Hilo and the Big Island.

It was like walking into a 1949 movie. Everywhere you looked, all the buildings, all the houses, had iron corrugated roofs, most of them painted bright blue or pale green. The main street, four blocks of tourist shops, was set back a considerable distance from the palm trees and the ocean, with a large triple lane parking lot in between. All the buildings that had once been there had been destroyed by a tsunami and, in the interest of safety, never rebuilt. When we walked into the Cafe Pesto, the ceiling fans were twisting at a slow, steady pace through the cool night air. I was the only one wearing a jacket, and almost the only one not wearing shorts.

"This is a 1949 movie," mused Tangerine after we had been led to a table next to the windows that looked out at the ocean across the street. "The waiter looks like Peter Lorrie and, don't look now, I think that's Humphrey Bogart standing at the bar."

"This is Hilo, not Casablanca," I reminded her as I started to laugh.

"Why, what's so—?"

"I don't know, but for some reason I started to think I should pull out a pack of cigarettes."

"Want me to ask the bartender if he has any?" she asked, watching me through those dark, enchanting eyes that, for a moment, made me forget why I was there. "The bartender," she repeated, this time with real curiosity. "He's the one who knows...?"

"If he isn't, it's been a long trip for nothing."

I asked Tangerine to order me something for dinner, and something to drink, and made my way across the crowded restaurant to the bar. Every stool was taken and everyone bunched into two rows behind them was trying to get the attention of the bartender. I nudged my way through to a place at the end of the bar and waited until the bartender, short and balding, with an easy smile, asked what I wanted.

"Scotch and soda. And Oscar Maddox. Archie Keeler told me to ask."

He did not change expressions and he did not say a word. He simply turned around and, a moment later, brought me the drink I had ordered. He searched my eyes in a silent interrogation.

"Archie Keeler a friend of yours?"

"I've never met him. My law partner, Albert Craven, knows him well. He talked to him yesterday, and as soon as he hung up had me booked on a flight. I'm in a trial, a murder trial, and Keeler agreed that it was important and that Maddox would want to know."

The bartender studied me a moment longer, and then, smiling in the direction of the next shouted voice he heard, quickly mixed another drink. I stood there, sipping on the scotch and soda, wondering what would happen, but nothing did. He kept about his business, taking orders, making drinks, passing glasses to their intended target through a half dozen raised hands. I finished my drink and started to turn away when I heard his voice reminding me that I had not paid. He handed me the bill, but there were no numbers on it, only an address.

It was somewhere out in Pahoa, a half-hour drive from Hilo along a long, lonely road where, off to the side, steam was coming up from vents in the ground from the volcano's last eruption. Less than a mile away, molten lava had flowed down to the sea, flowed faster than the fastest man had ever run. Molten red lava forty, fifty feet high, with so much heat trees five hundred yards away now stood dead and naked, like pale gray inkblots on a pad of paper. The morning sun was halfway up the morning sky when

I pulled off the road in front of a long line of majestic smooth-sided palm trees that stood like soldiers on parade. Running parallel twenty feet behind them, a four-foot-high lava wall marked the lower boundary of the place Oscar Maddox had come to hide.

There was nothing there, not a name, not a number, nothing but a simple black steel gate, an entrance that, when I looked beyond it, did not seem like an entrance at all. There was no driveway, no path, nothing except the bare outline of what might have been tire tracks across the high uncut grass. The land sloped upward until, several hundred yards away, a thick tangle of jungle with a few palm trees soaring high above blocked whatever might lay behind, a house, a tent, or perhaps nothing more than a tin roof to keep out the rain.

The gate was locked. I was not sure what to do. The wall was barely waist high. It would have been easy to climb over, but what then? Who knew what might be waiting on the other side—a guard dog, wild animals? Then I noticed, halfway down the left side of the gate, a small metal call box, rusty with age. I pressed the button. Nothing happened. I pressed it again.

"Yeah?" said someone. It was a man's voice, that much I was sure about; a voice that demanded an answer, an immediate reply, an explanation why I was there and, more than that, why I thought I had any right to be there.

"I'm Joseph—"

The static noise vanished. He had turned off the intercom. The gate could only be unlocked with a key. Was he coming to do that, to let me in, or had he just let me know with that sudden silence that he was not interested in who I was or what I wanted? I leaned back against the thick lava wall and looked down the road to the sun-splattered sea. There was not a sound anywhere. I had passed only three or four houses on the last mile I had driven; I could not see one from where I was standing. The grass between the road and wall, a space twenty or thirty feet wide, and at least four hundred feet in length, was cut close. The line of evenly spaced palm trees made the place look like one of those old tropical estates I used to see in black-and-white movies, a place where time did not matter and, if the volcano did not blow the island apart, life was easy and nothing much ever changed.

I was not sure how long I had been standing there, leaning back against the wall; a few minutes, I suppose. I bent down to pick up a coconut that had fallen on the ground. It surprised me, how heavy it was, as I tossed it from one hand to the other. Suddenly, I heard the barking of a dog, a vicious attack dog from the sharp, jagged sound of it. The wall was not high enough to keep a dog, a vicious attack dog, from bounding over it and going at my throat. I did not bother to look. I started for the car, parked just the other side of the street.

"It's nothing!" cried someone with a raucous, deep-throated laugh. "Rufus might lick you to death, but that is about the worst of what he'd ever do."

Embarrassed, and relieved, I turned around. Oscar Maddox—I was sure it was him—was sitting in an open Jeep. A grayish brown German Shepherd, too old to jump, was wagging his tail as he clawed at the top of the wall, beside himself with happiness at the chance to have someone new pat his head. Rufus might be glad to see me; Oscar Maddox was reserving judgment. He did not get out of the Jeep.

"I was expecting you. I got a call from the bartender who gave you the address. Archie wouldn't tell anyone how to find me until it was damn important. So tell me, what's so important you had to come all this way?"

He was not what I had expected. He did not look the way most lawyers—most San Francisco lawyers who never stepped inside a courtroom—looked. He was too large, too unkempt. His belly sagged over the faded blue Bermuda shorts he was wearing, and his arms, thick at the wrists, were covered with curly gray hair. His hair, thinning on top, was reddish gray, and he had at least two days' growth on his round, florid face. But his eyes were what really set him apart: bright—no, not just bright, incandescent—blue eyes that could be as cheerful, or as lethal and intense, as any I had seen. There was nothing shrewd or calculating, nothing that even hinted at a thought of his own advantage. I knew, I did not have a doubt, that I could trust him. He was that rarest kind of human being, a man who would not tell a lie whatever the truth might cost him. It was hard to believe he had practiced law.

"I'm defending T. J. Allen. He's accused of—"

"T. J. is in trouble?" he asked, bending forward, both hands on the top of the steering wheel.

"He's on trial for the murder of Matthew Stanton."

"Jesus Christ! And they think T. J...?" Muttering to himself, he climbed down from the Jeep and unlocked the gate. "Leave your car here," he suggested after we shook hands. "It might not make it up the drive."

Rufus managed to jump into the back of the Jeep and then started to crawl up next to me. Maddox, quite gently, ordered him to stay where he was.

"He likes company," Maddox explained. "That's one of the things we disagree about."

Clenching his jaw, he shook his head at the utter absurdity of it all, how stupid, how misguided, everyone was. He kept repeating Allen's name as if that, by itself, should have been enough to prove his innocence.

We started up what seemed a gentle slope, until the Jeep began to move along the rutted tire-tracked drive. There were no seatbelts, no restraints, nothing to hang on to except the roll bar above my head as we jolted our way forward, bouncing from one cratered hole to the next.

"It's because the soil is volcanic. It can rain forever, but there is never any mud. No dirt to start with, so there is nothing to fill up the holes. I could put in some gravel, smooth it out that way, but I don't go out that often, and..."

His voice trailed off, a thought, whatever it was, left unfinished. The drive, the pathway, the bare imprint of a designated route, whatever that helter-skelter, rollercoaster ride might be called, got us from the paved street in front nearly half a mile to the house. What need to make improvements, why hurry to do what was not essential, especially when, as was obvious, Maddox liked it just the way it was: a path, a road, that no one, no one of the kind he had left behind on the mainland, would have thought tolerable.

"T. J. didn't kill Matthew!" he shouted over the Jeep's crashing racket. "But you knew that already. That's why you're here, isn't it? To see what I can tell you about why Matthew was murdered, and why, one way or the other, Victoria Stanton was behind it."

We passed through the ragged tangle of palm trees and jungle vegetation that marked the end of the clearing and came out in another one. In the distance, a few hundred yards ahead, was a house that Frank Lloyd Wright might have built, a wall of glass, or rather, several of them, a series of rectangles beneath a green-colored corrugated metal roof. We parked under an enormous banyan tree in back and went inside. Maddox went straight for the refrigerator.

Holding a can of beer in one hand, he tossed me one with his other. He had not bothered to ask, and with that simple gesture made it seem that we had not only known each other a long time, but were good friends.

"You don't know Archie, but Archie and Albert Craven... Archie always had the greatest respect for him. So have I. I knew who you were. Hell, who didn't know who you were. But, you know, there are two kinds of lawyers: those who try cases and those who don't. I never tried a case in my life. I wouldn't have known what I was doing. I used to feel a little insecure about that, the fact that I was never in a courtroom. I didn't think I was a real lawyer, if you know what I mean. I was just a guy who waded through papers, made sure every line was in compliance with the rules; made sure, to put it in a little different way, that none of our clients ever had to go to court."

He tossed back a long drink and then put the can down on the lamp table next to the wicker sofa where he was sitting. He emitted a long, low, rumbling cynical laugh and his eyes burned with more than regret, a deep and unforgiving resentment.

"Then Emmett married that whore, and I discovered what it was like to be in the middle of a criminal conspiracy; what it was like to fight a battle with someone who doesn't think there are any rules at all. I tried to warn Emmett; I tried to tell him what she was really like, but... Did you know Emmett? No? Too bad. I'm not sure you would have liked him, but I think you would have been fascinated. I mean, if you had known him at the beginning, when we were first starting out, when he became one of the wealthiest men around and we created the foundation that was going to give it all away."

He noticed that I had not touched my beer.

"You're not drinking?" he asked, rubbing the back of his hand against his nose.

"Not this early."

My answer seemed to puzzle him, and then he laughed, a deep, booming laugh that echoed off the walls.

"You're right! It is too early. That's the problem: nothing changes here. Christmas, Fourth of July, it's still low eighties in the afternoon, seventies at night. Easy to forget what time it is."

He glanced at the can he held in his hand, wondering, as it seemed, why he had not remembered it was still morning and not even close to afternoon.

"I don't have a television, don't get a paper. I go into Hilo once or twice a month. I didn't just leave San Francisco; I left everything, everything I knew and used to think important. I could have stayed; perhaps I should have. I felt a little like a coward leaving. After what happened to Emmett, I was sure they would try to have me murdered, too. I'm not sure I would have left if it had only been a question of what Victoria might try."

What other reason could he have had, I wondered. Why would he have given up a successful law practice, leave everything he had and everyone he knew, if he had not felt his life was in danger? The reason, when he gave it, seemed too general, too vague, though perhaps good enough for its purpose. He had become so dissatisfied with everything he saw happening around him, he did not think he had any choice. He had to get away. If Victoria Stanton had simply been who she was—if she had married Emmett Stanton and had done nothing else—the influence she had, the way she wanted things to be, the changes she insisted had to be made would have been enough. If he had not had to run for his life, he would have done it for his own sanity.

"I've seen her in court," I remarked as he got up and, with a brief smile of apology, took my beer and his back to the kitchen.

"I can imagine what that must have been like," he replied when he came back into the room.

We sat facing each other. I was sitting on a white-cushioned wicker chair on the other side of a glass-topped coffee table with a Polynesian carved wood pedestal for support. On my left, twenty-foot-wide sliding glass doors were open all the way without a screen to blur the view or slow the trade winds that blew in off the ocean. His arms folded across his heavy chest, Maddox stretched out his legs and crossed his ankles. The straps of his leather sandals flapped, unfastened, against the tan tile floor.

"She would have acted like she owned the place. She came in —didn't she?—wearing something that cost a fortune, and with the attitude of some who thinks, really thinks, that she's only wearing what anyone else would have worn. That was what got Emmett's attention. He thought it meant that money didn't mean anything to her; that she was simply oblivious to what things cost. Emmett was a genius when it came to money; how, if you had it to start with, you could make a lot more. But when it came to her, when it came to Victoria, he was an idiot, pure and simple."

As if everything had for the first time just become clear—as if, just that moment, everything now made sense—the eyes of Oscar Maddox flashed with the certainty of a flawless intuition.

"You know what it was, what it really was? Victoria was all woman, in that old-fashioned country club sense: drop-dead gorgeous, with legs to her shoulders and eyes that, every time she looked at you, announced in bright new colors, 'I'm the greatest fuck you'll ever have.' Listen. Emmett's wife left him; left him, not for another man, but for a woman. His wife, the mother of his son! A lesbian! And the next woman he meets wants nothing but to spend all her time in bed with him! She knew what she was doing; she knew how to make Emmett crazy!"

Maddox studied me carefully, trying to decide how far he should go, how much of the truth he could tell me. It was not a question of whether I could be trusted, it was not that at all; it was the question we have all had to face at some point: what can we decently reveal about someone we had known and respected, or perhaps even loved, after their death.

"Make him crazy!" he repeated, shaking his head at what, looking back on everything that had happened, seemed a serious, and even grotesque, understatement. "Even crazier than he was, I should have said. He was, you know, crazy as a loon. Brilliant, quicker to get to the point, the central issue of an argument, than anyone I have ever been around. Maybe you have to be crazy to do what he could do. We would be in the middle of a discussion about something we were planning, some new project, some change in the way we were doing things, and then, suddenly, he was not there. He was still sitting in the same chair, he hadn't moved; he was looking at you the same way he had been looking at you before—but he was gone! I mean completely. A trumpet player, a whole marching band, could have come walking through the door and Emmett would not have heard it. He was catatonic, literally catatonic. But the thing was, a moment later, he was back, all excited, waving his arms around like some half-demented shipwrecked sailor who just sighted land. He had the answer, the solution, whatever we had been talking about, whatever difficulty we were dealing with, he knew what we had to do, and he was almost always right.

"He could not explain it. I don't mean how it happened, how he would fall into that trance-like state; he could not explain the reason for whatever answer, whatever solution, that had come to him. He just knew. It wasn't logic; it was not deductive or inductive reasoning. Emmett's mind moved too fast to trace out all the measured steps by which the rest of us try to prove a correspondence between thought and reality. That, I think—the speed, the astonishing quickness of his mind—was why he sometimes seemed as surprised as I was when, coming out of that state of almost suspended animation, he would start talking about things he was hearing for the first time. The last time I saw that look was the day before he flew off to Europe for that climbing expedition in the French Alps, when he suddenly said, 'They're going to kill me.' And then he smiled, smiled in that strange way he had at the knowledge that he knew things no one else could know."

FOURTEEN

I had heard enough stories about the strange, erratic behavior of Emmett Stanton to believe what Oscar Maddox had said was true, but no one had ever told me anything like this.

"When he said they were going to kill him, did you have any doubt he meant his wife and Michael Kensington?"

"No doubt at all. He knew about them. It would have been hard not to know about them." Maddox frowned at his inability to explain what, because I had not known Emmett Stanton, I would not understand. "That is misleading. It was not just that he was in and out of reality, the way I tried to describe; everything about him seemed to be separated into parts that frequently had no connection. I'm sorry, that is too vague, too abstract. Victoria —I told you this—was all about sex. That is what she was for Emmett. She was there whenever he wanted her, but, and this is the point, he did not think of her when he wasn't with her. When he wanted her, she was there; when he didn't want her, she did not exist. He did not care, he simply had no interest, in what she did. It just didn't register."

Maddox shrugged his shoulders. There were things about Emmett Stanton that could not be explained.

"Did you ever know a woman—we all knew a woman, probably more than one—you wanted to go to bed with, and then, when it was over, all you could think about was how to get away? That was kind of how Emmett thought of her. The difference was that he married her, afraid that if he didn't, she wouldn't be there when he felt the need. He did not care what she... No, that's not true. It's that he didn't notice that his wife was sleeping with practically every guy she met."

He seemed to scold himself for his reluctance to tell the whole truth, his continued resistance to disclose what, in any other circumstance, he would never have revealed.

"Again, that isn't right. He did notice. Because, you see, he liked it; liked the fact that she slept with other men. It gave him a sense of importance. The woman everyone wanted, the woman everyone had, was always there for him. She used to tell him the things she had done. They may have been the only truthful things she ever told him."

It had begun to rain. Maddox, for some reason, suggested we sit outside. There was no point protesting, the rain itself was the reason he wanted to do it. We sat on wooden lawn chairs with pale yellow cushions on a cement patio just outside the living room. A few miles east, the far side of the gray clouds moving overhead, the morning sun slid across the ocean in a haze of burnished bronze. The light warm rain fell softly on my face.

"The rain is different here," Maddox explained. "Mostly, it comes at night, but when it happens during the day, it's usually like this. When it is fairly heavy, it doesn't last. Rains almost every day, and I don't have an umbrella in the house. Sure you don't want a beer? Something? Anything?"

We sat there a few moments, staring at the brightly colored sea and the clouded, shining sky, the rain and the sun and the stars at night the only tangible reminders of time's existence.

"She was the reason Stanton bought the basketball team?" I asked, just to be certain.

I was not sure Maddox heard me. He kept gazing out over the palm trees and the thick green foliage of his private sanctuary. Answerable to no one but himself, he was free to think honestly about the past.

"I used to think it could only have happened in San Francisco, where there aren't any rules, where no one makes judgments, and everyone is free to live whatever way they want; where it didn't matter if you were gay or straight; where it did not matter if you slept with someone different every night. No one seemed to wonder what would happen when sex became no more than a moment's physical pleasure, or what would happen to the human heart when the human heart was empty; or what would happen when a young girl, like Victoria Stanton had once been, had her own heart broken."

I remembered what Albert Craven had told me, how the night before her engagement to Michael Kensington was to be announced, she had run off to Reno and married that marvelously romantic young man who wanted to move all around Europe living like a poet; and how, less than a year later, he had left her, alone in a hotel room, and vanished forever from her life.

"Is that what happened?" asked Maddox, intensely interested. "I had not heard that before. I knew she had broken off her engagement to Kensington when they were both young, and that she had married someone else. I never knew anything about her marriage, only that it did not work out and that, years later, she fell madly in love with Kensington, and that he wanted nothing to do with her."

Maddox locked his hands around his right knee and slowly rocked back and forth. His breath was labored, a thick, rasping sound from deep inside his thick, heavy chest. His eyes narrowed into a squinting gaze of strict attention as he concentrated on what he was picturing in his mind. He wanted me to see it, too; see it in the same detail and, as close as possible, from the same perspective.

"Nothing to do with her. That was the key to everything, really. Even when he started carrying on with her, when they were having their affair, he wanted nothing to do with her. Even after Emmett died," said Maddox, with a sharp, sudden glance that left no doubt how significant this was, "he wanted nothing to do with her."

Maddox got to his feet and stretched his arms high in the air. The rain had dwindled down into not much more than an occasional sprinkle. The sun was everywhere.

"Well, it feels like afternoon," he remarked with an affable sparkle in his still thoughtful eyes. He went inside and came back with two cans of beer. He handed one to me, "In case you change your mind," snapped open the other, and took a drink. He wiped his gray stubbled chin with the back of his hand and sank down into the chair next to mine.

"I can only guess, but I don't think Kensington ever got over what she had done to him. I knew a few people who had known him in college. He was a kind of innocent, interested in girls, but not obsessed with them. He wasn't one of those guys who bragged about all the women he had been with; it wasn't clear that he had ever been with any. Then he met Victoria, and he fell in love the way you do the first time it happens, when it is the only thing that matters, the only reason you're alive, when the girl is all you think about. Someone who was with him the night before the engagement was to be announced told me he had never known anyone that happy, that glad to be alive. And then, a day later, the only question was whether he would ever feel alive again. The only reason he did not kill himself—and this is exactly what he was supposed to have said—was that he wanted to find out what it was like to live when he did not care, one way or the other, if he lived or died."

Scratching his chin, Maddox raised his wire-rough rust-colored eyebrows and, flaring his nostrils, took a deep breath. He held it there and did not let it out, as if, more than his breath, he was holding on to a fragment of an almost forgotten time that, now that he had remembered it, he was afraid he might lose. Finally, he let it out, and with a quiet, helpless laugh, made an observation I had not heard before and could not contradict.

"It's the years between eighteen and twenty-one that, for most of us, decide our lives. I never had much use for those narrow-minded psychologists who insist that it is what happens in your childhood that makes all the difference. It is those three years, just after high school. Until then, there really isn't, for most of us, any real decisions; everything is decided for you—where you live, where you go to school, and most of what you study. The decisions you do get to make—what sports to play, what clubs to join, whether you are going to be in the school play—are mainly questions of what you have the aptitude or the physical ability for. But once you graduate from high school, you suddenly have to make decisions for yourself—are you going to college, and if you are, which school; and, more importantly, what do you want to be. The worst part—or maybe the best—it's when, in all probability, you first fall in love.

"Michael Kensington and Victoria Stanton might have both been virgins when he asked her to marry him; and even if they weren't, neither one of them would have been much experienced. Then, suddenly, the night before they were to announce their engagement, she runs off with someone else and everything he had looked forward to, every dream he had, is gone."

There was an urgency in Maddox's voice that suggested a new

insight into the human condition, something that precisely because it was so obvious, was easily missed.

"Love and sex; sex and love. We fall in love; we're drawn, physically and emotionally, to the other person. Physically and emotionally, but physically—think of the power that drive has, the need we have; that need, that drive, that, more than our own desire to live, keeps the whole thing going, generation after generation. It is the tyrant in our soul. But we're in love, and love restrains the wild beast; trains it, refines it, controls it. You fall in love and, if you're halfway decent, you sleep with only that one woman. Michael Kensington, a young man in his early twenties, falls in love with Victoria, a year or so younger. And then she runs off with someone else. Love has not just vanished; love has betrayed him. The drive, the need, is still there, greater even than it was before, because the source, the reason, for all restraint is gone. And there is now this: think what he feels, how devastated he must have been, how desperate he must have felt, not just the hurt, but the sense, the knowledge, that the pain is always going to be with him; it is never going to go away. His mind is a light show of excruciating, fragmentary thoughts: jealousy, rage, disbelief. He can't concentrate, he can't sleep. He had to free himself; he has to get some relief. Sex with any woman he can find; sex by himself, if he has to."

Maddox shook his head, remembering, as I now understood, more than what he imagined about Michael Kensington, remembering what had once happened to himself. He caught the look in my eye. With a quick smile that vanished even quicker, he acknowledged with the wisdom of his years his own not quite forgotten youth.

"Happened to a lot of people, I imagine," he remarked with a shrug. "It happened to her, Victoria Stanton. She didn't start sleeping with every man she met until, when, exactly? She woke up one morning in a small hotel—what you were just telling me

—and discovers that her husband has left her. Think how much chance decides our lives. If she hadn't run off with someone else, if she had married Kensington, what would they have become? One of the most admired couples in San Francisco, pillars of the community, with wonderful, promising children of their own? Who knows? But whatever they would have become, it would not have been what they are now: two amoral, selfish human beings who think murder only a crime if you get caught. Although, between the two of them, Kensington is the one most to blame. She would do anything for him, and he knows it."

Oscar Maddox kept talking, going back in time, viewing from first one perspective, then another, the parallel lives of Michael Kensington and Victoria Stanton. Finished telling one story, he would start on another episode of their known histories; then, remembering something he had left out, he would go back to tell me what he had forgotten and thought I should know. He had the gift of the born storyteller: a perfect sense of timing and no sense of time. He could have talked all weekend and never noticed. And why would he? He had not talked to anyone in months, and not to anyone for more than a few minutes, someone he met in Hilo on his occasional visits to town. The only conversations Oscar Maddox had now were with himself; serious conversations about how much had changed, and how nothing he had thought important, the things he and Emmett Stanton had wanted to do, had been achieved. Worse yet, none of what they had thought to accomplish was now thought worth doing.

"We were going to do great things for the city. Emmett had all this money, but—and not many people understood this—he had a lot more, a great deal more, money than he had. That doesn't seem to make any sense, does it?" he said, chuckling to himself. "But it's absolutely true. There were a hundred people in the city who contributed most of the money given to charitable causes. Most of them did it because it made them part of the city's elite, the people who get their picture in the paper, the people all the politicians, from the president on down, wanted to meet, the people every candidate wanted to know. They were the people who did not want to be left out, and the way to make sure that never happened was to never say no when the guy who had more money than any of them asked them to join him in some worthy cause. When Emmett made a million-dollar contribution, it meant there would be at least twenty million to go with it.

"We were going to do great things for the city: decent housing for the homeless and the poor, better schools, programs for music and the arts, preservation of the city's landmarks, restoration of old buildings, new landscaping for the parks. Emmett thought we could make San Francisco, if not a perfect place, a city where everyone felt welcome and no one felt left out. Emmett was what, years ago, the Rockefellers were for New York. They shared the belief that the only justification for great wealth is to use it to improve the world around you. Emmett understood that; he may have been the last man, the last rich man, who did. And then came Victoria, with those blazing eyes, that fire she had, making him feel that he was a man again. She convinced him that he could do even greater things for the public if the public knew who he was and what he wanted to do; convinced him that if he became the owner of a professional basketball team, a team everyone thought more important than almost anything else, he could have all the support he would ever need.

"More than money, she told him—and he would have more of it if he owned the team—he would have every elected public official on his side for everything he thought the city should do. It seemed to make perfect sense. How many owners of professional teams get the public to pay billions to build their stadiums? Instead of taking money, she explained, Emmett would be giving money—hundreds of millions—to the community; giving it now in conjunction with public expenditures for a common public purpose: better schools, better parks, more affordable housing. Emmett had used his own money to leverage the money of other wealthy people; now, simply by becoming an owner, he could leverage tax dollars, and in that way spend more than he had been able to spend before on making the city what it should be. It was irresistible. Emmett was mesmerized. He never believed a word she said."

I was not sure I had heard him right.

"He never believed...?"

"He was mesmerized by her certainty, by how excited she was at what she insisted would happen; mesmerized by how happy she seemed to be by this new project that would give them both something to look forward to; something, an idea of her own, that would help him with what he had always wanted. And what would be the worst that could happen? The team might not make much money. What was there to lose? So Emmett bought the team and everything changed. Everything got pushed back. Instead of thinking about what the foundation was going to do for the city, everything was about what had to be done to make the team more competitive: what coach should be hired, which players should be signed and how important it was to pay them more than they could get anywhere else.

"Victoria didn't care what anything cost; she didn't care what it meant for the things Emmett wanted to do. She didn't want to be active behind the scenes, spending her time on good works. She wanted what she got: to be famous, the face of the franchise, the woman everyone knew, the woman everyone wanted to know. Every home game, before the introduction of the players, the spotlight would shine on her, sitting in her luxury box, and as soon as her name was announced, she would flash that glittering smile of hers and wave to everyone like she was waving to all her best friends.

"She loved the crowd, and the crowd loved her. Applause was

so much her aphrodisiac you had the feeling that she was having an orgasm each time she heard it. And if she didn't have one, then she probably had one later, with one of the players," he remarked with a careless shrug. "I don't know that for certain, you understand, but there were rumors. There isn't any question she was sleeping with someone on the side. It's what I said before: she may have been a virgin when she was almost engaged to Kensington, and she may have been, and probably was, faithful during her first, brief marriage, but sex soon took the place of love. It's the same thing, isn't it?" he asked with a slow, sideways glance as if I knew already what he was going to say. "The need to have everyone know you, the need to have everyone think you're desirable. What is the desire for celebrity except a kind of sexless nymphomania?"

I had to confess I had never quite thought of it like that.

"But that must have changed after she and Kensington were finally together. He might not have been in love with her, but she was in love with him, wasn't she?"

"Changed? Stopped sleeping with other men? No, I doubt it. She had the same need; probably more so. You're right, she was in love with Kensington, but he was not in love with her and did not pretend that he was. Or perhaps he did at first; long enough to convince her that they had to get rid of Emmett if they wanted to get married."

"Not divorce, because of the money and everything that came with it: ownership of the team, the life she had to have?"

"I'm not sure that is quite right. It underestimates the hold he had, that he still has, on her. Read all the bad novels ever written, see all the tear-jerking movies ever made, you'll never come across anyone who played his part more perfectly. Remember, he had been only twenty-one or twenty-two when she not only broke his heart, but humiliated him. All their friends, all their relatives, knew they were about to announce their engagement and she runs off and marries someone else. She doesn't see Kensington again until he's in his thirties. They boy who loved her, the eager innocent, has become a worldly adventurer, distant, self-possessed, and with the kind of dark-eyed good looks that made every woman stare whenever he walked into a room.

"Kensington had been hopelessly in love with her and she destroyed his one great chance at happiness. He became disciplined, driven, willing to try anything that might bring some excitement into his life, anything that would help him forget what had happened. He drove race cars at Laguna Seca, skied at Aspen, acquired a reputation as a brash, free-wheeling, independent-minded man eager to make his mark. He had a production company in Hollywood, made a few movies, but he was too impatient, too much in a hurry, to stay very long with anything. It was the same thing with women. He was always seen with someone new, usually some young actress, one of those not quite famous faces you know you have seen but cannot quite remember where.

"And they were always looking at him. It was uncanny. Whenever a photograph was taken, the girl was never looking at the camera, she was always looking at him. The other thing you noticed was that no matter how he was dressed, he always looked exactly the same. That was what made him stand out: however large the crowd, your eye was invariably drawn to him. He could have walked out of the pages of Hemingway or Fitzgerald, broad-shouldered with thick, powerful legs, a mustache that could have been drawn with a pencil, and black, shiny hair parted neatly on the side. There was nothing weak or sensitive in that look of his, nothing of the false equality that women who want to be men think a man should be. He had predatory eyes. Any feminist, man or woman, would have hated him for what he was. It was precisely women who knew he would never be faithful who most wanted to be with him, and no one more than...well, I don't have to tell you who that was.

"When she saw him after all those years at some event in the city, or some wedding in the Napa Valley, it seemed a matter of chance, an accidental meeting, but I would not be surprised if Kensington had planned the whole thing. He must have known that they would inevitably find themselves together. Whatever people may think, San Francisco is a small town. Whenever it happened, the moment she saw him she knew that what she had done to him had been a tragic mistake. She was, like most of us, a prisoner of first impressions. She remembered, or thought she remembered, that she had always been in love with Michael Kensington. She remembered, or thought she remembered, that what had happened had been a youthful indiscretion, a young girl's excusable confusion. All she could think of now was how much she had missed.

"Missed, but not forever. Like everyone who believes in the great American myth, she believed in second chances. Michael Kensington did not. He had fallen in love with her and had been destroyed. She was married, he reminded her, a second time. Her second chance was with her husband, Emmett Stanton. Believe in second chances all you want, there is no more desperate feeling than knowing that your second chance, your last chance, at happiness, that happiness you have never known, is gone forever. She became frantic; he became, not just indifferent, but angry that she could not seem to understand that he simply was not interested."

The large, luminous eyes of Oscar Maddox flew open. He seemed, if not to reconsider, to re-examine, what he had been telling me. He did not want to leave me with a false impression.

"I don't know what was said, but I've no doubt this is how they felt; no doubt at all that she was in love with him, desperately in love, and that he was not in love with her at all. He probably even hated her, not just for what she had done to him, but for what she had become. It was not just his innocence that had been lost, but hers as well. The girl he had fallen in love with, the girl he had wanted to marry, the girl he would have loved forever, was on her second marriage, married to the richest man in town, and, according to all the stories, sleeping with anyone she found halfway attractive. Think what that must have been like. Two kids, pure at heart, now all grown up, he an unrepentant womanizer, she a dedicated whore. He would have done anything for her when he first fell in love with her, and now, years too late, she wanted to go back to how things could have been and do anything for him. It became, I think, a strange, evil kind of revenge; a way to get even, to see how far she would go; to see if there was any limit to what she would do."

A scowl hung heavy on Maddox's wide mouth as his head moved slowly side to side, measuring like a metronome the insanity of the world, the cruel indifference with which men and women ignored and, more than that, rejected, a decent regard for the sanctity of other people's lives.

"That was how it happened, how a boy and a girl, a young man and a young woman, who, but for one night's unfortunate decision, an otherwise blameless change of heart, a girl's longing for the kind of love young girls read about, became, together, willing, and, willing, able, to do whatever they thought they had to do to get what they wanted, and do it without a moment's sense of guilt or remorse."

The rain had stopped and we sat in the sunlight's midday warmth. A gentle breeze lifted the fronds of the palm trees down below and sent them swaying in a slow-motion dance of their own devising, like thoughtless men and women for whom tomorrow has no meaning. Nodding to himself, a reminder of what he had to do, Maddox put his hands on the arms of his chair and pushed himself up to his feet.

"I thought you should know this about them, what they were; what, in their different ways, they became," he said, looking down at me with a grim, determined expression on his aging, well-lined tan face. "They killed Emmett. I don't have any proof of that, and I'm not sure there is any. I'm not sure they committed murder in the legal sense, but if one of them didn't shove him off that mountain, they found some other way to make him fall—dared him to jump a few feet from one hand hold to another, told him a snow-covered crevice was solid ice. I don't know what happened, only that they're responsible. What happened to Matthew, that, of course, is another story. I don't know anything about how it was done, how it was arranged. I know nothing about his murder. But I know why they did it, why they thought it had to be done, why they did not think there was any other choice. It was why I left when I did, why I made sure no one could find me, why I came here, in the shadow of the volcano. Matthew and I had come up with a way to put an end to all the madness; a way, the only way, we could make the dream Matthew's father Emmett always had become a reality."

Fifteen

Leonard Silverman walked briskly to the bench, smiled briefly at the jury, looked down to where I was sitting next to the defendant, and, in a quiet, but firm voice, asked, "Is the defense ready to call its first witness?"

"Yes, Your Honor," I replied as I rose slowly from my chair. "The defense calls Thaddeus John Allen."

No matter how eager a defendant may be to testify, to tell the jury what really happened, to tell the world that they are not guilty, that they did not do what they are accused of doing, they are usually nervous, a little uncertain of themselves, as they walk toward the empty witness stand. T. J. Allen almost knocked over his chair as he rushed forward, raised his hand, and in as loud a voice as I ever heard, swore to tell the truth, the whole truth, and nothing but the truth. He did not just swear it, he repeated it, every word of it, a one-man chorus to the clerk's routine recitation. T. J. Allen owned the courtroom. Every eye was on him, everyone on the jury leaned forward.

"Mr. Allen," I began in a calm, formal voice, "the first question I want to ask is—"

"I didn't do it! I didn't kill Matthew!" he fairly shouted as he turned to the jury. "I didn't murder Matthew. We were friends, we were..." He remembered where he was. "Sorry," he apologized in a soft, chastened voice. "I didn't mean to..."

"It's all right," I told him. "You didn't kill Matthew Stanton. But you were there, the night it happened, weren't you?" I placed my hands on the jury box railing and, as if I were reconsidering the line of questioning I wanted to pursue, peered down at the floor. "Before we talk about what happened that night, the night Matthew Stanton was murdered, we need to know—the jury needs to know—how it was, as you just testified, that you and Matthew Stanton were friends. We know from other witnesses that Matthew Stanton was born into a life of privilege. His father was one of the wealthiest men in the country. Is that what happened to you? Was your father a wealthy man?"

I had asked questions of thousands of witnesses in my career, but, I suddenly realized, this was the first time the witness chair had disappeared, vanished beneath the prodigious length and breadth of Thaddeus John Allen. Six foot eight inches, two hundred forty-five pounds, over seven feet fingertip to fingertip when he stretched out his arms, he looked less like someone sitting in a chair than a man crouched beneath some invisible weight, like Atlas without a globe.

"My father?" Allen replied. "I never knew my father. My mother raised me by herself. Worked two, sometimes three jobs; any work she could get." Turning toward the jury again, close enough, as it seemed, to reach out and touch them, a smile full of sympathy and understanding for what he had experienced as a child spread across his wide, friendly mouth. "Wealthy? There were times we didn't have enough to eat. I mean," he added, quick to correct himself, "times my mother didn't, times when there was only enough for me. She always made sure of that; made sure I had what I needed, even though, sometimes, it meant there was nothing for her. I grew up poor, but I always had what I needed."

The smile flashed again, brighter than it had before, bright enough to light up a room. His shoulders pulled back, his hands and arms shot straight up.

"That didn't mean she wouldn't slap my little...whenever I did something or said something I shouldn't. She should have been in the Army or the Marines. You would have felt sorry for anyone who had to serve under her. You give a hundred and ten percent or you weren't trying. First time I had a job, delivering papers before school, I started complaining about how early I had to get up. She tells me that in that case, I can start getting up with her, an hour earlier, and make my own damn breakfast!"

Pausing, his shoulders came forward and he leaned on his elbows, that brilliant smile of his replaced by a sullen look of confused frustration.

"She died my first year in college. Cancer, the doctors said; cancer that could have been treated if she worked somewhere where she could have had insurance. Cancer, the doctors said; but what really killed her was being poor and overworked."

Allen was as mercurial as anyone I had ever known, moving at times from one emotion to another with such speed you had to wonder how much of it was real, how deep any one emotion really went; wonder whether it was not simply the way he instantly reacted, as it were, to what was happening right in front of him. He was, after all, an athlete, expert at a game in which everything depended on how quickly he could forget what had just happened and get ready for the next thing he had to do. His eyes could light up with admiration for something someone had just done, and then, half a second later, stare with rage at someone who had failed to do what they were supposed to have done. He could love you, hate you, view you with complete indifference, before he took a second breath. The memory of his mother, what she had endured, the sacrifices she had made for him, filled him with depression and remorse. With the next question I asked, his large brown eyes began to sparkle like all the stars in heaven.

"You went to college on a basketball scholarship, didn't you?"

It was a perfectly useless question. Everyone knew the answer. There was not anyone in the courtroom, there was not anyone in the city, there was not anyone anywhere who did not know T. J. Allen and where he went to college.

"Michigan State. They offered me a scholarship my junior year."

He reported this fact with evident pride. He had not had to wait until he was a senior in high school before major universities were trying to recruit him.

"You went to Michigan State on a basketball scholarship. What did you go there to study?"

Allen looked at me in helpless wonder.

"I didn't go there to study anything; I went there to play basketball."

He knew why I had asked the question, the point I was trying to make. We had discussed at some length what it meant that he had gone to college and, if anything, knew less when he left than when he started. The jury had to know his history to understand the basis of the friendship he had with Matthew Stanton. Everything depended on this, on convincing the jury that Matthew Stanton was the last person he would have thought of killing.

"You must have majored in something; you must have gone to class," I remarked as I walked idly in front of the jury box, dragging my fingers along the railing. "History, political science, economics?" I stopped moving and looked directly at him. "You didn't really go to college, did you?"

"No, not the way you mean. I went to play ball. I had to take some courses," he explained, scanning the line of jurors seated in the box with an earnest look. He wanted them to understand what he had done, and why he had come to regret it. "If you were an athlete, they set you up with courses to take. Physical education courses, mainly; courses in things like Theory of Basketball. You didn't have to do anything, just show up. There wasn't any work."

"But there are courses every undergraduate has to take, course required for graduation," I insisted with an innocent expression.

Allen's mouth curled down at the corners. He shrugged his shoulders in what seemed a sad lament for what he had missed.

"I didn't go to college to graduate; it was all about basketball. When they recruited me, all the college coaches told me that if I came to their school, I would be a high draft pick after I played two years, and maybe only one, and could turn pro. Course work? Are you kidding? Who had time for that? I was going to be making millions, tens of millions, my first year in the NBA. Why would I waste time in a classroom? I was never going to need a job, and wasn't that the reason everyone seemed to think you should get a college degree?"

Shaking his head in a slow, wide-spreading arc, he smiled at how little he had understood, and how arrogant he had been.

"If it hadn't been for Matthew, I'd probably still be as ignorant as I was then. He was the only person I knew—I mean that: the only one, except my mother—who ever talked to me about anything except basketball. It's why we became such good friends, why he was the only person I trusted: we both knew the whole thing was a fraud, a kid's game, nothing serious; a game I loved to play, the way other people like to play tennis or golf, but still a game. It doesn't mean anything; it's just an escape, entertainment for people who don't have anything better to do. We're all famous, everyone knows our names, and because we're celebrities, everyone wants to know what we think, and not just about basketball, but everything, politics, the state of the world. Me? Who never read a book, never studied anything in college. You going to tell me this isn't a fraud? But, you know," he went on, speaking in a confidential tone, as if he and the twelve jurors were all alone, "it never occurred to me that it was—a fraud, I mean. I didn't know anything, but I thought I did. It was only after I got to know Matthew, only after we started reading things together, that I began to realize that there are more important things than playing a game in front of a screaming crowd of twenty thousand, and twenty million more watching on television."

He could have talked for hours, talked for days, and no one on that jury, no one in that courtroom, would have gotten tired of listening. He was that good, that compelling, that, to use a word seldom used to describe a witness, charismatic. He might, as he admitted, have been talking nonsense when, as a player, he answered a reporter's questions about the great issues of our time, but those answers had no doubt been more believable than the same thing said by a seasoned politician. I could almost sense the disappointment in the courtroom when I stopped him in midsentence with a question that brought his testimony closer to the issue in the case.

"Let me go back to where we started. You did not murder Matthew Stanton, but you were there the night it happened. Tell the jury why you were there that night."

"There wasn't any particular reason. We were friends, close friends, as I tried to explain. Sometimes I would just drop by; sometimes one of us would call and we would decide when we would get together. That night, Matthew called and asked if I would come over. He sounded worried, upset about something. I got there around seven, we had dinner, we talked. He was angry, upset, like I said, but he wouldn't talk about it, wouldn't tell me why he was so angry. And that got me upset. I told him we were supposed to be friends, but that if he wouldn't tell me what had him so upset, well, then he could just go to hell. And I stormed out of there, as angry as he had been. By the time I reached the street, I realized what I had done, that I had made a bad situation worse."

The lines in Allen's forehead deepened and became more pronounced as he went back in time, wondering whether, had he never left, his friend might still be alive.

"He was so angry, so depressed, that for a moment I thought that maybe he... I called him on my phone, and when he didn't answer, I went back, hoping he had not done anything stupid, that I wasn't too late. I burst through the door, and that's when I saw him, lying on the floor, the gun laying next to him, and then I realized it wasn't suicide. The gun was too far away. Someone had shot him and just dropped it as they ran out of the room. I had only been gone a few minutes. The killer might still be there. That must have been why I picked it up, because I thought I heard something. That's why I fired, why there was gunshot residue on my hand; why I was still holding it when the police arrived."

"Yes, the gun," I remarked, scratching my chin as my voice trailed off. "The prosecution insists that the gun, the murder weapon, belonged to you. Did it? Did the gun belong to you?"

"Yes, it was mine. Until it was stolen."

"Stolen from your locker?"

"That's right. I bought it because... It was stolen from my locker. I reported it. I filed a stolen property report."

I was about to ask the next question when I realized what he had left out.

"You bought the gun because...because why, exactly?"

Allen looked down at his hands. He seemed reluctant, embarrassed even, to explain.

"A lot of players have them; I never did. But then I started getting a lot of threats when I started talking about playing somewhere else. There are a lot of crazy people out there, and they say a lot of crazy things. They probably don't mean it, but when they started writing about how anyone as ungrateful as I was, willing to turn down millions because I thought I could get more somewhere else, didn't deserve to live, then I decided that..."

"You bought the gun to protect yourself, and then it was stolen from your locker. Who would have had access to your locker? Could anyone have just walked into the locker room?"

"No one was allowed in there, only players and staff, and after games, members of the press. But during practice, no one who did not have authorization. There were always security people."

"Would Victoria Stanton or her husband, Michael Kensington, have been allowed inside?" I asked, moving a significant step closer along the long, low jury box railing.

"Anytime they wanted."

"Because they owned the team?"

Allen's mouth, closed tight, shifted far to the right as he rubbed his left hand from high on his cheekbone down to the point of his chin where he held it while he pondered the question.

"Yes, and then again, no. They didn't own the team; Matthew's father, Emmett, owned it, and then, when he died... You see," he said, interrupting himself to give the jury the background they needed, "the team isn't owned by an individual; it's owned by a trust, the Stanton Trust. After Mr. Stanton died, Matthew ended up with more than eighty percent of the shares; Matthew's stepmother, Mr. Stanton's wife, Victoria Stanton, had a little less than twenty percent. But that doesn't tell you anything about who was really running things. Matthew's father was never very involved, and Matthew wasn't interested. Victoria Stanton ran everything, and she did it exactly the way she wanted to; or the way Kensington told her to. He was really the one with all the power; she never did anything without clearing it with him first."

There are few things Americans take more seriously than the confirmation that there are mysterious forces in control, someone nameless and all-powerful behind the scenes. I did not have to turn around to measure the reaction of the courtroom crowd.

Victoria Stanton was a figurehead, the public face of an organization run by someone else. Everyone knew, or thought they knew, that this happened in politics and government, but sport, even professional sport, was supposedly held to a higher standard. That someone, a name the public knew nothing about, had somehow gathered in his hands all the strings of power was almost as much a disillusion as learning that the games themselves had been fixed. Allen insisted that Victoria Stanton and Michael Kensington had done something even worse than that.

"It's a game, a game we all love," Allen began. "The game, if you play it right, has a purity. I mean that. It may sound odd, purity, but that's what it is. There isn't any argument, there isn't any disagreement, about what happens on the court. You make the basket or you don't; you're called for a foul or you're not. At the end, when time runs out, you win the game or you lose it. And everyone knows—if you're a player, you know—who the great ones are. We make a lot of money; we understand it's a business, but if they disbanded the league tomorrow, if there wasn't any pro basketball anymore, there isn't one of us who wouldn't be back on a court somewhere, playing the game with anyone we could get to play. Emmett Stanton understood that. He liked the game; he used to come to practice just to watch. Victoria Stanton didn't care anything about it. She didn't come to watch; she wanted everyone to watch her."

Dressed in a dark blue suit and a pale blue tie, Allen turned up the palms of his enormous hands as if to weigh in the balance an allegation more serious because more universal.

"We weren't playing a sport anymore; we were in the entertainment business. The game became part of something bigger, a television spectacle. You can't have any dead time on television. Remember when you were a kid," he said, facing the jury that was hanging on his every word, "and you went to a high school game. You took a seat in the stands, watched the players warm up, then the game started and at half time you maybe got up, walked around, talked to the people you came with. No one is going to watch that on television; the entertainment has to be nonstop. The players get introduced to music, music so loud it hurts your ears, and when the game starts and there is a timeout for commercials on television, there has to be something—a juggler, a dance group, a trick rider on a bicycle—to keep the people who paid a fortune for tickets from getting bored.

"The game is bigger than the game. When you go down to LA to play the Lakers, half of Hollywood is there. It's where you go to be seen. It's why a guy who made billions at Microsoft bought the Clippers and moved them from San Diego to Los Angeles: it made him one of the rich and famous people everyone wants to know. That's what Kensington and Victoria Stanton have done: become the producers and directors of a television show, a whole damn network; and not only that, in her case, the leading actor, the woman everyone wants to interview. That's why they did what they did to me!"

Allen left his mouth half open, as if he were daring everyone to disagree. Swept along by his own insistent voice, his passionate belief that no one could possibly doubt what he was saying, he assumed that everyone knew as well as he did what he was talking about. I stared back at him, and then slowly turned away, and with both hands on the jury box railing, studied each of the jurors long enough to change their frame of reference from Allen to me; long enough to stop him from becoming any angrier than he seemed in danger of becoming. Finally, my hands still on the railing, I looked at him again.

"What did they do to you? Can you be more specific?"

"What did they do to me?" he cried as his eyebrows arched higher. "You want to know what they did to me? Not much, just framed me for murder, a murder they arranged! That's all! Just that!" He laughed, tossed back his head, and laughed again.

"Don't you get it? Doesn't anyone understand? You have to give them credit. It's pure genius," he remarked as his eyes narrowed into a searching glance. "Think about it! They turned a sports team into a multi-billion-dollar entertainment empire. Everyone, all round the word—China, Europe—watches it; not just the game, but everything about the team, everything about the players, on and off the court: how they spend their time, where they go on vacation, their wives, their kids; everything they think, everything they think they think. What more could they do? How about a murder trial? A trial in which a black man, a famous black athlete, murders a rich white guy! A black player murders a white owner! What could you invent that would have more appeal? The great American sin, the original sin, the deep, unhealed subconscious drive, the conflict between white and black, master and slave. Listen! It's been there all along, and everyone, if they're honest with themselves, knows it. Years ago—you all remember Malcolm X, what you probably didn't know is how he used it, how when he spoke to a black audience he talked about how 'the white man wants the black woman,' and when he talked to a white audience, he told them how 'the black man wants the white woman.' Victoria Stanton and Michael Kensington understood that. They understood they could get rid of Matthew and own the team and all the billions themselves, and blame it on a black man because who is going to believe that a black man could ever be friends with a white man, or believe that a black man, because a black man is always violent, wouldn't be willing to kill?"

His chin held high in defiance, Allen's eyes blazed with indignation. This was not just a trial, this was a war of the races, a black man once again the victim, a lynching anyway you looked at it; worse than a lynching, because sanctioned by the law. Four members of the jury, three of them women, were black, but they were not the only ones mesmerized by what they heard.

I was not mesmerized, but I was surprised. We had spent

hours going over his testimony, and he had never mentioned race as a motive for what we were both convinced Kensington and Victoria Stanton had done, framed him for the murder for which they alone were responsible. Under the pressure of the moment, it had all come pouring out. He was right when he said that it was always there, lurking just below the surface. However civilized, however tolerant, we might be in our normal, everyday lives, the anger, the resentment, the sense of grievance, the belief that without the legacy of slavery everything would be different, was embraced or rejected with the kind of emotion that left little room for compromise. The prosecution would have none of it.

"Is it really your position, Mr. Allen, that the only reason you're on trial for the murder of Matthew Stanton is because you're a famous black athlete?" asked Samantha Longstreet with her mocking, long-lashed eyes as she rose from the counsel table on my left to begin her cross-examination. "Never mind," she said before he could start to answer. "We all heard what you said. First question, Mr. Allen: you owned the gun with which Matthew Stanton was murdered, did you not?"

"Yes, I did; but as I testified—"

"You owned the gun. Good. But you say the gun was stolen, taken from your locker. Is that your testimony?" she asked, a thin, skeptical smile on her red-colored lips.

Allen watched her carefully, trying to anticipate what was behind the questions she was asking. He was smart, easy to teach. I had told him to keep his answers on cross-examination as brief as possible.

"Yes, it is."

"You testified that only people directly connected with the team could enter the locker room, correct?"

"Yes."

"Your locker, like all the lockers there, had a code, a code you could change as often as you liked, correct?"

"Yes, but I never changed mine. And, besides, half the time I didn't even bother locking it."

"Really? Even when you left your gun inside it? That wasn't a very safe thing to do, was it, Mr. Allen?"

"The locker room was safe," insisted Allen, clenching his jaw. "No one could get in who wasn't authorized to be there."

"Yes, I understand," said Longstreet in a tone that suggested she did not. "The gun was stolen, and you reported it to the police. But it was never found, was it?"

"No."

"I take that back," she said with a sudden, withering glance. "It was found, wasn't it? The night the police found it still in your hand after you shot and killed Matthew Stanton!"

I was on my feet, objecting, but she had made her point, and nothing a judge ever told a jury made them forget what they had heard. Silverman sustained the objection almost before I finished making it. Longstreet was ready with her next question.

"You had been in a very public dispute over your next contract, isn't that correct? You wanted more money than they were willing to offer, isn't that true?"

"It's true we didn't agree on what I should be paid."

"You negotiated with Mrs. Stanton, didn't you?" she asked without any great interest as she began leafing through some papers on the table in front of her.

"That's right, I was negotiating with her; though it was really Kensington who was holding things up."

Her hands still on the papers, Longstreet looked up.

"You mean it was Michael Kensington who refused to give you what you wanted?"

"She never did anything without his permission."

Longstreet let go of the papers and slowly smiled.

"Which means there was no point in talking directly with Michael Kensington, was there?"

"I'm not sure what you mean."

"You didn't talk to Kensington. You talked to the only person who could overrule Mrs. Stanton, the person who, after his father died, was in almost complete control. You talked to Matthew Stanton, and when he turned you down, when he refused to give you the money you wanted, you killed him! Murdered him in cold blood with the gun you reported missing, the gun that had never been stolen at all! Isn't that true, Mr. Allen? Isn't that what happened? No one cares what color you are, Mr. Allen. All anyone cares about is that you're a murderer who deserves to spend the rest of your life in prison!"

Sixteen

Leonard Silverman left the bench, the twelve jurors filed out of the jury box, and the courtroom slowly emptied. Samantha Longstreet packed up her briefcase and her papers and walked away, and I was left alone with my client for a few minutes before the guards took him back to jail.

"How did I do?" asked T. J. Allen, watching me with worried eyes. "Did I do all right?"

He had done better than I expected, though I was not sure why I had expected anything less. For all his disparagement of sports as entertainment, he was a born performer. He had dominated the courtroom. Even had you wanted to, you could not have looked away. I could have kept him on the witness stand for a week, longer had I wanted to, and no one would have become tired of listening. Which is the reason I thought he had made a mistake.

"You didn't need to turn things into a question of race. Do you really believe that...?"

The question died on my lips. He was looking at me in a way that suggested not just a distance, but a gap so wide between our experience that, no matter how hard I might try, could never completely be bridged. I was white, he was black, and that difference would always remain. I did not agree. I sat back and gave him a look of my own.

"I don't give a damn what color you are. You don't think I can understand you because I'm white and you're black, but you think you can understand me? And don't bother with that nonsense about how the victim can always understand the oppressor. I heard what you said, and you'll have to forgive me if I'm a little, let's just say, disappointed that I had not heard anything like this from you before, not once in all the time we spent getting ready for this. I told you at the beginning... Well, it's too late for that. But if I had known, I wouldn't have—"

"Taken the case? You're not the one on trial; your life isn't on the line. Listen, Antonelli, I'm grateful for what you've done, what you're doing. I didn't know I was going to do what I did. I didn't plan it; it just came out. And that's what I mean. What I said, what just came out, that's what black people really feel, that's what we think, what we've learned. So, yeah, you're right: I didn't say anything like that to you. Why would I? I believe you; I believe you don't have a racist bone in your body. When you think of me, your first thought isn't that I'm black, but, let's face it, you aren't exactly the proverbial man in the street. Those four jurors, the four black ones, they know what I'm talking about."

Allen was right. I was not the one on trial for my life; he was the one with everything to lose. He had to have been spending long, sleepless nights in his cell wondering what he could do, what he could say, that would make the jury feel that, whatever the evidence might suggest, he should be set free. How often, sitting in obligatory silence at the counsel table in the chair closest to the jury box, must he have studied the faces of the jurors? How often must he have searched the faces of those four black jurors, four people who felt a closer bond than just his celebrity, and, aware that he was watching them, felt drawn even closer by what they had in common?

I went directly from the courthouse to my office and had barely settled into my chair when Albert Craven walked in, anxious to hear what had happened.

"When did you get back?" he asked, sliding sideways onto the overstuffed wingback chair on the other side of my desk. He learned forward slightly, hoping the trip had not been a failure.

"We missed the flight we were supposed to take. Just landed an hour ago and came straight from the airport," I reported with a shrug of indifference. "Missed the trial today. Don't know what happened. Probably went straight to closing arguments, which means the jury, hearing only the prosecution's side of things, must have found Allen guilty. I guess I'll go tomorrow and argue he should be given life in prison instead of execution."

The sensitive mouth of Albert Craven, which had begun to open in astonished alarm, closed tight into a dismissive smile of friendly scorn. I smiled back in a way that suggested there was still some truth in the lie, something serious in the absurdity.

"Once I put Allen on the stand, I might just as well have been somewhere else. Some witnesses—most defendants, if you want to know the truth—you want to get on and off the stand as quickly as you can. Ask the two or three questions you have to ask and hope they survive what the prosecution will do to them on cross. But T. J. Allen? The more he talked, the more everyone wanted to hear."

Loosening my tie, I turned and casually folded my arms across my chest. My eyes traced the long line of bookshelves full of reported cases and books of both ancient learning and classic works of fiction.

"What?" inquired Craven, following my distracted gaze.

"*Anna Karenina. The Great Gatsby.*" I shook my head, embarrassed that I had not thought of it before, the two stories that together told another story, one that had not yet been written. "Suppose that, in *Anna Karenina*, Tolstoy had changed the story. Everything, or almost everything, stays the same. Bored with her husband, the tried-and-true husband who puts in all the hard work necessary for the tsar's government, she runs off with the reckless adventurer who lives only for the moment, and then, after leaving her husband, is abandoned by her lover. But instead of throwing herself on the railroad tracks, a suicide, she goes back to her husband. And this is where the story, the new story, really begins. Her husband takes her back because he loves her and is glad she is once again his wife. But, gradually, he begins to remember what she did, the scorn she felt for him, the humiliation he suffered, the looks he got from his friends and colleagues, the things said behind his back. He had always loved her; now he begins to hate her. He takes his revenge, not in some single, dramatic moment, but slowly, a gradual drifting apart, a cutting word, a lethal silence. In all the ways he can, he makes her understand that everyone thinks him a saint for taking her back, and for the very reason that everyone thinks her a soulless whore. She had dominated his existence; now he dominates hers."

With his hands folded in his lap, Albert followed, or rather, in his mind, raced ahead of what he heard.

"And *The Great Gatsby*? If Gatsby had not died, hadn't been murdered, is that what...?"

"Didn't die, yes; but more than that. If Daisy had left her husband and gone off with Gatsby with whom she had once, remember, almost been engaged. Remember what Gatsby was, or rather, what he became, what he wanted. Money. That wonderful line that in six words tells you everything you need to know: 'She had a voice like money.' I've read *Gatsby* at least half a dozen times. That line, that is the story. Daisy falls in love with Gatsby when he is a soldier. She marries Tom Buchanan who is rich and from a prominent family. Gatsby knows—he never seems to doubt this—that the only way he can ever have her is to have more money than anyone else. He doesn't want money for what money can buy; he wants it because it represents success. It is the measure of success, what everyone looks up to. Everything in America, even the World Series, has a price.

"What happens if Fitzgerald changes the story the way I said? Daisy leaves Tom Buchanan, and, after a divorce, marries Gatsby. What happens to him? The green light, that beacon of undiminished hope, that unfulfilled dream, isn't there anymore. He has everything he ever wanted to have. And now that he has her, he remembers what he had once heard her remember with Tom: how much they had loved each other when together they made their child. And he remembers she could have done the same thing with him years earlier when, instead of waiting for him, she had married Tom Buchanan and all his money. How long before that careless indifference of hers, that willingness to let others, to let him, take the blame for her own negligence—the hit-and-run killing of Tom's mistress—would have begun to poison him against her? How long before Daisy realized that all the love Gatsby said he had for her had vanished with the past?"

Albert tapped his fingers together just beneath his chin.

"Michael Kensington and Victoria Stanton. Is that who you're talking about? Is that what you learned from Oscar Maddox in Hawaii? Something that explains why they murdered Matthew's father and then Matthew himself?" he asked, pushing himself forward with his left hand on the arm of the chair.

"Probably more *Anna Karenina* than *Gatsby*," I allowed. "Kensington, if Maddox is right, never got over the hurt and humiliation when Victoria ran off with someone else. It changed him, an innocent boy who loved a girl, into a hard-driving grown man who hated her for what she did to him, and despised himself for ever being that vulnerable. Like *The Great Gatsby*, in that the two of them together, like Tom and Daisy Buchanan, were careless of everything except their own selfish need for money, power, and, in her case, celebrity."

"So that's all there is to it?" asked Craven, disappointed. "They wanted money and power and the only way to get it was to get rid of Matthew and Matthew's father?"

Turning toward the window, I looked out at the lingering scarlet light of the evening sun, marveling at the willingness, the sheer audacity of what, before his death, Matthew Stanton had decided to do. I glanced back at Albert, who understood immediately there was something that changed everything, something I had only just learned. I reached down into my briefcase on the floor next to me.

"Here," I said, handing him a thin typed document. "This is why Matthew Stanton had to be killed, and why Oscar Maddox thought his own life was in danger."

Craven glanced at the first page, and then, a question in his eyes, looked at me again.

"There is no mistake," I assured him. "It's exactly what it says it is."

Craven's faded blue eyes brightened with recognition. With the penetrating gaze of a well-trained lawyer, he proceeded to read, word by word, a legal document he seemed to admire more with every page. When he finished, he held it in his hands with all the veneration of a priest cradling a chalice during a Sunday service.

"There isn't a word in it I would change," he remarked, measuring what he said by the stringent standard by which he judged his own, always individual work. He was the last of a breed, a lawyer who drafted every document from scratch; too proud, too good, ever to use a pre-prepared form. "This is what Matthew decided to do. No one would ever have guessed, no one would even think it possible." He handed the document back to me. "You understand, I take it, that the way this was done, it can't—"

"I know. That's what makes it so ingenious. If he had done it any other way, the way most people would have... Well, then there wouldn't be...."

"Exactly. But now there isn't anything..." Craven threw up his hands and with a laugh looked past me to the window and the darkening sky. "It's a lost art; it's what I like most about being a lawyer, the kind of lawyer I am. We fight our battles with documents, well-drafted documents like this." Wrinkling his nose, his chest quivered with laughter. "You fight your battles in the courtroom," he added, getting up from the chair. "Those of us, the few of us, who know how to write with precision are far too subtle for such cheap theatrics!"

"Sit down, Albert," I insisted, motioning toward the chair with my hand. "I have more to tell you, and more to ask."

He sat down, his expression now more serious.

"What is it you think I can tell you? With that document, with what you learned from Oscar Maddox—how was he, by the way? I forgot to ask. Forced to go into hiding, that can't have been easy."

"Easier than you might think. He told me someone told him that if you live there, you don't have to die because you are already in heaven. He said he thought that was pretty close to the truth. Everything is exactly how you would like it to be, nothing to complain about, and yet, though he would not say it, he misses the life he had. He misses San Francisco with all its tragic flaws. He must have asked a hundred questions about what was going on here. It was not that direct. It was always in connection with what he was telling me about Kensington, or the Stantons, or some of the others involved in the trial. He seemed especially interest in Elizabeth Burroughs."

Craven's gray eyebrows rose in two half circles, hunched around his eyes like a private audience eager for gossip.

"As a coroner or as a writer?"

"As a woman."

"You mean, whether she and Victoria Stanton...?"

"He wasn't sure; he thought they had."

"Burroughs is a lesbian; everyone in town knows that. She doesn't flaunt it, the way a lot of them do now," said Craven with a distant smile, remembering, as it seemed, a different time. "Not that she was trying to hide it; she just seemed to think it better, given her position, given her national audience as a best-selling writer, to keep her private life reasonably private. Victoria, on the other hand...I wouldn't be surprised if she occasionally went to bed with a woman. But why was Maddox so interested in that? He was never, so far as I know, much interested in what went on in the lives of other people."

"I was there all day; I didn't leave until close to ten at night. I told him everything about the trial, everything that had happened. He told me everything about the Stantons. He was very close to Emmett Stanton, almost his alter ego. They worked on everything together. Stanton was even smarter than I had thought. Smarter?" I cried, laughing at the blatant insufficiency of the word. "Makes it sound like someone good at school. Smarter isn't the word; shrewder, more insightful than anyone else in the way the world really works, the way in which everyone, or almost everyone, wants to be known by other people; the way everyone, or almost everyone, wants to belong to something, some group, that sets them apart from all those others who don't have whatever it takes to get in. He understood what money really means, that it is really all about the absence of a limit."

Craven was not surprised. It confirmed what he had always known himself, about money and about what Emmett Stanton had done.

"I'm sure I told you this before, there are really only a hundred people in San Francisco who have the kind of money that counts, the kind that makes the difference between success and failure when it comes to charitable or political contributions. The Stanton Foundation, the members of the board—it tells you everything you need to know about who is important. You pay to get on that board; you contribute, contribute large sums, to have that privilege."

"That's what Maddox tried to explain, how a million-dollar contribution from Emmett Stanton was worth twenty or thirty times that amount."

Craven nodded eagerly. "Gatsby's parties. It's the same principle at work. If you're not invited, you're not anyone."

"Right, and it's what made Emmett Stanton crazier than he might have been."

Craven's gentle eyes filled with doubt and confusion. He waited for an explanation.

"Maddox was sure of it." I picked up my fountain pen that lay next to a yellow legal pad on my desk and scratched Maddox's name on the top line. I then wrote the name Emmett Stanton on the line just below. "This will sound strange, but if I understood what Maddox was telling me, it was all about numbers. I don't mean a number, or the numbers, connected with the amounts involved; the way Emmett Stanton used the fact that he had more money than anyone else to get other wealthy people to put their money where he wanted it to go. It was something simpler—or perhaps much more complicated—than that."

I grabbed a half dozen paper clips out of a blue ceramic container and spread them out on the legal pad.

"Stanton thought of money in relation to things, things you can touch and feel. Look at it this way. What do you see? Six silver paper clips. Or rather, an assemblage of paper clips. That is what you see first—things, objects, things you can count. Now, what happens when I do this?" I reached inside the desk drawer and pulled out a handful of rubber bands and placed six of them on a line next to the paper clips. "Another half dozen things you can count. Simple, yes? Every child can do it. But notice what no one ever notices. The things are different—paper clips and rubber bands—but the numbers are the same: six of each. The numbers, in a manner of speaking, exist by themselves, separate and apart from the things that are counted."

Precisely because it was not at all clear where I was going with this, Craven was interested.

"Emmett Stanton had a genius for numbers, an understanding of how the numbers of the financial markets moved. Like any real form of genius, it could not be taught, but it had something to do with understanding the differences between numbers and what numbers are used to count. What he gradually came to understand, again according to Maddox, was that for all those other people, always so eager to follow his lead, the numbers, and only the numbers—not what they were used to count—were important. No one cared, no one shared his vision of what the city could be. They cared, of course, but only in the general way of people who want to find themselves on the right side of things. What they really cared about was what others thought of them. That is what their money meant, how it made them part of the only group, the only circle, that counted—that same word in its double meaning—the circle of the really wealthy, the ones who could afford to give enough to get on Stanton's board."

"And that, according to Maddox, made Emmett crazy?"

"Crazier," I said, reminding him of exactly what Maddox had told me. "Crazier, which may be nothing more than saying that Emmett Stanton was one of the few really sane people around. Think about it. Everyone out there, spending all their time trying to figure out the market, which means trying to figure out what everyone else—all those millions of traders and investors—are going to do, and Emmett Stanton just knew. And then everyone trying to become rich and famous so everyone will know who they are, and Emmett Stanton sits there with all his money and lets everyone come to him. What drove him crazy, if he was crazy, was the knowledge of how hollow, how meaningless, how fraudulent these people really were. Don't you think his son had to have thought the same thing as well?"

His chin sunk down on his chest, Craven stared at me for a long, silent moment. The light from my desk lamp gave the corner of his face the yellow parchment tint of a forgotten ancient page, a new discovery of something old and immensely valuable.

"Yes, but I think in a different way," he replied in a voice so quiet I could barely hear him. "Emmett's problem—his disillusionment, if you will—was with the empty-minded people who measure everything in money; in numbers, as Maddox told you Emmett came to see it. Matthew's problem was more specific, more concrete."

Craven's eyes flashed with the recognition of something he had just now understood. He sat straight up, perched on the edge of the chair.

"What Emmett understood, what he came to despise, was this need for acknowledgement and the belief that the only way to get it was by having more money than other people. We used to call it greed, but it isn't that at all. It is the fame, the celebrity, money can buy. It was the corruption that followed from this that was at the heart of Matthew's troubles. Victoria Stanton and Michael Kensington, her new husband, wanted what Matthew had, full control, because, unless they had it, he had the power to sell the only thing that made them—that made her—someone everyone wanted to know."

Craven paused and shook his head. Everyone, everyone except Matthew Stanton, had been a fool. He gave me a knowing glance.

"Can you imagine what they must have thought when they found out what Matthew really had in mind?" He nodded toward the document Oscar Maddox had drafted for Matthew Stanton's astonishing use. "Any reservations, any doubt, gone the moment they found out about that!"

Looking away, I tapped three fingers in a slow, methodical rhythm on the hard wooden surface of my desk, the measure, not so much of a doubt, as of an uncertainty, a sense of something missing.

"But why T. J. Allen? It can't have been sheer coincidence: a hired killer just happens to murder Matthew Stanton, murder him in his Nob Hill apartment, just minutes after Allen left. Why murder Stanton at all? And why anything that obvious? Why not an accidental death? His father was killed while mountain climbing. Instead of an accident—a hit-and-run on a San Francisco street, or a boating accident, a drowning in the bay—he's shot to death and Allen, who had just left, decides to come back."

"They wouldn't have known he was coming back," Craven reminded me. "They would have known—the killer would have known—he was there. Why doesn't that make perfect sense? They didn't have to be thinking that they would have someone else to blame. The killer knows someone is there and just waits until he is sure Matthew is all alone."

"You're forgetting the gun. The killer—whoever the killer was—didn't use a gun that couldn't be traced; he used a gun that would immediately be traced to Allen. What other reason would he have to drop it and leave it in plain view for the police to find? They wanted Allen to be blamed. That is what keeps gnawing at me. Why? Why go to all that trouble: steal his gun; steal it, by the way, weeks before the murder? Because he was giving them trouble over a new contract? It makes no sense. There had to be another..."

I glanced again at the document Craven had prized as a model of legal craftsmanship. "Matthew!" I exclaimed, chagrined at my own dull stupidity, my failure to see everything that crucial, decisive document proved, or might prove.

"Yes," Craven agreed, his eyes shining as he realized what I meant. "They were friends. Allen had been the only real friend Matthew had. He would have told him, or he might have told him. Victoria and Kensington had to assume he had. They had to kill Matthew to stop him from doing it; and by making sure Allen was blamed, nothing he said about what Matthew was going to do would have any credibility." He gestured toward Maddox's drafted document. "Without that, it would not matter if he had any credibility or not. No one would ever believe it."

Seventeen

"The defense calls Michael Kensington," I announced with quiet understatement.

Everyone knew why Kensington was important; there was no point in overdramatizing it. He took the oath with none of T. J. Allen's eager flamboyance, and none of his wife's dismissive arrogance. When it was over, he smiled politely at the clerk, and when he seated himself on the witness chair, he smiled the same way at the jury. With a cool, expectant gaze, he looked at me like a professional gambler welcoming a new player. It was remarkable how confident he seemed to be.

I walked the few short steps to the corner of the jury box farthest from the witness stand. The jury would have to turn their heads a full half circle to watch when he answered a question I asked. I was about to ask my first question, but Kensington would not let me ask it.

"I didn't do either of the things you have accused me of doing, Mr. Antonelli. I did not kill Emmett Stanton and I did not murder, or have anything to do with the murder, of Matthew Stanton."

He was actually smiling at me. I smiled back, but not at him, at the jury.

"He's new at this," I explained. "We'll give him a second chance. The question, Mr. Kensington—and you're not here to do anything except answer the questions you're asked—is what, precisely, is your position, your formal position, with the professional basketball team owned by the Stanton family?"

He studied me a moment, trying to hide his irritation. With powerful arms and shoulders, a thick neck and broad forehead, he was what you would imagine someone who played football in college would look like when he turned forty-five. A pencil-thin mustache ran across his upper lip as straight as the signature of a wealthy man with too many checks to sign to worry whether his signature might be legible.

"My wife, Victoria, is the team's CEO," he replied finally. "I don't have a formal position. I serve only in an advisory capacity."

I went over to the counsel table and opened a manilla file folder. I looked up at Kensington and almost started to laugh.

"An advisory capacity? I have a whole file here, Mr. Kensington, a whole file of contracts in which your name, your signature, appears on behalf of the organization."

"You asked if I held a formal position—chief financial officer, general manager, something like that. I do not. I have, however, from time to time acted on behalf of my wife, acted with her power of attorney. I'm sure you're familiar with that term, Mr. Antonelli, whatever your particular line of work," he remarked, his baritone voice filled with derision.

"My line of work?" I asked, as if I were puzzled by the meaning of his remark. "Are you referring to the fact that I try cases in a court of law, that I don't spend my time drafting contracts and other legal documents? You're right when you say that," I admitted, turning to the jury with a look of injured innocence, an apology, or at least an explanation, for my incapacity.

"I've never done that, drafted a document, a complicated document, that involves a lot of money, the kind that makes a rich man poor and a poor man rich. I'm afraid all I know how to do," I said, staring at him with as lethal a look as I knew how to give, "is defend people who have been set up to take the blame for what other people have done!"

Longstreet bolted to her feet with such force her chair fell backward onto the floor.

"Objection!" she shouted, clenching her fists tight against her sides to keep herself from using them on me. "This is outrageous! This is—"

"True?" I asked, smiling my indifference.

"Your Honor!" she cried with white-faced fury.

Leonard Silverman flapped his hand, motioning for her to get control of herself. Pursing his lips as he decided how far he should go, whether simply to sustain the objection or reprimand me for what I had done, he began to move his head from side to side.

"He did not say that that was what he was doing in this case," he began in a thoughtful voice that might have reminded a student of medieval philosophy of Thomas Aquinas, starting a critique of one of Aristotle's more difficult works.

Whatever Longstreet might be a student of, it was not that. Her eyes were bulging so far out of her head, I halfway expected her to fall forward, dead, onto the floor.

"On the other hand," continued Silverman, as if he were alone in chambers wrestling with the question, "it would be easy, not to say inevitable, that some might draw that inference and assume that he was doing precisely that. On that ground, and for that reason, I will sustain the prosecution's objection."

Nodding his satisfaction with what he had done, and how he had done it, he instructed me to continue my questioning of the witness. The courtroom, after all the commotion, had gone quiet again. Longstreet, too appalled to speak, picked her chair off the floor and sat down. She held her hands together on the table, staring with barely suppressed rage at a point straight in front of her.

"What would you have done if your objection had been overruled, thrown the chair at me?"

Her head snapped up. She threw me a venomous glance.

"Who do you think you're talking to?" she demanded, halfway out of her chair. Bracing her hands on the table, she started to say something else, and then, changing her mind, she turned her wrathful gaze on Silverman. "Are you going to allow...? Are you going to just sit there and do nothing? Are you—?"

The harsh, strident sound of a beating gavel stopped her from saying another word. The look in Leonard Silverman's eyes stopped her from even moving.

"That's enough! Both of you! Mr. Antonelli, direct your questions to the witness. Ms. Longstreet, if you wish to make an objection, you make it to me."

He nodded twice decisively, the mark of finality, the end of all discussion. He started to sit back, but suddenly stopped. With the serious smile of a learned judge, he explained to the jury the real meaning of what they had just witnessed.

"'First thing, we'll kill all the lawyers,'" he quoted with apparent approval. "You may have heard that line. It's from one of Shakespeare's plays. Everyone blames the lawyers. No one likes them very much. Unless, of course, we find ourselves in trouble, or we have in some way been injured. Then we need them to prosecute those who have broken the law; we need Ms. Longstreet to make sure the guilty are brought to justice. We need them to defend the accused, because, as William Blackstone wrote almost two hundred fifty years ago, it is better that ten guilty people go free than that one innocent person be convicted. We need Mr. Antonelli to make sure that someone accused of a crime gets the best defense possible.

"This is what we all learn in school; this is something on which we can all agree. The problem is that the law's greatest strength is also its greatest weakness, and lest you think this is too abstract, it is, let me assure you, the same thing with each of us individually. The law is nothing more, and nothing less, than reason, the long thought-out attempt to control ourselves, to force us to act toward one another the way we should. The problem, the great difficulty, is that while the law may be reasonable, reason does not act alone. It is the very definition of a human being: the animal with reason. But our reason is never complete. We are also burdened with emotions: the desire to survive, the desire to acquire, the desire to have what we have no right to have. We get angry, we get depressed; we want to win, we hate to lose. But we also know that we are wrong when we yield to what we feel. Reason, if we try hard enough, and if we have others around to remind of us our better selves, will hold its own.

"The law is reason. A trial is a kind of competition, a struggle to get at the truth. It is not perfect; we make mistakes. But it is the best we have been able to come up with. So, I would ask you not to think too badly of the lawyers when tempers flare and angry words are spoken. View it instead as a measure of how deeply, how seriously, they take their responsibilities. Let me add one last thing. I have been on the bench a good many years, and I have seldom seen two lawyers as good as the two arguing the case you have to decide."

He was Thomas Aquinas, lecturing on Aristotle to an eager, grateful room of students.

"And as for the two of you," Silverman continued as he leaned back against the tall black leather chair, "do that sort of thing again, I'll have you executed."

He did not mean it, and the jury knew he did not mean it, but from the cheerful looks on their faces, they might not have minded if he had.

"Mr. Antonelli," said Silverman, again all business, "you may continue."

Everyone in the courtroom had followed with intense interest the heated confrontation between Longstreet and myself, and the court's dispassionate explanation of the connection between reason and the law. Everyone except Michael Kensington. His hands held together in front of him, his fingers interlocked, he tapped his thumbs in measured irritation.

"You may not hold a formal position of authority, but you were directly involved in the decision to move the team from Oakland to San Francisco, were you not?"

His thumbs stopped moving. He sat straight up.

"Yes, I was involved in that decision."

"The team had been in Oakland more than forty years. Why move across the bay?"

"The facility was old; a relic, by today's standards. We needed an arena with all the modern conveniences."

"It isn't more convenient for the fans, though, is it? The arena in Oakland was just off the freeway, and if you didn't want to drive, you could get there by rapid transit from almost anywhere in the Bay Area, isn't that true?"

"There is adequate parking in the new facility," he replied defensively.

"More than adequate—concierge parking for those who can afford it; underground parking for those who spend the night at the hotel which is part of the new arena complex. And, of course, plenty of space for those who get there on their yachts. They can dock less than a hundred yards from the new arena, can't they, Mr. Kensington?" I asked, drily.

"If you're suggesting that the new arena is state of the art, that it has the most advanced technology, the most comfortable seating, the most desirable—"

"The most desirable? You mean the luxury suites? There are thirty-two of them. Or did I get the number wrong?"

"No, that's correct: thirty-two."

With a slow, deliberate quarter turn, I looked at the jury.

"And if I, or someone on the jury, wanted to buy one of them, what would we get—a seat high above the crowd, maybe a television set so we could watch a replay?"

Kensington eyed me with the suspicion the rich always feel when forced to defend what they have to those who don't have much of anything.

"More than that," he replied, quietly vague.

"Much more than that, isn't it? If you buy a suite—how much does that cost, by the way?"

"Two million," he said reluctantly.

I turned toward him as if I could not believe the number he had just given me.

"Two million? I assume you have it forever. You can pass it on to your children, if you don't sell it."

"Two million a year."

"Two million a... That must buy a lot more than a chair to sit on and a television to watch. Yes, now I remember! You get a courtside seat so you can watch the game the way the players watch it, and, of course, be on television yourself whenever the cameras point that way. And, of course, you get all the food and drink you want. Each suite comes with its own wine cellar, doesn't it? Who could watch a game without access to your own favorite vintage? But never mind that. How much did this modern state of the art arena with all its advanced technology end up costing?

"A little less than one and a half billion. But," he quickly added, "it was paid for with private money. It didn't cost the city anything, and it will add millions, hundreds of millions, to the local economy."

"To the local economy? You mean San Francisco?"

"Yes, of course: San Francisco."

"Not Oakland, because, why, exactly? You haven't yet explained why you thought it was necessary to move."

"Yes, I did. The Oakland facility was too old: it had to be replaced."

"It's cheaper to build in Oakland, so it was not because of the cost. You built in San Francisco because San Francisco is a world-famous city. You, and your wife, become the owners not just of a professional basketball team, but of a sports and entertainment complex the envy of the world. Isn't that the reason you left Oakland?"

Samantha Longstreet, tense and nervous, tapped her long, sharp fingernails on the wooden counsel table. Kensington, neither tense nor nervous, could not wait to respond.

"San Francisco is a world-class city. It was important, from a business perspective, for the team to be part of that. Professional sports—football, basketball, baseball—are not the leisure-time activities they were twenty or thirty years ago, games that people would watch in their spare time. Professional sports are now the most important things we do. They have become our identity, our common interest; our common cause, if you will. Do you have any idea how many million shirts and jerseys, how much athletic paraphernalia, are sold every year, the names of your favorite team, you favorite player, written across the back? Who do you think everyone looks up to? Politicians, scientists, poets, novelists? They look up to athletes, entertainers, the men and women who perform on television, the celebrities, the movie stars! That is what San Francisco is all about: people who other people want to see, people everyone wants to watch! So, yes, that's why we made the move, why we left Oakland, why we came to San Francisco instead."

"'All the adventurers in the world, blown there by the winds of heaven,'" I said in a quiet, distant voice.

"What? I'm sorry, I didn't hear you."

"Just a line I remembered; something Robert Louis Stevenson once wrote about the city and what it meant. There is another line," I added with a look that suggested there might be more than one meaning in what I was about to tell him, "a line from Gertrude Stein. Ever heard of her?"

"No," replied Kensington without any apparent regret. "I'm afraid I haven't."

"Something she once wrote about Oakland, a line that though written a hundred years ago captures perfectly what you and Victoria Stanton decided when you moved the team: 'There is no there there.' The interesting question is what Gertrude Stein might say now about what, thanks to you and people like you, San Francisco has become. Is there still a there there? I wonder. But never mind that now. We have some other, more immediate, things to settle. How many people does the new arena seat?"

"Eighteen thousand."

"The old arena in Oakland, how many?"

"Twenty thousand."

"You're going to lose money. Two thousand fewer seats to fill."

Kensington was too intelligent, too shrewd, to think I meant it. He knew I was trying to expose the excess involved. He tried to deflect it by an appeal to civic pride.

"We wanted the new arena to be the best ever built. We thought the city deserved that; we thought we owed it to our fans who have supported us through all the years, good and bad."

My hands dropped to my sides as I looked up at the ceiling and rolled my eyes.

"The fans? Who supported you all the years! They're in Oakland. And even if they wanted to see a game in your brand new, state-of-the-art arena, most of them could not afford it! Eighteen thousand seats, two thousand less than you had before, and the revenue from ticket sales two, maybe even three times what it was before. And that is just the beginning, isn't it, Mr. Kensington? Basketball is just one of the things that will be played there. It's already booked for more than a hundred events in the next year alone, events from which you will make millions, hundreds of millions of dollars, isn't that true?"

"It's a business," replied Kensington, bolting forward. "No one is denying that. The new arena will bring things—conventions, performances—the city has not had before."

"And the people who own it—the team, the arena—will become some of the wealthiest people in the country, won't they, Mr. Kensington? Too bad that you and Mrs. Stanton won't be among them," I added, almost as an afterthought, as I went back got the counsel table and opened a file folder.

He thought, he must have thought, I meant that both he and his wife would be unmasked and found guilty of their crimes, the murder of Emmett Stanton and the murder of his son. The only reaction was a smile of indifference, a smile that suggested that, as far as he was concerned, it was nothing more than a lawyer's desperate attempt to save his client, the real killer, from getting what he deserved.

I pulled out a seven-page document and studied it for a few moments. Then I put it down and began a new line questioning.

"You married Victoria Stanton within a year of her former husband, Emmett Stanton's death, is that correct?"

Kensington raised his chin and squared his shoulders.

"Yes, that's correct," he replied warily.

"You had known her for some time, hadn't you?"

"Yes."

"You knew Emmett Stanton as well, didn't you?"

"Yes, I knew him."

"Knew him well enough that you were invited to go along with him and his wife on a mountain climbing expedition, correct?"

Kensington shook his head. He wanted to be clear about something.

"The word 'expedition.' It makes it sound like climbing Mt. Everest. None of us were mountain climbers in that sense. There is a place in France I like to ski. Emmett and Victoria had not been there before. We agreed to go. The skiing wasn't very good, and one day we decided to go on a climb instead. It's usually quite safe. The views are spectacular. But, all of a sudden, a storm blew up and we found ourselves in the middle of a whiteout. Emmett must have become disoriented, stepped through the ice or slipped on something. We never really knew."

It was perfect, a murder no one could ever prove; an accidental death that could have happened to anyone. Kensington waited for the next question. I let him wait. The silence became the accusation for which I had no proof to offer. I kept looking at him, staring at him eye to eye, the look I gave him more dismissive, more derisive, with every moment that passed. The silence became intense, unbearable, repeating every muted instant the refusal of my belief.

"Emmett Stanton died on a climbing expedition, with only you and his wife, the woman with whom you were having an affair, as witnesses. That's true, isn't it, Mr. Kensington? The two of you had been sleeping together!"

The tendons on his thick muscled neck drew taut as bowstrings. His mouth went rigid. He glanced past me to Samantha Longstreet, sitting at the counsel table, expecting her to do something. She tried.

"Your Honor, the question about the witness's private life, I don't see where this—"

"Overruled," Silverman announced. He looked down at the witness. "You may answer the question."

Kensington seemed almost relieved. Perhaps, forced to answer, he no longer felt the burden of a secret. He had, for once, the luxury of being honest.

"Victoria and I had known each other for a very long time. We should have waited, but, it's true, we did start to see each other, to have an affair, as you suggested."

"You had known each other a long time," I remarked pensively. "Starting when you were both in college, when you, and all your friends and relatives, thought the two of you were going to get married."

Studying the floor as if it were an open page from which I was reading his unknown history, I began to pace slowly, a few steps away from the jury box, a few steps back.

"Everything was set, everything was agreed. You had asked her to marry you, and she had said yes. Everyone knew it; everyone was looking forward to it: Mr. and Mrs. Michael Kensington, the lovely young couple starting their new life together. The engagement had been made, the rings purchased, the dinner of family and friends where the formal announcement was to be made scheduled. And then, the night before the announcement, the night before your bright new future was to begin; the night before..."

I stopped and looked up.

"What happened? Tell us, Mr. Kensington. What happened that night, more than twenty years ago, the night that, if it did not ruin your life, changed it forever?"

I almost felt sorry for him. His eyes, though still bold and defiant, were burdened with the memory of an unbearable sadness; a wound that, no matter how often or how long it was put out of mind, was always there and would never be healed.

"She decided she was in love with someone else," he forced himself to admit. "And she married him instead."

There was an undertone of cruelty in his voice he could not quite hide. Nothing, not even a later reconciliation, had ever, or could ever, erase the feeling of disappointment, the sense of betrayal, at what she had done.

Sympathy was the last thing I wanted the jury to feel, but what had happened to him—the marriage that never took place, the heartbreak he experienced—had to be brought out if I was to show the jury what he had become: a man who cared for nothing except his own advantage, someone willing to commit murder if it became necessary.

"She married someone else, and you didn't see her again until, years later, she was married to Emmett Stanton, correct?"

"Yes, that's right."

"You had never married?'

"No."

"You lived for a number of years in Los Angeles, didn't you?"

"Yes, I did."

"You had your own production company, you made movies. According to the tabloids, you were one of the most popular men in Hollywood. Would that be a fair characterization?"

"It would be a fair characterization of what the tabloids reported," he replied with a dismissive shrug.

"You were single, you were famous, and you were rich. And then you came back to San Francisco and became part of the same crowd as Emmett and Victoria Stanton. Isn't that the reason you left Los Angeles, because you knew she was here?"

He looked at me as if I were mad.

"No, of course not. I came back because I got tired of LA. I came back because I was born and raised here and have always loved San Francisco."

"Where you met, and almost married, Victoria Stanton.

Whatever the reason, you came back, and you began to run into her at various events around the city, isn't that how it started?"

"How what started?" he demanded in an angry, cutting voice.

My eyebrows shot straight up, as a knowing gin raced across my mouth.

"You just admitted you were having an affair with her! I'm only asking when it started. But forget that," I said, stepping sideways from the table. "Forget when it started. Tell us whose idea it was."

His eyes, drawn back behind half-closed lids, mocked me with my incompetence.

"Whose idea...?" he repeated, trying not to laugh. "When two people fall in love—"

"It was her idea," I insisted with such confidence that his eyes flashed open with surprise. "She was in love with you. She told you she was in love with you, told you that she had never stopped hating herself for what she had done all those years ago, running off with someone else, marrying someone else. She told you that it wasn't too late, that the two of you could still make it work. She told you all that, and what did you reply? That you weren't interested, that, and I believe this is exactly, word for word, what you said, she could believe in second chances all she wanted, but there weren't going to be any second chances with you. Isn't that what you told her, the woman who is now your wife, when she said she wanted a second chance with you?"

I was not sure a witness had ever looked at me with more real hatred. Kensington now knew that I knew more about him than anyone ever had. No one likes to feel that vulnerable, all their secrets, shared with those they trusted, shared with others they did not know. Whomever he had told about what had been said between him and Victoria had passed it on until it had come into my possession, and now, through me, out to the world at large. He could only wonder what else I might know.

"She told you that she was still in love with you. She told you she wanted to marry you. And she said all this while she was married to Emmett Stanton, correct?"

He did not answer. He just looked at me with a blank stare.

"She was married to Emmett Stanton, correct?" I insisted.

"Yes," he replied grudgingly.

"The two of you started an affair, but she didn't start divorce proceedings?"

"Not that I'm aware of."

"Not that you're aware of? You were quite aware of that, Mr. Kensington. Just as you were aware that under the terms of her prenuptial agreement, Victoria Stanton would have gotten only a cash settlement, which meant she would have had no share in the ownership of the basketball team in the case of a divorce. You were aware of that agreement, were you not?"

"I knew there was a prenuptial agreement; I didn't know much about the details."

"Really? But then you didn't need to know anything about the details of that agreement to know that in the event Emmett Stanton died while he was still married, Victoria Stanton and Emmett Stanton's son, Matthew, would be his only surviving relatives, his only heirs. And that meant—did it not?—that once Emmett Stanton was out of the way and you were married to his widow, only Matthew Stanton would stand in the way between you and everything Emmett Stanton ever had. That would be one reason to want Matthew Stanton dead, wouldn't it, Mr. Kensington? But there was another reason, an urgent reason, why Matthew Stanton had to die. The reason you and Victoria Stanton could not wait, isn't that true?"

He was gripping the arms of the witness chair as tightly as he could. His voice, when he tried to speak, was jarring, on the ragged edge between anger and contempt.

"T. J. Allen murdered Matthew. I had nothing to do with it;

Victoria had nothing to do with it. We didn't have any reason to wish him harm. Because Matthew had eighty-one percent ownership of the team? Is that your motive? We have all the money we'll ever need. Murder Matthew? What kind of people do you think we are?"

EIGHTEEN

Albert Craven shoved his hands deep into the pockets of his dark blue cashmere overcoat and shook his head.

"You didn't use the document, the one Oscar Maddox gave you, the one that—?"

"No," I tried to explain. "I'm saving it. Kensington knows I know something, but he doesn't know what it is. He doesn't know I saw Maddox, and even if he did, he wouldn't know anything about the document itself. They must have known what Stanton was planning to do, but not that he had already done it."

We were standing together at Fisherman's Wharf, waiting for the Sausalito ferry. The sky was heavy with gray clouds and the air wet with fog.

"Just like summer," said Craven, "and summer is still months away."

Bouncing up on the tips of his shiny black shoes, he was so delighted with this remark, the kind that only a native San Franciscan would make, I thought he might start to dance. Instead, he looked past me and started to sing. I turned to follow his eager, cheerful, and thoroughly smitten stare. Tangerine, her name echoing in the mist-covered light, was standing on the deck of the ferry as it hovered into view, waving her hand with bright-eyed excitement.

When the ferry docked, she hurried down the ramp and, first thing, kissed Albert on the side of his face.

"Leave this criminal lawyer," he laughed, rather shyly. "Run off with me. I'll take you to every romantic senior citizen golf course community there is."

"You don't play golf, Albert," she reminded him, smiling with her eyes.

"No, but all my friends do; the ones who aren't dead, the ones still in Palm Springs bragging about all the money they made."

"Promise me you'll never do that," she said with a look of real affection. "You wouldn't anyway. You're much too intelligent, too nice, to become one of those awful people who think what they have is what they are."

The soft, easy sympathy in her voice, changing, became teasing, breathless, the words brushing past me, as she touched me gently on my nose.

"Why would I want to be around people with money when I can go barefoot in the kitchen, barefoot and..."

The baffled expression on Albert's face vanished as he remembered the phrase. He started to laugh.

"We'll name the first one after you," she promised.

The ferry was getting ready to pull out on the passage back across the bay to Sausalito.

"I just came to say hello," explained Albert as he kissed Tangerine on the cheek. He patted me on the shoulder. "I'll see you tomorrow."

He started to head back to the street where he would catch a cab for the short ride home. He stopped and looked back.

"You're lucky, both of you, to have each other. It's really the only thing that matters, isn't it?"

Humming the lyrics to the old, classic song that Tangerine had been named after, he stepped away as if he really were about to dance.

"He's really quite wonderful, isn't he?" said Tangerine, clutching my hand. "Quick, we better hurry," she said, tightening her grip. "The ferry!"

There was not any danger we were going to miss it, but we dashed the few yards to the gangway as if our lives depended on it. It was all Tangerine, the effect she had. She made Albert Craven think he could dance like Fred Astaire; she made me imagine I was still too young to drink. She made everyone crowded on the inside of the ferry want to do nothing but stare at the gorgeous creature with the black silk scarf wrapped around her head and the black wool coat thrown around her shoulders, someone, a movie star, an evening mirage, drifting past them as we headed, the way we always did, to the deck outside.

"It's cold as hell out here," I grumbled cheerfully.

"That's all right; pretend it's summer," said Tangerine as she led me to the white-painted bench from which we could watch the city as the ferry churned away from the shore.

"That's what Albert said: summer in San Francisco is just like winter."

"Everyone says that if they live here long enough." She held on to my arm with both hands, snuggling close. "Or if they heard it's what Mark Twain once said: that the coldest day he ever spent was a summer day in San Francisco. It's like the things you read in a novel. Once the words are in your head, it's how you think of things."

"It's pretty damn obvious Mark Twain never rode the ferry on a night in winter!"

"Would you like to go inside?"

"Then I wouldn't have anything to complain about. Besides, we always sit out here, every time we do this, once a week, when you take the ferry over so we can ride back together. It's become a tradition."

"Is that why you do it? Because it's a tradition, and you're so traditional?"

"No, it's because, with no one else around, we can sit here and make out."

I pulled her closer and kissed her. She kissed me back, and just for the fun of it, I slid my hand inside her dress, just far enough so my icy cold fingers could touch her naked thigh.

"You...!" she cried, laughing so hard I thought she might choke.

She took my hand and held it in front of her mouth, blowing on it to get it warm. She crossed her legs, in case, she explained, I might think it an invitation.

"It would be kind of fun, wouldn't it?" she asked with a whimsical sparkle in her eyes. "To conceive a child, our child, on the passenger deck of a San Francisco ferry."

The ferry began to pull away. Fisherman's Wharf was a brightly lit silhouette. Behind it, towering in the distance, the tightly packed downtown buildings shined their lights like stars in the dense, gray fog-bound night. Moments later, the lights had all but disappeared, vanished like a vessel lost at sea, the fog so thick as we headed out onto the bay that the pale illumination from inside the ferry was barely visible on the deck outside.

"Let's!" she said suddenly in an eager, breathless voice. She opened her coat and pulled up her dress. "Let's do it, right here, right now!" Her mouth was on mine, and mine was on hers. I felt her hand unbuttoning my shirt. I felt her hand slide inside, onto my bare skin. I felt—

"Christ!" I shouted, jumping back from her icy-fingered act of revenge.

She leaned back, happy as a child on her birthday at what she had done.

"Look at it this way, Antonelli," she said, suddenly all analytical. "What if we had done it right here, on this old wooden bench? I saved you from a splinter. Now, tell me all about—"

"The trial?" I buttoned my shirt and tried, and failed, to give her an evil look. "I'm getting killed."

"No, you're not," she insisted with utter confidence. "Have you ever lost a case when the defendant was really innocent?"

"What makes you think Allen is innocent?"

"You told me he was. You said that—"

"That I thought he was." I nodded toward the unseen city buried in the fog. "The trial is like that. All sorts of things are going on, people are living their lives, but I can't show you who they are or what they are doing. I don't have any evidence; I can't prove anything. If it weren't for the noise of the engine, the slight breeze blowing against my face, I couldn't prove we were actually out on the bay and not still tied up at the dock.

"Allen innocent? There isn't any proof of it. Stanton is shot to death; Allen is found there with the gun, his gun, still in his hand. Stanton and Allen were friends, but most murders don't happen between strangers, and Allen admits on the stand that there had been an argument. What have I got? Only a theory, which means a motive, a reason why someone else, Victoria Stanton and Michael Kensington, might have wanted Matthew Stanton dead. A motive, that's all. Not a single provable fact that they were responsible. But, yes, you're right," I laughed into the cold smoke colored air, "now that I think of it, I don't have anything to worry about."

"But you're not sure, really not sure, that Allen is innocent?"

"I was at first, and I still think he probably is. But one hundred percent absolutely sure? No. It's the race thing. What he did the other day, what he said about what was being done to him by Kensington and Victoria Stanton."

"Strange, when you think about it," said Tangerine, resting

her head against my shoulder. "If he wasn't a famous black athlete, would anyone be that much interested in the trial? Everyone loves him, everyone loves to watch him play. If you wanted someone to blame for a murder, isn't T. J. Allen about the last person you would think of? Race, the fact he is black, doesn't mean anything anymore. Not here, anyway."

"It meant everything when he was growing up. He lived in public housing; guns, drugs everywhere. He had a brother—he doesn't talk about him—gunned down on his way home from school. Everyone loves T. J.—or at least they did before Matthew Stanton was murdered—but he understands that it is only because he became the famous basketball player everyone wanted to see. What he said in court, that hard-edged cynicism about what is being done to him, that is the real world as he understands it. He told me once, when he was trying to explain why he and Stanton became such close friends, that the night after they won the championship, Matthew wanted to take him to dinner, but he wouldn't go. He did not want to walk into a restaurant and have everyone start to applaud, the way he knew it would happen."

"I don't understand. Why would that bother him? He must be used to it," she said, looking up to search my eyes.

"Because he was used to it. He's an athlete. Everyone admires his skill, what he can do on a basketball court. That is what they see: what he can do. They don't see him. He plays a game, and everyone thinks him a hero. Fraud—that's what he keeps calling it, the mindless addiction to what by itself has no importance. Allen's real problem is that, unlike most people, he is not superficial. Like the rest of us, he sees what he remembers; unlike the rest of us, his memory goes back a lot further than yesterday, or the end of last season. He sees black kids getting killed, not just by white cops, but by other black kids, kids trying to prove themselves important by becoming part of some gang. He sees a lot of white people spending millions every year on seats in an arena so they can watch black guys like him try to beat another team whose players are mainly black. And it doesn't matter that he, and a lot of the other players, make more a year than the rich white people watching. They're still black performers paid to play in front of a crowd in a place most black people can't afford to buy a ticket."

The fog, so thick Tangerine's upturned face shined like a winter ornament on a Christmas tree, began to dissipate. A few random stars made a surprise appearance in the sky overhead, and a moment later the ferry emerged into a clear, cloudless night. The lights at the northern end of the Golden Gate Bridge glistened in reflection off the dark still waters of the bay. In a few minutes, we would be docked in Sausalito.

"Home, or shall we go somewhere?" I asked. "Let's go somewhere. First place we pass that isn't crowded." I changed my mind. "Some place crowded. Everyone will turn to look at you, and then you'll know, if you don't know already, what T. J. Allen meant."

I did not have to explain to her what I meant. There was no more false modesty than vanity in the way she saw herself.

"I know people look at me; I can feel the way everyone turns to look when I walk into a restaurant or some other crowded place. But why should that be thought some kind of fraud? T. J. Allen is a gifted athlete, what anyone who thinks athletics important, or just appreciates the movements of the human body, would like to be. Isn't that what we admire in anything: how close to perfection it is? Isn't his complaint as if an artist, someone like Rembrandt, were to complain that the only reason people admire him is because of how he can paint?"

With a loud, thumping noise, the ferry slid up against the wooden pilings of the single berth at the open dock.

"There's a difference. Rembrandt, artists altogether, make

something lasting, something that has a depth of meaning. Basketball is just a game."

"And the way a woman looks?" she asked, tilting her head in the way of a question that answers itself.

"Beauty, the idea of it, never dies."

"And is that what attracts you, what you want to go to bed with, an idea?"

"Yes," I replied, to her vast amusement, as we headed inside. "But only because, to quote Aristotle, you participate in it."

We were just inside the metal door, where we joined the line waiting to disembark. She put her hand against the side of my face and looked deep into my eyes.

"That, Antonelli, is the least seductive line I ever heard! Aristotle?"

I shrugged off her complaint. With my hands on her shoulders, I turned her around so we could join the others in a slow march toward the wooden plank dock outside.

"You keep talking about being barefoot and pregnant in the kitchen," I whispered in her ear. "I thought I better start thinking about children and their education."

"Aristotle?" she laughed helplessly, stumbling forward onto the gangway.

"You think I'm kidding. One thing I've learned from T. J. Allen is how intensely curious someone can be, how eager to learn, when they understand that there are serious things worth learning. It's why Albert thinks you and I should have a child."

She held my hand as we walked across the tree-lined parking lot where she had left her car. We kept walking down the street, as it ran along the bay, until, a few blocks later, we were at the restaurant once called Valhalla when it belonged, years ago, to Sally Stanford, one-time mayor of Sausalito and the owner of a brothel.

"Nice of you to bring me to a whore house," Tangerine chided me with an impish grin.

"Saves money," I replied as I held open the door. "I only have to pay for dinner."

"And dinner is probably all you're going to get."

Removing her silk scarf, she shook her long dark hair free and took off her coat. In a long black dress, she walked with me behind the maître d' through the packed restaurant and seemed not to notice when the room went silent. I never could quite explain it. There were other beautiful women, women everyone noticed, but nothing like this. It was how she carried it off, without any self-awareness, without any sense that she deserved any particular attention, or that she would have lost a moment's sleep if no one noticed her at all. That was it, really. It was not just that she was the most gorgeous woman you had ever seen; she was the most likable. If half the men in the place would have left their wives to be with her; their wives, or most of them, would have approved of their decision.

I remembered what T. J. Allen had told me, and as I looked around at the way everyone was looking at Tangerine, I could only wonder why they did not start applauding.

"Albert thinks we should have a child? Is that what you were telling me?" she asked after we had sampled the wine we had ordered.

"Yes. I didn't know it before this evening. He's never said anything about that sort of thing before. I think he really meant it when he told us how lucky we are. He's extremely fond of you. You're the reason he was there. I happened to mention when I was leaving the office that I was meeting you at the ferry. He asked if he could come along, that he had not seen you in weeks. You should have seen the way his eyes lit up when I said how much you missed seeing him. He lied a little. He told me he wanted to talk to me about his testimony when I call him as a—"

"Albert is a witness? And he's worried, isn't he?" she asked, sympathizing for what she assumed was his nervousness.

"Not as much as he would like me to believe. I think he's actually looking forward to it."

"But why are you—? Oh, I remember. What Matthew Stanton told him that time he went to see him."

I drank a little more wine and thought about how Albert could help; and then I took another drink, and without quite knowing why, began to laugh, a quiet, bitter laugh, the sign of my own growing frustration.

"I keep thinking about what Leonard Silverman said, when he asked me to take the case. That line he used."

"How 'all of American contributed to the making of Matthew Stanton,'" said Tangerine, quoting the line perfectly.

"I'm still not sure what he meant. What does Conrad's novel, what does *Heart of Darkness*, have to do with any of this? Some of it is obvious: all the things that happened to him. Born into all that wealth, no necessity to work, to try hard at anything; what happened when he was in college: watching, feeling responsible for the death of a young student because he told some of his so-called friends about a story he had heard from a girl he liked, a story about forcing someone to commit suicide, the gun that was not supposed to be loaded, loaded because the boy is gay. He tells the truth about what happened, and what does that get him? A lesson in the hypocrisy of the one place where the truth is supposed to matter. He isn't even twenty-one and his life is ruined. And then his mother, whom he apparently adored, leaves his father because she decides after all the years married to Emmett Stanton that she is a lesbian.

"But things are only just getting started, aren't they?" I said with a rueful laugh. "Because now his father, a financial genius who may very well be totally insane, marries Victoria Stanton who has slept with half the men, and maybe half the women, in San Francisco, who then falls in love with another man, Michael Kensington, whose life she once destroyed. They murder his father, though no one can ever call it that, and then, he has every reason to believe, they're going to murder him. What is that, if not a normal, American, made for television life?"

The waiter came. Tangerine ordered for us both. I was too busy pondering all the things I did not know.

"That's one part of what—however much he may have known about any of this—Silverman must have meant. Then the other part, the part where Allen comes in. The game, the multi-billion-dollar spectator sport that made Matthew Stanton, after his father's death, one of the richest and most famous men around. The game, America's compulsive need for entertainment, made him more than an owner; it made him a victim; a victim to what others thought they had to have, a victim to Victoria Stanton's belief, a belief she shares with almost everyone now, that it isn't how much money you have, it is having more than anyone else; what it takes to set you apart, to own a team, to make you famous; a celebrity, someone everyone wants to see on television. All of America contributed to..."

Suddenly, it came to me, what that line meant, and I wondered why I had not thought of it before.

"Race," I said, staring straight ahead. "That's what I forgot. *Heart of Darkness*. Kurtz, the white man, part of the governing class of a colonial power, sent into darkest Africa to bring civilization to the savages and becomes more savage than any black native ever thought to be. Here, now, in this new, modern age of barbarism, what happened? A black man, T. J. Allen, who has a sense of how bad, how corrupt, things really are, becomes friends with a white man, and the two of them try to bring some decency and civility to the way we live. 'All of America contributed to the making of Matthew Stanton.' All of America contributed to make the two of them, Matthew Stanton and T. J. Allen, turn their backs on the world around them and read about the great things people were once able to do, and how those same things might be done again. What they read together, what they talked about together, it made Stanton see the importance of what he finally decided he had to do."

Dinner came and I was not hungry, but I ate anyway because I did not want Tangerine to think anything was wrong, and because I simply liked being there with her. There is something intimate, something romantic, about being alone together in a crowded room.

It was only later, while we were walking from the restaurant to the car, that I remembered the last remaining connection.

"Kurtz had nothing to be proud of when he died. Matthew Stanton, on the other hand, had..."

"Everything to live for," said Tangerine, walking next to me, her head lowered in silent meditation. "They're going to get away with it, aren't they?"

"For the murder of Emmett Stanton? There isn't any question. For the murder of Matthew Stanton?"

I did not know. The defense of T. J. Allen might depend on convincing the jury that Kensington and Victoria Stanton had the only real motive to murder Matthew Stanton, but motive by itself was not proof of anything. Allen might walk out of that courtroom a free man, but the two of them would be free as well.

"I changed my mind," I said when we reached the car.

"About what?"

"When I said I wasn't a hundred percent absolutely sure Allen was innocent."

"You're that sure now?"

"Yes. *Heart of Darkness*. What Silverman said. It all makes sense now. And all because of you."

"Because of me?" she laughed. "What did I do?"

"You listened."

She smiled and started driving and did not say anything else while we wound our way up the hill to our chocolate-colored shingle-sided house with a view of the Golden Gate and, on the other side, San Francisco, still covered in fog.

"In a few minutes, when we're inside and all the lights are out," she whispered in a soft, lilting voice, "I'll listen some more to what you say, if you think of something you would like to tell me."

I almost lost my voice.

Nineteen

A trial, a jury trial, is not what everyone seems to think it is: a way to get at the truth, a way to find out what really happened. A trial is a way to find out whether the state can actually prove beyond that famous reasonable doubt that someone accused of a crime is guilty. It is not enough that the police arrest you; it is not enough that you are indicted and charged. The prosecution has to produce witnesses, evidence that you did what they say you did. I did not have to prove that someone else murdered Matthew Stanton; I did not have to prove that T. J. Allen was innocent. I just had to convince the jury that even if he was guilty, the prosecution had not proven it.

This was why I had asked every juror whether they would return a verdict of not guilty even if they thought the defendant was guilty, but that the prosecution had not proven it beyond a reasonable doubt. They had all said they would. Jurors always said that. They were sworn to obey the law, sworn to follow the judge's instructions as to what the law requires. This is why the main job of the defense attorney is to tear apart the case for the prosecution. Victoria Stanton did not think it was fair.

"I've already testified!" she protested. "I've already said everything there is to say."

She had just taken the stand. Either no one had told her that she had dressed too much like a woman who flaunted her wealth in her first court appearance, or she had refused to listen. Everything she wore, from the bright green silk dress to the pointed high heel shoes had the look of things bought to be worn once and then discarded for something else new and expensive.

"Already said everything there is to say?" I remarked with a knowing glance at the twelve average-looking and inexpensively dressed men and women in the jury box. "Why don't you assume we're all a little too slow to understand things the first time we hear them. Or, if you prefer, just imagine we like hearing what you say so much we couldn't wait to hear you say it again."

Glaring at me through her black-lashed eyes, she lifted her smooth, powdered chin and waited.

I stood at the side of the counsel table, my left hand resting on a thick stack of typed papers, selected portions of the trial transcript. I picked up the page on top.

"When you were here before, when you were called as a witness for the prosecution, I asked you on cross-examination about your relationship with Michael Kensington; specifically what that relationship had been at the time your husband, Emmett Stanton, died while climbing with the two of you in the French Alps. I asked, let me read it to you, 'You had been having an affair with Michael Kensington, isn't that correct?' And you answered," I said, looking up, "let me read this as well, 'No! Well, I mean...'"

I placed the single sheet of the transcript back on the table, next to the stack of the other, unread pages, and looked at her as if I was expecting a reply.

"'No! Well, I mean...'" I repeated from memory. "Your first impulse was to lie, wasn't it, Mrs. Stanton? 'No,' and then, catching yourself, you started to explain it away. But I stopped you, remember? I immediately asked you another question. Here it is," I said, grabbing the same page again. "'A year, slightly less than a year, after your husband, Emmett Stanton, died, you remarried, correct?' Let's go back to that question you started to lie about. You had been having an affair with Michael Kensington, isn't that correct?"

"I'm not sure I would call it that,' she replied tentatively, as if she had to think it over. She was not being deceptive; she was honest in her uncertainty.

"You're not sure? What you would call it? Are you going to tell us that you were not sleeping with Michael Kensington while you were married to Emmett Stanton?"

She shook her head, confused, for some reason, about how to answer.

"No, I'm not going to tell you that we never slept together. But it wasn't that often, just once in a while. It wasn't the way you usually think of what happens when people are having an affair."

Suddenly, I understood.

"Because not only were you not faithful to your husband, you weren't faithful to your lover, either, were you? You only slept with him sometimes because you were also sleeping with someone else. Is that what you are trying to say? We can certainly understand now your inability, or should I say your unwillingness, to put a name to what you were doing."

She could have sold herself in the street and still been offended had anyone called her a whore.

"It's still called an affair, Mrs. Stanton," I reminded her without the slightest show of tolerance. "No matter how many of them you are having at the same time. I won't ask you about the others, only the one you were having with Michael Kensington. He testified that the two of you had known each other for years, and that you were once engaged. Tell us what happened, why you didn't marry, why the engagement was broken off."

"You know that already," she replied in a highly irritated voice. "Michael told you."

"We know what he said," I remarked sharply. "We haven't heard your version."

She looked at me with contempt. I looked at her with indifference.

"You were in love with someone else, isn't that what happened?"

"I thought I was in love with someone else," she replied, drawing a distinction that had importance for her. The guilt of what she had done in some measure absolved by this retrospective doubt of what she had felt.

"You married someone else."

"I made a mistake. I was young; I didn't know what I wanted. I was always in love with—"

"With Michael Kensington. Even when you married Emmett Stanton?"

"I was barely twenty when I fell in love with Michael. I met Emmett a long time after that. Michael was gone, out of my life. I had not seen him since the day our engagement ended."

This was what I wanted the jury to see: the connection, the unbreakable connection, between them; how, if in different ways, they were each dependent on the other.

"You had not seen him in all this time, and then, the moment you ran into him again, you knew you were still in love with him, is that how it was?" I asked, pretending a skepticism I did not feel.

"Yes," she insisted eagerly. "As soon as we met again. It had always been there, just below the surface, I suppose you could say. Michael had always been the love of my life. I had just been too young, too stupid, to know it."

My right hand on my hip, I tapped the trial transcript with

three fingers of my left, marveling at how easily the truth of her feelings came through the practiced facade she wore in public. She might care only for herself and what she wanted, but there was no doubt that what she wanted more than anything was Michael Kensington and his approval.

"It must have just about killed you," I remarked sympathetically.

"Must have just about... I'm not sure I understand."

"When he told you he didn't want anything to do with you."

She started to deny it, but she saw the look on my face, the way I was watching her, and held back.

"What was the line he used? That you could believe in second chances all you wanted, but there wasn't going to be any second chance with him. Isn't that what he told you? Isn't that what he said to make you understand that he wasn't the Michael Kensington you used to know, the young man whose heart you had so cruelly broken?"

Staring into the middle distance, she tried to swallow, the way someone does who is not sure they can.

"You would do anything for him now, wouldn't you? Anything to make up, to try to make up, for how you hurt him all those years ago."

The doubt, the vulnerability, the memory of what she had once been capable of feeling, vanished with her next breath. She was in full control of herself, the disciplined celebrity she had always dreamed of being. She was not about to answer the question I had asked without first qualifying her response.

"Anything it was reasonable to do. Nothing like what you keep trying to suggest. Michael would never ask me—I would never ask Michael—to do anything we shouldn't. And let me repeat," she added, turning to the jury in that effortless way she had, "I had nothing to do with the murder of my stepson, and neither did my husband."

"So you say. But certainly no one had a better motive."

"What do you mean by that? You're not going to try that again, are you? Insist that I must have been involved because with Matthew's death I inherit what he had. You're not going to—"

"Your Honor!" said Longstreet, raising her hand in protest as she rose slowly from her chair. "Mrs. Stanton is right. This is the same ground the defense attempted to cover during cross-examination. Calling a prosecution witness as a witness for the defense doesn't mean the defense gets a second chance to ask the same questions it asked before."

Leonard Silverman placed his elbows on the bench and leaned forward. With a pensive expression, he tapped his fingers together.

"Mr. Antonelli?"

"I'm allowed to call a prosecution witness when the testimony of subsequent witnesses have called into question what the witness said before, or when subsequent witnesses provide a new and different basis for cross-examination."

"That's my point, Your Honor," insisted Longstreet, batting her long index finger up and down. "He's asking questions he asked before. Asked and answered."

Silverman looked at me again.

"The beginning of my inquiry may sound the same; the ending won't. This is a murder trial, Your Honor. I would beg the court's indulgence."

Nodding his agreement, Silverman waved off the objection and sat back. Longstreet muttered her displeasure and took her chair. Victoria Stanton watched me through half-closed suspicious eyes, waiting to see what I would do next. I moved a step closer.

"I asked you about the ownership of the team. Do you remember your reply?"

"Do you mean about the trust?"

"Yes. The team is owned by the Stanton Trust. What did you tell us about how the shares in the trust are divided?"

"Originally, my late husband, Emmett Stanton, had a controlling interest, fifty-one percent. His son, my stepson, Matthew Stanton, owed thirty percent, and I owned nineteen percent."

"Exactly. And when Emmett Stanton died, his shares, fifty-one percent, passed to his son, Matthew. That left you with your nineteen percent. But now that Matthew Stanton is dead, what happens? How was it set up under Emmett Stanton's will?"

She sat still as a statue, motionless, distant, remote, ready to rule the world with a snap of her finely manicured fingers. She was not embarrassed, and she certainly did not feel guilty; she was actually quite proud of what she had acquired. After all, it had been her own hard work that had built the organization, the sports and entertainment enterprise, into the great commercial success it had become.

"All of it came to me. I am now the sole shareholder."

I reached over to the table and the top page on the pile.

"When you were here before, I asked you how much money you would make once you owned everything. Do you recall your reply? You were quite angry."

"No, I'm afraid I don't."

"You said...here, let me read it." I held the page up to my eyes. "'The money doesn't matter. Four billion, ten billion; nineteen percent, a hundred percent: we were never going to sell. What for? To buy something else?'"

"That's true!" she cried, wagging her finger for emphasis. "The money doesn't matter. The team is never going to be sold."

"Unless Matthew Stanton decided he had to sell it. He could have done that, couldn't he? He owned more than four-fifths of it. You couldn't have done anything to stop it. The money might not mean anything to you—that wasn't the reason you owned the team—but it might have meant something to Matthew Stanton!"

"Matthew owned eighty-one percent. He had no reason to sell. He did not need money, not with all the money the team was making. Why would he ever think—?"

"Because of you! Because he was certain you and Michael Kensington had murdered his father! Because he was certain you and Michael Kensington were going to murder him next!"

"Objection!" screamed Longstreet at the top of her lungs. "He can't possibly know what Matthew Stanton did or did not believe!"

"But I do know, Your Honor. And I have a witness to prove it, a witness who will testify that shortly before Matthew Stanton's death, this was exactly what he was afraid was going to happen!"

The courtroom erupted. The jurors looked at one another, trying to understand what it might mean. Silverman slammed his gavel hard on the bench, and with a warning glance quieted the crowd.

"You have a witness, Mr. Antonelli? Very well, you may continue."

"But, Your Honor!" protested Longstreet, to no avail.

"Matthew Stanton hated you for what you had done! Didn't he, Mrs. Stanton?" I demanded with a withering stare.

"Matthew didn't hate me!" she insisted with a show of anger. "I told you before, I loved Matthew as if he were my own son."

"Is that what you told him the night he was killed, when you called him?" I asked, suddenly as calm as if I were talking to an old friend. She hesitated, not sure how to answer. "I have the phone records," I said quite casually, as if a thing of no great importance. "You called him on his cell phone at six forty-seven, just a few minutes before T. J. Allen came to see him; when, as Mr. Allen testified, Matthew Stanton was angry, extremely upset. What did you talk to him about, Mrs. Stanton? What did you say that made him so angry, so upset?"

She hid behind her eyes.

"Nothing. I just called to say hello, to see how he was."

I leaned back against the table and crossed one ankle in front of the other. I smiled gently, the way a silent assassin might say goodbye to his latest victim.

"You spoke to him about what you had learned he was going to do with the team. You told him it was his last chance to change his mind."

"What he was going to do with the team? I have no idea what you're talking about, and neither, I suspect, do you!"

The smile on my mouth grew broader, and more deadly.

"You didn't know—you hadn't heard—that he was making plans, that he had gone so far as to have the document drawn up; that it was only a matter of time before you wouldn't have nineteen percent, or any percent, of the ownership of the team?"

"There were always rumors, stories people invent. The team was worth a lot of money, and so there was always talk about how much it might bring on the open market and who would be most likely to buy it. But, no, we were never going to sell. Matthew was never going to sell."

"And you would have known if he had changed his mind? You would have known if he had decided to do something like that?"

"Of course I would have known. I knew everything that went on, especially about the business side of things."

"You signed contracts, things like that?" I asked with only mild-seeming curiosity, a routine question that did nothing more than follow up on the answer she had just given.

"Yes, of course, I signed contracts."

"And your husband, I gather he had the authority to sign them as well?"

"Yes, he has that authority."

"And, of course, Matthew Stanton, the owner of four-fifths of the shares and the principal trustee, could have done that as well, correct?"

"Yes, of course," she replied, becoming impatient with what seemed an unnecessary and tedious line of questioning.

"But none of you, I assume, drafted the various contracts and other legal documents you were signing. Lawyers do that sort of thing. What was the name of the lawyer who did the legal work for the trust?"

She dismissed it with the same impatience, as a matter of no consequence.

"The trust has a law firm in the city. It's been the same one for years."

"No, Mrs. Stanton, not the firm, the lawyer. His name is Oscar Maddox, is it not?"

She acted as if she could not quite remember, that she had to think about it for a while.

"Yes, that's right," she said finally with an apologetic look. "He left the firm a few months ago. Retired and went to live somewhere in Europe, if I am not mistaken."

"A few months ago! A few months before Matthew Stanton's murder, wasn't it? And you're wrong. Oscar Maddox isn't living in Europe. I spent the better part of a day with him just last week. It turns out that Matthew Stanton had decided to get rid of the team, Mrs. Stanton. Oscar Maddox, the trust's lawyer, drew up the papers. He started working on it, making all the arrangements, about the same time, as it turns out, that T. J. Allen's gun, the one he kept in is locker, went missing. Matthew was murdered, Mrs. Stanton, not very long after you made your call, the one you claim had nothing to do with what he was planning to do. Now, tell us, did you make any other calls that night, any that might just have a bearing on what happened, the murder of Matthew Stanton you say you know nothing about?"

Ashen faced, as angry as I have ever seen anyone, her eyes shot wide open and, like the furies, seemed to dash everywhere at once.

Her right hand, curled into a fist, beat three times in a hard staccato rhythm on the arm of the witness chair.

"I didn't—! How many times do I have to tell you? I called Matthew to say hello," she said in a bristling, metallic voice. "Check those phone records again! Tell the jury, tell everyone, not just about that one call, give an honest account! I called Matthew at least once a week. I was worried about him; I was always worried about him, worried he was spending too much time with...with him! T. J. Allen. I kept telling him, telling Matthew, that he was dangerous!"

"Answer my question!" I shouted back at her. "Did you make any other calls?"

"I spend half my life on the phone!"

I waved my hand; enough was enough. There were other things, other questions, still to be dealt with.

"Remind us again. Who are the members of the Stanton Foundation board of directors?" I waved my hand again to stop her from answering. With my head bent low, I began to pace back and forth in front of the two counsel tables. "It would take too long to name all twenty-four. They fall into two categories: those with money, and those, fewer in number, who occupy positions of power and influence. I'm interested in this second category. Elizabeth Burroughs, the county coroner, that isn't why she is on it, is it?" I asked, stopping long enough to look up.

"She's a world-famous author," she replied, glad to be talking on what she assumed was safer ground.

I waved my hand for the third time.

"She's also your sometime lover, but we'll let that go for the moment. And the lead investigator in this case, Owen Chang, the homicide detective who lives in the same Nob Hill building in which Matthew Stanton was murdered. He isn't on the board, but his wife, Marilyn Chang, owner of the largest real estate company in the city, she's on it, isn't she?"

"She's an extremely successful businesswoman."

I went over to my briefcase, sitting on the floor next to the counsel table, and pulled out a copy of a loan agreement.

"Not only an extremely successful businesswoman, an apparently extremely good credit risk. The Stanton Foundation, which you described as committed to making the city a better place to live for everyone, gave her an unsecured loan for fifty million dollars."

She did not bat an eyelash.

"It's a short-term arrangement, part of a commercial development for which financing was needed."

"The board takes care of its own. I see. Everyone takes care of everyone; everyone is indebted to everyone else. It helps to be rich, doesn't it? Elizabeth Burroughs, Marilyn Chang, and—I almost forgot!—the district attorney, the prosecutor in this case, Samantha Longstreet. As I said, everyone takes care of everyone else!"

"Your Honor!" Longstreet was on her feet, red-faced with rage, but not just that, embarrassment.

If, as she must have thought at the beginning, T. J. Allen was guilty, her membership on a charitable board, funded by the family of the victim, was not a disqualification; but if Allen was innocent, if Victoria Stanton herself was involved in the murder, her position was untenable. She was more angry with herself than she was with me, but I was the only one she could take it out on. She started to add to her complaint, but Silverman stopped her with a quick motion of his hand.

"Chambers," he instructed quietly, but firmly.

The three of us sat together in Silverman's threadbare office like three revelers at a wake. Silverman thought it almost funny.

"It's a strange business, jury trials. I'm never quite sure who I should feel sorry for: the defense attorney losing a case he should win, or the prosecutor discovering too late that she is prosecuting the wrong man. Or, sometimes, the defendant, who never meant to commit the crime for which he is now facing prison. I would not say this in public, but I almost never feel sorry for the victim. You know why? Because they're dead. Nothing we do in court, nothing we do in a trial, will do anything for them. Everyone talks about getting justice for the victim. Really? The victim will never know anything about it. The relatives, the friends, of the victim, if the victim had any, may get some sense of something having been done, but it usually doesn't bring that much relief or sense of satisfaction. Revenge only has meaning when you haven't yet got it."

Leonard Silverman looked at both of us, sitting in the two armless chairs in front of his spartan desk, and then he looked at Longstreet alone.

"I've given the defense great latitude in this trial. I've done it for more than the usual reasons. This is a murder case, but it isn't just a murder case. It's a case that goes to the question of who we are, of what we have become. It involves a whole set of circumstances that go far beyond the proof of a few determinative facts. Every once in a while, we have a case—and this is one of them—where, in a very serious sense, we're all on trial. Look, I understand this may not make much sense to you. You're a prosecutor, a very good one, if I may be permitted to say, and you have a crime, a murder, and a suspect. You have what you no doubt honestly believe is sufficient evidence to convict. But imagine a trial in the South in the days of segregation, imagine a black man on trial for the rape of a white woman. A black man is on trial, but the trial is a fraud. What is really on trial, if they had wit enough to know it, is their whole way of life. Don't misunderstand. I'm certainly not suggesting that we're dealing with anything like that here. But we are dealing with the question of what kind of people we have become. Would any of this have happened if Matthew Stanton had not been born rich, if everyone, all of America, had not become so wrapped up in watching games on television? Would Matthew Stanton still be alive if we were not all living in the age of celebrity? That, it seems to me, is a question worth considering.

"I have given the defense considerable leeway, and I thought I owed it to you to tell you why. I do not believe, however, that I have in any way failed to interpret the rules of evidence properly. Now, is there anything you would like to tell me?"

"No, Your Honor. I think I understand. I'm not sure I agree," she added thoughtfully. "But in your position, acting as a judge, I can't quarrel with you. Maybe I would be doing the same thing myself."

"Now, Mr. Antonelli, how much more do you have? When you're done with Mrs. Stanton, how many more witnesses do you intend to call?"

"Just two, Your Honor."

"You mentioned Oscar Maddox. Is he one of them?"

"No, I'm afraid not."

"I used to know him, when I was still practicing. I used to kid him about the way he drafted documents. He never met a comma he didn't like. I never knew anyone more thorough."

"You have something, don't you?" asked Longstreet with a sudden look of interest. "What you were saying in there. Maddox drafted a document for Matthew Stanton. He was really going to sell the team?'

I turned up my hands and shrugged my shoulders and did not say a word. Silverman asked how much longer I would need to keep Victoria Stanton on the stand.

"Just a few more questions," I replied.

I had only two.

"You testified that you thought the defendant reported his gun stolen so that the police—let me read exactly what you said—'so the police would think someone else had used it to murder

Matthew!' Is that still your testimony? Is that still what you believe?"

"He murdered Matthew! He shot him with his own gun. What other explanation could there be?"

"You insist, then, that the defendant, T. J. Allen, planned the murder weeks in advance, so that, as I think I observed at the time of your testimony, he could save himself the trouble of getting a gun that could not be traced back to him, and could make sure he would be holding it when the police arrived so that, and I think I remember word for word what I said, 'he could claim that he must be innocent because no one guilty of murder could ever have come up with a story that stupid.'

"One last question, Mrs. Stanton. Is it still your testimony that the defendant 'told people, friends of his, that Matthew was treating him like some ignorant fool who did not even know how to read. He said he was—and this is what I could never forget—treating him like the house nigger, and no one could treat him like that'? I ask you that question, Mrs. Stanton, because not a single one of those people, those friends of his has come forward to testify for the prosecution. And don't you think, on something as important as the question of motive, one of them would have been called to support your outrageous allegation if it had ever happened?"

Twenty

Albert Craven bought a new suit for court, elegant and understated, the tailored perfection on which he always insisted. It was a mark of distinction, a point of honor, a way to remind himself that there were standards that should be observed, an obligation all the greater when those standards had been all but forgotten by everyone else. He stood with his right hand raised, listened as the court clerk recited the oath, solemnly swore to tell the truth, the whole truth, and nothing but the truth, and walked with measured steps to the witness stand. He looked up at Leonard Silverman and nodded, but only once.

Silverman, as always, was wearing a black judicial robe. There were at least two hundred spectators who had come to watch, and, of course, the twelve men and women in the jury box. Only three of us were wearing suits and ties.

"He looks almost as good in a tie as you do," I whispered to T. J. Allen, sitting next me in a dark gray suit and a dark gray tie. "Remember when you asked me if I always wore one? Watch the way the jury watches him."

"Mr. Antonelli, if you're ready," said Silverman.

I left Allen to ponder the advantages of doing things in a formal way when a witness, or anyone else, tries to persuade others that he is not just telling the truth, but knows what he is talking about.

"Mr. Craven," I began after he stated his full name for the record, "how are you employed?"

"I'm an attorney in private practice," he replied in a surprisingly strong voice.

Despite all the stories about how nervous, how really terrified he had been the few times he had made an appearance in court, he was in complete control of himself. He was direct, on point, every word decisive as he described his background in the law and the history of his firm.

"You left something out, didn't you?" I asked, suppressing a grin. "You failed to mention that I'm one of the partners in the firm."

A wistful sparkle in his pale blue eyes, he turned to the jury.

"For some reason, I often find myself forgetting that," he admitted with a rueful smile

And with that one remark, Albert Craven became their trusted friend. You could see it immediately, the way they all seemed to shift their weight and move closer; the sense of recognition that this impeccably dressed, clearly intelligent older man understood what the world, what they themselves, thought of lawyers as a class. More than that, they knew that he had a sense of humor that showed affection in a way no formal tribute ever could.

"We're partners in the same firm, or rather, I'm a partner in the firm you started. But the reason you're here today is because of some independent knowledge you have about the case. A short time before his death, you met with Matthew Stanton. Would you please tell the jury why he came to see you and what you discovered?"

The lines in his forehead, though barely visible, stretched tight as a spider's web. He became quite serious.

"He did not come to see me; he invited me to lunch. I was surprised when he called. I knew him, but not very well. I had known his father, Emmett Stanton, but, again, only in the way of people who see each other at social events. Emmett, as you must have heard," he said, looking at the jurors, "was involved in a great many charitable causes. There was always some dinner, some fundraising event. So, as I say, I knew him, but it would be going too far to suggest we were good friends. Anyway, Matthew called, said he wanted to talk to me, that it was important, and could I meet him for lunch at the Fairmont."

I had taken a position at the end of the jury box, farthest from the witness stand, where I would be right in front of him, and he could see the encouragement in my eyes. But he did not look at me; he was too busy telling his story to the jury.

"He told me a lot about his father. It was really quite extraordinary. He said his father had probably been insane—yes, he said that. The proof of it was that his father had always been completely honest! You see," he added confidentially, as it were, "he didn't think his father had been insane at all. He was responding to what everyone liked to say about Emmett. Everyone knew he was a genius, someone who somehow understood the way the financial markets worked the way you and I know when we go outside whether the sun is shining or whether it is hot or cold. We don't consult the weather report, we don't have to look at the thermometer. That was how Matthew's father knew what no one else, for all their research, all their measured graphs, ever knew as quickly. Perhaps because he knew things that way, had that kind of intuition, Emmett Stanton's behavior was, at times, well, let's just say erratic.

"Matthew told me these things about his father because he wanted me to understand, to believe, what he was convinced had happened, the reason his father had died. He did not think his father's death had been an accident. He did not have any proof that it had not been an accident, there wasn't any evidence, but he knew, he was certain, that his father had been murdered, and that he was going to be murdered next. And that wasn't all," he went on, aware that everyone on the jury was listening intently to everything he told them. Everyone else —the judge, the lawyers, the courtroom crowd—the silent audience for their private conversation. "He knew who had murdered his father and who was going to murder him. They murdered his father so they could get what Emmett had; they were going to murder him because it was the only way they could get all of it."

"They? Who did he mean? Who did he think murdered his father? Who did he think was going to murder him?"

"His stepmother, Victoria Stanton, and her husband, Michael Kensington."

I started back toward the counsel table. Samantha Longstreet thought I was finished with the witness. She started to get up, ready to begin her cross-examination. She seemed startled when I picked up two copies of a printed document and handed one to her. I gave the other one, the original, to Albert Craven.

"Would you tell the court if you have seen this document before?" I asked with a serious, straightforward expression

"Yes, you had me look it over in my office a few days ago."

"Do you know who drafted this document?"

"Oscar Maddox. His name and signature appear on the last page."

"And would you tell us who signed this document, the authority for the transaction this document memorializes?"

"Matthew Stanton. He signed on behalf of the Stanton Trust, the owner of the professional basketball team on which the defendant, Thaddeus John Allen, played."

"Is it a contract of sale? Does the document transfer ownership of the team for an agreed upon price?"

"No, it does not."

Leonard Silverman leaned forward, eager to hear what Albert Craven would say next. Samantha Longstreet stared at Craven with puzzled eyes. The jurors seemed to hold their collective breath. If it was not a contract of sale, if no one was buying the team, what had Matthew Stanton done instead, and how could it possibly affect the outcome of a murder trial?"

"Matthew was not going to sell the team," reported Craven, lifting his gray eyebrows in tribute to the astonishing thing Stanton had done instead. "He gave it away."

Everyone in the courtroom turned to look at someone, hoping that somewhere in a stranger's eyes they might find the meaning of what, if they had heard right, seemed nothing short of impossible.

"Gave it away?" I asked, as if I were more surprised than anyone. "You said he gave it away. You mean he did this, gave the team away, before his death?"

"It's not a contract of sale," insisted Craven, as if this fact alone explained everything. "In a contract of sale, both parties, the seller and the buyer, have to sign the contract for the contract to be binding." He spread his hand open, as if to show the jury that it was all very simple. "It was not a contact of sale; it was a gift. His death does nothing to invalidate the gift. It was signed and dated before he died. A contract of sale requires two signatures: buyer and seller. This document, making a gift, requires only the signature of the person who owns the gift he wishes to give. The professional basketball team is no longer owned by the Stanton Trust. The Stanton Trust gave it away."

"But Victoria Stanton, because of the death of Matthew Stanton, now owns a hundred percent of the Stanton Trust, does she not?"

"Yes, she does, but the basketball team belongs to another party."

"She cannot, as sole trustee, revoke the gift and get the team back?"

"No, it's gone, gone forever. She won't even have season tickets, unless she buys them," added Craven with a blank expression that could not hide the vast amusement in his eyes.

I paused, enjoying the suspense, the question everyone wanted answered. If the Stanton Trust, if Victoria Stanton, no longer owned the team; if Matthew Stanton, in a moment of inspiration, or perhaps a moment of hereditary insanity, had given up more than four billion dollars he could have had, who owned it now? Who was the beneficiary of this bizarre act of unfathomable generosity, or this desperate act of revenge for what had been done to his father and what, he was convinced, might be done to him?

Craven clasped his hands together, relishing the moment. He glanced briefly at the document drafted with such painstaking precision by Oscar Maddox, the document Maddox had taken with him when he realized how far, if they learned of its existence, Victoria Stanton and her husband would go to make sure no one would ever know about it. He looked at me with as proud a look as I had ever seen.

"Who owns the team, Mr. Craven? Who did Matthew Stanton give it to?"

"The team is now owned, owned as of the date of this document signed by Matthew Stanton two days before his death, by the Oakland school district. The team, the new arena in San Francisco, all the games and events that will take place there, all the advertising, all the television revenues—in short, all the money that will ever be made will now be used for the education of the children of the city of Oakland, California."

There was absolute silence. No one said a word; no one could think of a word to say. And then, from somewhere far back in the courtroom crowd, someone shouted, "Good for him; good for Matthew Stanton!" Everyone started to cheer. They might have cheered the roof off if Leonard Silverman had not, though with some reluctance, gently beat his gavel until, gradually, the cheering stopped.

"I knew he was going to do something," said T. J. Allen with a broad grin on his face and a sad, distant look in his eyes. "Only Matthew could have thought of doing something like that."

None of this changed the evidence. Except for a deeper understanding of the kind of human being Matthew Stanton had been, nothing now was different. Samantha Longstreet still had her job to do.

"Mr. Craven," she began, rising from her chair but not moving from the spot, "you said that Matthew Stanton told you that he thought his father had been murdered, but that he had no proof, no evidence, that's correct, isn't it?"

"Yes, that's what he said."

"He had no proof, no evidence; only a suspicion?"

"Yes."

"And then, because of what was nothing more than a suspicion, he suspected something might happen to him, correct?"

"I would not put it like that. He had more than a suspicion; he had a certainty."

Longstreet's head snapped back. She could not conceal her surprise.

"A certainty? You just said he did not have any proof, any evidence."

Craven smiled indulgently. He had the great advantage of not just his age, but his manner. It was impossible not to trust him.

"We all know things we can't prove. Emmett Stanton knew things that had not happened yet. He wasn't a fortune teller; he just had a sense of things, a sense of what was going to happen.

Matthew had that same sense of things when it came to his stepmother. He knew what she was capable of when it came to getting what she thought she had to have."

"But, again," said Longstreet, trying to regain lost ground, "no proof, no evidence, of anything?"

"Not of the sort you mean, that's correct," replied Craven succinctly.

"And I take it from your testimony that Matthew Stanton said nothing to you about making a gift of the team to the city of Oakland?"

"No, we did not discuss the basketball team at all."

"And, so far as you know, no one knew what Matthew Stanton was planning to do?"

I understood what Longstreet was trying to do. If no one knew what Stanton was planning, it could not be a motive to kill him. I tried to give her question a different meaning on re-direct.

"This was the only conversation you had with Matthew Stanton?"

"Yes, it was."

"So you wouldn't know to whom he might have spoken about his plans?"

"No, I wouldn't."

"You wouldn't know, for example, when he first started talking with the trust's lawyer, Oscar Maddox, about doing what the document he drafted and Matthew Stanton signed accomplished? But it is safe to assume that someone connected with the team would have been in the best position to find out, is it not?"

Then, before Longstreet could object, I announced, "No more questions."

I had one more witness to call, one more prosecution witness to help make my case. Owen Chang seemed less certain of himself than when he had been called by Longstreet as the lead detective. Everyone now knew that he was not just a homicide detective, but part of the wealthy crowd that decided much of what happened in the city.

"Detective Chang, when you testified earlier, the district attorney asked you to describe what happened the night Matthew Stanton was murdered. Let me read your response:

"'We had a call. Someone in the building where Mr. Stanton lived heard what they thought was some kind of fight, loud voices, things being broken. The two officers who responded discovered Mr. Stanton dead from a gunshot. The defendant, Mr. Allen, was standing there, the gun still in his hand.'"

I put down the trial transcript and looked at Chang.

"The gun—you admitted this—had been reported stolen several weeks earlier. You remember that, don't you?"

"Yes, I remember."

"It was your conclusion that he had made a false report, that the gun hadn't been stolen, that he had only pretended it had so that, when he used it to kill Matthew Stanton, he could explain that someone else had used it to commit murder. Do I remember your testimony correctly?" I asked, smiling my disbelief.

Owen Chang sat the way he had before: back straight, one pressed pant leg crossed over the other. Though his eyes stayed fixed on mine, they moved ceaselessly back and forth, searching my eyes, one after the other; trying, as it seemed, to find the real meaning behind the questions I was asking.

"We discussed the defendant's stolen gun report," he replied in a dull, bureaucratic voice.

"Discussed at length, as I remember, how improbable it was," I remarked with a slight, but serious laugh. "But do you know what surprises me even more? That there was a gun there at all. Do you remember when you testified that the defendant often came to see Matthew Stanton, when you implied they were gay lovers, that I asked why, if he was going to kill him, he didn't use his bare hands? T. J. Allen is six foot eight and extremely strong.

Matthew Stanton was not quite five foot ten and rather thin. How tall are you, Detective Chang? Five foot eight, five foot nine? I could understand why you might need a gun to do something like that, but T. J. Allen? Why do you think he needed a gun? It had to be because he had been planning it for weeks, wouldn't you agree? Otherwise, why go to all the trouble of reporting the gun missing?" I asked, my voice echoing my skepticism.

"I don't know why he reported the gun stolen. I don't know when the defendant decided to murder Matthew Stanton, whether it was when he reported the gun missing or the night he went there and they got into some kind of argument. All I know is that his gun was the murder weapon and he was holding it when the two officers arrived."

"When you arrived at the scene, the defendant was already in custody? That's when you came, isn't it? After the two patrolmen who had been just a couple of blocks away arrived?"

"Yes, that's right."

"And the reason you came…? No, never mind. Let me make sure this is exact."

I picked up the trial transcript and read the passage out loud.

"'And you were already there, weren't you? You weren't on duty that night; you were home, with your wife, in the apartment you own on the second floor of the same building. Isn't that the reason you were called, because you were just an elevator ride away?'

"Is that the reason you went there, Detective Chang?" I asked as I looked up. "Because you were just an elevator ride away?"

"That, and the fact that I'm a homicide detective," replied Chang with a cursory nod.

"That's the reason you were called?" I asked, as if I wanted to be doubly sure.

"Yes, of course."

"Who called you?"

"Who called me?"

"Yes, who called to tell you there had been a homicide in the building where you lived? Who called to tell you that Matthew Stanton had been murdered?"

He looked at me like I was a fool.

"Dispatch called me."

I looked at him like he was a liar.

"No, Detective Chang, no one from the police department called you."

"Then it was probably one of the patrolmen, once they got there and saw what happened; once they had the suspect in custody."

"No, Detective Chang, they did not. No one called you. No one connected with the police," I added with a withering glance. I looked at the jury to make sure they understood the implications. "Victoria Stanton testified that your wife, Marilyn Chang, has an unsecured loan of fifty million dollars from the Stanton Foundation. You're aware of that, aren't you?"

Chang shifted uneasily in the witness chair. He tried to look indignant.

"It isn't unsecured. She often has lenders as participants in real estate projects, especially ones as large as the one for which that loan was provided."

"She owes fifty million dollars, borrowed, not from a bank or some other financial institution, it isn't even borrowed from the Stanton Foundation. It is borrowed from one individual—Victoria Stanton. No one called you from the police department," I said suddenly. "No one called you after Matthew Stanton was murdered. But you did get a phone call, didn't you, Detective Chang?"

"I don't know what you mean."

"Victoria Stanton called you," I said, moving closer. "I have the phone records. She called you a few minutes before seven, just a few minutes after she hung up from the call she made to her stepson, Matthew Stanton; the phone call that left him angry and upset. You didn't get a phone call from the police; no one called to tell you Matthew Stanton had been murdered. The only call you got came before he was killed. What was the reason you kept insisting that you, and not some other detective, had been called? What was it I said? Because you were just an elevator ride away?"

Longstreet was out of her chair before I was back in mine. Holding her head high in defiance of what she was quick to assert was one of the most desperate attempts to subvert the cause of justice she had ever seen, she smiled apologetically at Owen Chang and asked if anything the defense attorney had insinuated was true.

"It's true I live in the same building as the victim, Matthew Stanton, did."

Longstreet became more specific.

"Did you receive a phone call from Victoria Stanton the night Matthew Stanton was killed?"

"Yes, I did," he replied, as if he could not wait to clear up any confusion. "She called to tell me that she had just spoken to her stepson and she was worried. She asked if I would mind checking to see if he was all right. He had been saying all sorts of strange things, and she was afraid he might do something to himself. She thought he was getting paranoid, the way his father had been."

"Did you go to check on him?"

"Yes, but it was too late."

"You mean that when you got there, he was already dead?"

"When I got there, the two patrolmen were there and Allen was under arrest."

"So you didn't get a phone call from dispatch; no one from the department called. Why did you say you had when you first testified?"

"I should have, but I didn't think it was important. I would have been called, if I had not gone up to the apartment when I did. And I suppose I didn't see any reason to cause Mrs. Stanton any more grief than what she was dealing with already."

"But you know now that it was a mistake?" asked Longstreet, willing to forgive a minor error of judgment.

"Yes, I'm sorry; I should have known better."

Longstreet nodded in the legal equivalent of absolution and thanked him for confessing his small, unimportant sin.

I sprang out of my chair.

"Victoria Stanton told you that Matthew Stanton 'had been saying all sorts of strange things.' Is that your testimony, Detective Chang?" I demanded. "Did those strange things happen to include anything about getting rid of the basketball team? Anything about depriving her and her husband of any share in the new ownership; anything about making sure she would never have anything like the same fame and celebrity she had before?"

"She was worried about her stepson. That's all she told me."

"Really? What did she tell you in the next phone conversation you had with her, the one that took place just a few minutes after her stepson was murdered?"

"She did not say anything. She was crying too hard. I was the one who had to tell her that her steps had been murdered!" Chang shot back.

"Was that after the first, or the second time, you went up to Matthew Stanton's apartment? Before or after you killed him! No more questions, Your Honor," I said as the courtroom exploded with noise.

Twenty-One

Some cases are won at the beginning, on voir dire, when the jury promises that even if they think the defendant is guilty, they will not convict him unless the prosecution has proven it beyond a reasonable doubt. Some cases are won at the very end, on closing argument, when the jury is persuaded that the prosecution has not proven guilt at all. There are some cases, however, when the only way to win is to prosecute someone else for the crime.

I thought of that as I sat listening to Samantha Longstreet summarize the evidence against T. J. Allen. She was good, very good, as good as any prosecutor could have been. The case against the defendant, she insisted with unwavering assurance, was straightforward, open and shut. There was nothing that, despite the best efforts of the defense, left any room for doubt, reasonable or otherwise. Allen owned the gun, the gun that was used to murder Matthew Stanton, the gun the defendant had in his hand when the police arrived and found Matthew Stanton's dead body.

"The defense has spent a lot of time ridiculing the suggestion that anyone would be dumb enough to report a gun stolen so they could use it later to commit a murder. Mr. Antonelli went to great lengths to argue that it would be not only the most stupid, but the most convoluted murder plan ever devised, to report the gun's theft so when the police found it in your hand after you shot someone to death, you could insist you could not have done it, committed murder, because it had been stolen by someone else.

"Let's assume Mr. Antonelli is right. Let's assume that the defendant did not plan any of this. Let's assume that he reported the gun stolen, but that it had only been misplaced; left in the glove compartment of his car, or in a closet or a drawer at home. He finds the gun, but he doesn't report it to the police. Why should he? The police hadn't done anything when he reported it stolen. He has the gun; he carries on just the way he has before. He carries it with him when he goes out at night; he brings it with him when he goes to Matthew Stanton's apartment. The gun stolen, the gun lost and found; a murder planned weeks in advance, a murder planned moments before it happened. It doesn't matter. The only thing that matters is what the evidence, the incontrovertible evidence, has shown: the gun belonged to Thaddeus John Allen, he had the gun when the police arrived, and the forensic evidence, the gunshot residue on his hand and clothing, prove that he, and he alone, fired it!"

For the next forty-five minutes, Longstreet outlined the testimony that had been given by the witnesses for the prosecution; for ten minutes after that she took apart what she called the self-serving testimony of the defendant. And then she came after me.

"From the very beginning of this trial, the defense has attempted to convince you that the defendant is the victim of a conspiracy. Everyone with political power or influence, everyone who has tried to make San Francisco a better place to live, has joined forces to convict an innocent man. T. J. Allen did not murder Matthew Stanton—the board of directors of the Stanton Foundation did! And the conspiracy did not start with the murder of Matthew Stanton. Oh, no! It started long before that. It started, apparently, when Victoria Stanton and Michael Kensington, years after they first knew each other, became reacquainted. It started when they decided to murder her husband, Emmett Stanton, by throwing him off a mountain somewhere in the French Alps. It's all quite dramatic, this conspiracy, the stuff of daytime television.

"Mr. Antonelli should be writing novels," said Longstreet as she wheeled around to point a long, accusatory finger at me. "A conspiracy that includes every prominent man and woman in the city, including, and I confess I feel a little flattered, even me! Why? Because I'm the district attorney and a member of the Stanton board, where, when we're not discussing how best to spend the money that has been contributed to make the city a better place, we decide who we're going to murder next!

"The prosecution's case rests on solid evidence. The defense knows that. And so, without any evidence of its own, the defense appeals to fantasy, our too eager desire to believe the worst of people who have achieved a certain degree of fame and fortune. It is interesting that the one exception to this, the one individual who doesn't fit this pattern, is the most famous person of all—the defendant, T. J. Allen. Everyone knows who he is; everyone loved to watch him play.

"The defense is right. Nothing, not fame, not money, puts anyone above the law. This is a trial. The only thing that matters is the evidence, and the evidence in this case is overwhelming. T. J. Allen is guilty of murder, and guilty is the only verdict you can possibly return!"

I waited until Silverman asked if I was ready to give my closing argument, and then I waited some more. I sat there, as if I were lost in thought, staring straight ahead. Then, with a solemn glance at Silverman, I took a deep breath and got to my feet. Standing behind T. J. Allen, I placed my hands on his shoulders.

"This is T. J. Allen. He was arrested and charged with the murder of Matthew Stanton. He did not confess to the crime; he insisted that he had not murdered his friend. He was arraigned in court, and when he was asked how he pled to the charge, he announced, in no uncertain terms, that he pled not guilty and demanded a jury trial, a trial by his peers." I let go of his shoulders and took a step closer to the jury. "And that is the problem. He is a defendant on trial. It narrows our vision as to what is really at issue. This shouldn't be a trial at all. It should not be a trial to determine whether the defendant is guilty, or not guilty, of the charge; it should be an inquest, an examination, into everything involved. At the very beginning, before I started representing the defendant, someone far wiser than I will ever be, observed that, as he put it, 'All of America contributed to the making of Matthew Stanton.' Through much of this trial, the meaning of that remark remained a mystery to me, but now, finally, I have come to understand it.

"Matthew Stanton was murdered. The prosecution and the defense agree on that. No one, including especially the district attorney, has been able to tell us why. Why did Matthew Stanton have to die? What did he do, or what did he not do, that made someone think he had to be killed? It is, in some ways, the wrong question; it is not the question that, by itself, tells us what we need to know. The question we should be asking is: who was Matthew Stanton? The answer, if it had to be given in a single sentence, is Matthew Stanton was an extraordinarily wealthy man who thought the only important thing about money was how well you spend it. It is an old-fashioned idea, one he got from his father. The best thing you can do if you have money is to die poor, not because you spent it all on useless pleasures, but because you invested it in other people to help them live better lives. He had no use for those, like his stepmother, who thought money should be used to become one of the famous people, the people you see on television, the people everyone thinks important because they provide the spectacles, the sporting events, the entertainment too many of us think important.

"Matthew Stanton did not go to games, and he did not watch them on television. As far as I know, he didn't watch television at all. What did he do with his time? What we should all be doing. He tried to educate himself, to learn more about the world. He read books, serious books, books that have through the ages taught us what is important, what is worth knowing. He read them, some of them, with his one close friend, T. J. Allen. You heard T. J. Allen testify; you saw the look in his eyes when he talked about what he and Matthew Stanton did together. You know—we all know—when someone is lying and when someone is telling the truth. You know how T. J. Allen felt about how important a part of his life Matthew Stanton had become.

"At the beginning of the trial, Judge Silverman gave you a very interesting, and a very important, instruction. He told you that you were not to discuss with anyone, including other jurors, anything about the trial. The reason for that instruction should now be obvious. You didn't know—no one knew—until the testimony of one of the last witnesses what Matthew Stanton had done, made a gift of the team to the school district over in Oakland. It was not until then that, finally, we discovered the motive, the reason why Matthew Stanton had to die.

"The prosecution has given its closing argument, a summary of the evidence that, according to the district attorney, proves beyond a reasonable doubt the guilt of the defendant. But in that open and shut case of hers, she never mentioned motive. The prosecution's entire case rests upon two facts, facts we have never disputed: the defendant owned the murder weapon and he was holding it when the police arrived. That is it, two facts; but two facts which are decisive for the prosecution only because the defendant is on trial."

I moved away a few steps. My back to the jury, I shook my head at the strange incongruities in the things we do. Shoving my hands into my pants pockets, I turned slowly to the jury's waiting eyes.

"Imagine that instead of T. J. Allen, someone else, Victoria Stanton, was on trial. Consider what those two facts would mean then. Think what the prosecution's case would be. Remember the evidence, everything you learned. Victoria Stanton, the defendant, a grasping, ambitious woman who started an affair with the man with whom she had, years earlier, broken off an engagement to marry someone else. The marriage was a mistake. She realized, too late, that Michael Kensington was her one true love. She'll never know a love like that again. She becomes involved with who knows how many other men until she marries Emmett Stanton, one of the richest men alive. With his money she becomes the very public owner of a world-famous professional basketball team. She is famous now, someone everyone wants to know. Then Michael Kensington comes back into her life. She's desperately, hopelessly in love. She'll do anything to get him back. They start an affair. It's not enough, for either of them. She could divorce Emmett Stanton, but that would mean she would lose all that power, all that attention. Her husband dies in a climbing accident, the only witnesses the two of them. Less than a year later, they marry. But there is still an obstacle—Matthew Stanton.

"Victoria Stanton testified, here, in court, under oath, that it did not matter if Matthew had eighty-one percent and she had only nineteen percent of the trust that owned the team. Neither she nor Matthew would ever sell. That is what she testified, but it was not true. Matthew was going to get rid of the team, and if he did, she would be left with nothing, or rather nothing she really needed. She would still have money, and plenty of it. The team was not the only thing the Stanton Trust owned. She would have money, but she would not have what meant more than life to her

—celebrity, fame, notoriety, her picture in the papers, her face on television, all the false tinsel of her existence.

"She did not know—only Oscar Maddox knew—that Matthew Stanton was going to give the team away; but she knew, she must have found out, that he was planning to get rid of it. She would have assumed—anyone would have assumed—that he was going to sell it. That meant it could still be stopped, if she could convince Matthew not to do it, not to sell. Because, remember the testimony, a contract of sale is not any good until both seller and buyer have signed it.

"She called Matthew, remember, just a few minutes before T. J. Allen came to see him. Matthew was angry, upset after that conversation. He wouldn't tell T. J. Allen why he was angry, and they got into an argument because of it. Allen leaves, and then, a short while later, when he is out on the street, realizes what he has done and tries to call Matthew, but Matthew doesn't answer. Allen goes back and finds his friend, his close friend, shot to death, the gun laying on the floor. He picks it up. He hears something, or thinks he does, and fires the gun out the open door to the terrace outside.

"Remember the evidence, part of the case, what the prosecution's case would be, against Victoria Stanton. Right after she called her stepson, right after she did not get what she wanted—a promise that he would not sell the team, or that he would at least wait until they could talk about it in person—she made another call. She called Owen Chang, the husband of a woman who just happened to owe her fifty million dollars; a detective, a homicide detective, a man who knew all about murder who just happened to live in the same building, an elevator ride away.

"What happened next? Remember, this is the prosecution's case, not against T. J. Allen, but against Victoria Stanton. Is there any evidence that ties Owen Chang to the murder of Matthew Stanton? Anything beyond that phone call? The gun, the murder weapon, had been reported stolen. There isn't any evidence where it ended up, or who had possession of it before Allen found it laying on the floor. Is there any evidence against Detective Chang? There is this: he lied about why he came to be in the apartment. He testified, under oath—a police detective who knows better than anyone the importance of telling the truth at a trial—that he was called by dispatch, that he went there under orders. He lied when he said that. He told the truth when he admitted that he went because Victoria Stanton sent him there. Why, you should ask yourselves, would an innocent man think he had to lie about something like that?

"And, finally, remember this: if Victoria Stanton was on trial, what would the prosecution say about those two facts we keep talking about: that T. J. Allen owned the gun and that he was holding it when the police arrived? I'll tell you exactly what the prosecution would say: T. J. Allen had no reason to murder Matthew Stanton, but Victoria Stanton had all the motive in the world."

I walked to the jury box, placed my hands on the railing, and looked at each juror in turn.

"Do one more thing. Look at T. J. Allen. Remember what you were thinking when he was testifying, and ask yourselves just this one question: is it even possible that he could ever have even thought about killing the only good friend he ever had?"

It was over; there was nothing more to do. Silverman gave his instructions to the jury and the life of T. J. Allen was now theirs to decide. It was impossible to know how long it would take; it might be hours and it could be days. There was nothing anyone could do now but wait. Leonard Silverman had other pressing matters on the docket that needed his attention. Samantha Longstreet had other trials for which she had to prepare. Everyone had other things to do; everyone except T. J. Allen, who was left to ponder the question of whether twelve men and women he had never met would set him free or send him off to a life in prison.

Restless and exhausted, I went back to my office and collapsed into my chair. The trial kept running back and forth, disconnected memories, in my mind. I sat there, the idle spectator of my own disordered thoughts, trying to imagine how the jury would make sense of everything they had heard. It was, of course, a useless endeavor that served no purpose. It was out of my hands. I had done what I could; I needed to think about something else.

I found Albert Craven, sitting alone in his office down the hall, reading a newspaper.

"Curious, the times in which we live," he remarked when he heard me enter. He invited me to sit down. "I was reading about the trial. Most of what they write about is the reaction to what Matthew did with the team. It's probably the first murder trial in San Francisco that has ever gotten the attention of the sports writers. What does it mean for the future of pro basketball? What will public ownership mean for the future of the sport? That is what everyone wants to know. That other question—did T. J. Allen murder Matthew Stanton, or is he innocent—what difference does that make for the future of the one thing everyone cares about?"

Craven gave me a knowing look, and then shrugged his shoulders at the idiocy of the world.

"How is he, by the way?" he asked as he pushed the newspaper off to the side of his glass-topped desk. "I can't imagine what that would be like, having to wait while a jury decides whether you are ever going to be free again."

"He's scared. He won't admit it, but he is. I could see it in his eyes. He thanked me for what I had done, thanked me for believing in him. That's the part that always amazes me. They all do it, nearly everyone I have ever defended. They think it is so important that I believe them when they tell me they did not do it. I always tell them that it doesn't matter, that the only thing that matters is the evidence, what the prosecution can prove. I never tell them what they want to hear; I never tell them that I believe they're innocent. I refuse to say it."

"Why?" asked Craven with a serious interest. "Why not give them that assurance? Why not let them know you believe in their innocence?"

"Because they're not always innocent, and even if they are, it is a mistake to let them think that if I believe them, so will everyone else. There's another reason. You have to keep a distance; you can't get involved. That doesn't mean you don't; it doesn't mean you don't feel more pressure, that you don't feel everything more intensely, when you're convinced someone is innocent and you're the only one standing between them and prison or worse."

I stopped, suddenly aware of my own hypocrisy, the false impression I was creating, I threw back my head and laughed at my own pretensions.

"You want to know the real truth? Those are the cases I live for, when it is just me, all alone, trying to save someone's life. I never feel more alive, more certain of what I am doing. I said I feel pressure. That isn't true, not when I'm in court. I don't feel anything, nothing, not a thing. There isn't any time for it. Question, answer, the next question after that; everything, every word, comes like something someone else has written; your mind too concentrated on what you are doing to think about whether you should have asked a different question or done something else. What did you once tell me about great writers? That they start writing, and before they know it, they're so lost in what they're doing they don't know that time has passed. It's like that. I started closing argument today with a few ideas, a few points I wanted to make, and before I knew it, the argument took on a life of its own, and instead of the twenty or thirty minutes I thought it would take, I talked for more than an hour."

Albert looked past me to the window and the pale winter light of the dwindling sun, remembering perhaps his own diminishing time.

"Tell me, strictly between us, do you think Allen is innocent?"

I did not say anything; I just looked at him.

"You don't think Victoria Stanton...?"

Too tense, too much on edge to sit still, I got up and started walking aimlessly about Craven's expensively furnished office, full of photographs of San Francisco's legendary past. There were photographs of the aftermath of the earthquake of 1906, photographs of the Golden Gate Bridge under construction in 1937, photographs of Willie Mayes and Joe Montana, Willie Brown and other once famous politicians. Albert Craven was so much a part of the city, and San Francisco was so much a part of him, that I could not imagine him anywhere else. Whenever he came to visit us in Sausalito, he seemed something like a refugee, desperate to go home again. He knew what I was thinking.

"Yes, you're right," he said with a gentle, modest laugh. "There is something about Oakland now owning part of San Francisco—the arena, the team—that doesn't seem quite right. On the other hand, I can't think of anything Matthew could have done that would have been a better thing to do. What better use of all the money we spend on sports than the education of children who would otherwise not have much of a chance in life? I used to think we could not have heroes anymore. Technology has made it almost impossible. The warrior leading his troops into hand-to-hand combat; the explorer on his own, without the ability to communicate, lost in the jungle or in the middle of the desert. Everything has become mechanized, dehumanized, the world reduced to mathematics. The individual and what he wants, or what she thinks she needs, is the only standard. And what does everyone want? That everyone look at them and acknowledge them for who they are. Isn't that what Victoria

Stanton was all about? But who they are has no singularity anymore, nothing that has not been seen a thousand times before; everything an average, and everyone like everyone else, just a little more so. But then, all of a sudden, out of nowhere, something like this happens. Matthew Stanton happens, and, at least for the moment, everything changes. What was that line I heard you use? 'All of America contributed to the making of Matthew Stanton.' It would be nice to think so."

He started to say something else, when the telephone rang.

"Yes, he's here. I'll tell him."

He put down the phone and looked at me, a question in his eyes.

"The court called. The jury has a verdict. That's rather fast, isn't it?"

"Two hours, in a murder trial? They must have thought there was nothing to decide. If you're asking me what it means, I don't know."

"Not guilty. It has to be that. It couldn't be anything else," he insisted, though more, I suspect, for my benefit than because he really believed it.

Half an hour later, I was back in court, sitting next to T. J. Allen, waiting for Leonard Silverman to enter the courtroom and take his place on the bench.

"What do you think?" Allen asked me nervously. His hands were shaking and his palms were sweating. He looked at me intently for a moment and then looked away. "It doesn't matter, does it, what anyone thinks is going to happen? But I want you to know—it's important to me that you know—I never lied to you, not once; I always told you the truth. I didn't murder Matthew; I swear I didn't."

I could not help myself. I broke my rule and told him what I really thought.

"I know you didn't. I never believed that you did."

His huge hands stopped shaking. His mouth began to tremble.

"Thank you."

That was all he said, all he needed to say. The trembling stopped. We sat there, and waited.

Leonard Silverman entered from the side and without so much as a sideways glance at the courtroom, now crowded with reporters, walked straight to the bench. He looked to make sure Samantha Longstreet was in her place and that, alongside the defendant, I was in mine, and then immediately ordered the bailiff to bring in the jury.

I did not need to have the verdict read to know what the jury had decided. Before the last juror had taken her chair in the jury box, several jurors looked at T. J. Allen. Jurors never look at those they vote to convict.

There is always something anticlimactic in an acquittal. There is not so much a sense of victory as of relief. It is finally over, the long, desperate wait behind bars, the twists and turns of the trial. All anyone wants is to get away and try to get back to what had been their normal life, knowing it will never happen.

Nothing will ever be quite the way it was. T. J. Allen had been acquitted, the jury had found him not guilty of the crime, but no one anymore would ever think of him without remembering that he had once stood trial for murder. Victoria Stanton did not own a sports team anymore, but the Stanton Foundation was still the most important civic organization in the city, and she still had more money than almost anyone else. Everyone still wanted to be her friend. They marveled, or claimed to marvel, all those great good friends of hers, at her resilience, the way she had risen above the vicious accusations that had been made against her during the trial. It reminded Albert Craven of the end of *The Great Gatsby*.

"Daisy's cousin, who narrates the story, runs into Daisy and her husband, Tom Buchanan, on the street in Manhattan. Gatsby had taken the blame when Daisy killed her husband's mistress in a car accident, and the husband of the mistress had murdered Gatsby in revenge. There they are, Tom and Daisy, responsible for the deaths of two people and completely indifferent to the point of forgetting what they had done. And now Victoria Stanton and Michael Kensington, the same careless attitude toward what they have done with the lives of others."

Albert was right. They were careless in their disregard for other people and all the rules of decent, civilized behavior; but it seemed to me that the book that explained everything was that brief novel Leonard Silverman had first mentioned. It showed us, if we read it carefully, that in this lunatic carnival, this heart of darkness of our own, Victoria Stanton and Michael Kensington were the kind of savages we are all in danger of becoming.

THE END

About the Author

D.W. Buffa was born in San Francisco and raised in the Bay Area. After graduation from Michigan State University, he studied under Leo Strauss, Joseph Cropsey and Hans J. Morgenthau at the University of Chicago where he earned both an M.A. and a Ph. D. in political science. He received his J.D. degree from Wayne State University in Detroit. Buffa was a criminal defense attorney for 10 years and his ten Joseph Antonelli novels reflect that experience. The *New York Times* called *The Defense* 'an accomplished first novel' which 'leaves you wanting to go back to the beginning and read it over again.' *The Judgment* was nominated for the Edgar Award for best novel of the year.

D.W. Buffa lives in Northern California. You can visit his Official Website at dwbuffa.net.